The Last Words of
James Joyce

James Broderick

The Last Words of James Joyce

Addison & Highsmith

Addison & Highsmith Publishers
Las Vegas ◊ Oxford ◊ Palm Beach

Published in the United States of America by
Histria Books, a division of Histria LLC
7181 N. Hualapai Way, Ste. 130-86
Las Vegas, NV 89166 USA
HistriaBooks.com

Addison & Highsmith is an imprint of Histria Books. Titles published under the imprints of Histria Books are distributed worldwide.

Library of Congress Control Number: 2021952724

ISBN 978-1-59211-142-8 (hardcover)

Contents

Prelude

St. Andrew's Hospital, Northampton, England, December 1982

All the floor nurses agreed it was the oddest thing they'd ever heard. Days later, when the story got around to the doctors, they all assumed Nurse Ballard had embellished the tale. Of course, in her defense (they reasoned) what else is there to do when almost all of your patients are sedated, barely animate, lolling in their chairs in the common room (or strapped down, in extreme cases), staring blankly at the black-and-white television clamped to the wall as the BBC unspools the same b-roll of Mrs. Thatcher's recent visit to Washington to dine with the Reagans?

Leontyne Ballard, the recent hire, was on lock-down duty at the time. "I thought I was having a vision," she would later tell the investigating medical officer, a neurologist named Pederson. "She hadn't stirred since I'd been assigned to that floor."

"And then?" Pederson asked, eyeing her above his rimless spectacles.

"Like a ghost, she floats into the hallway. That's the only word. She floated. And then, she begins dancing-like."

"How so?"

"You know, moving her arms, but not like wild, like an octopus or anything. But you know… what's the word? Angular."

"Go on."

"Well, I was stunned. Here's this 75-year-old woman who hasn't left the chair by the window in her sitting room in the month that I've been assigned here, and suddenly she's gyrating and flailing, but, um, controlled, if you know what I mean."

"Controlled."

"Wild, but on purpose. Like she was executing some sort of pattern. I called Mrs. Lang because I wasn't sure what to do."

"You didn't try to stop her?"

"Stop her dancing? No sir. I didn't think there were rules against dancing."

Pederson sort of wrinkled his nose.

"By the time Mrs. Lang got here, she had twirled around several times, stuck out her arms like she was reaching out for something, trying to touch something. And then —"

"And then?"

"She looked right at me, smiled, and said, `Archimedes! I see you!'"

"Archimedes? The ancient Greek?"

"I can't say what she meant. But that's what she said. `Archimedes.' And then Mrs. Lang got here, and she and an attendant grabbed her, and that's when she started shaking."

"Going into stroke, you mean."

"It was very ugly, sir. She went from this beautiful thing, dancing and smiling, to convulsing, and then she couldn't seem to move at all, and they took her away."

"You do know she has since died of the stroke she suffered, yes?"

"Oh yes, sir, I heard. I couldn't believe it."

"And why is that?"

"Well, sir, she was so happy when she was dancing. And I was happy too. It was like a moment of pure joy."

"She was mad," Pederson said, scratching away in his notepad.

"Well, I can't say. But I can tell you I know happy. And that dancing made her — made both of us — very happy."

"Thank you very much. That's all. You may get back to work."

"Yes, sir." She rose to go but then stopped and turned back. "Do you know what she meant by it? Archimedes, I mean. Do you know what she was thinking about?"

"Nonsense, most certainly. Don't trouble yourself about it."

Pederson walked over to a filing cabinet, opened a drawer, took out a manila file folder, tore a few pages out of the spiral notebook he'd been writing in, stuffed them dutifully into the folder, and re-filed it. He closed the cabinet drawer securely, and by the time he exited the office, he couldn't even remember what the name was that Nurse Ballard said the patient had uttered before she collapsed, never to speak again.

Part One

Like Water Through a Sieve

Russell Padget paused in his reading and looked up from his leather-bound edition of *Frankenstein*, his "Introduction to Literary Genres" students slumped in their seats like so many cadavers in some mad scientist's laboratory. Here and there, a book lay open on one of the tiny tongues of desktop that jutted out like a silent rebuke, far more likely to prop up a latte than a notepad. *Oh hell, they don't take notes anyway*, he thought. *This is 2019 — they write with their thumbs, for Christ's sake!* On this mid-spring morning, Dr. Padget stared out the grimy windows facing the visitors' parking lot, his mind wandering almost as far afield from Mary Shelley's classic tale as his students' thoughts — but always circling back to his *idée fixe*: "How did I end up here?" Hackett County Community College's motto was "Where learning meets life." It sounded impressive, but what did it mean, really? And why, after an academic career of seemingly all the right moves, was he sentenced to re-enact, like the Ancient Mariner, his rehearsed exhortations about "the transformative power of imaginative literature" to a population of students far better at marking time than marking up literary texts?

"Well, it seems you can all use a bit more time digesting nineteenth-century animism," Professor Padget said, turning his back on the class, holding the book aloft like a preacher and audibly slamming it closed with one hand, the dramatic clap raising a tuft of dust and rousing a few of the day dreamers back to consciousness. His students had become adept at reading the signs of a pending early dismissal. The scrape of backpacks being zippered and the crinkle of power-bar wrappers and cardboard coffee cups being crushed soon filled the room. There was no getting them back now, he knew. Once upon a time, earlier in his career, a gaggle of students would have gathered around his desk at the end of class, asking about various passages in the work or making an appointment to see him later in the day. But over the years, fewer students seemed able to resist the siren song of complete escape once class ended. The long-tenured professor had come to wonder whether he'd lost his edge, a verdict that seemed confirmed by his discovery last semester of a bit of ball-pointed poignancy inscribed on one of the desktops: "If I only had an our to live, I'd spend it in this class. It would seem like 10 years." He wasn't sure which made him feel worse: the sentiment or the "our."

He tried to think happier thoughts as he headed to his office. It was a short walk — Hackett County Community College ("Northern New Jersey's gateway to opportunity" the website proclaimed) comprised only three buildings: Eider Hall, a 1960s glass-and-chrome eight-story box where the administration, student services, and professors' offices were housed; Rumboldt, the neo-classical-style classroom building where the windows didn't open and the noisy HVAC system rattled one's fillings during seasons of extreme heat and cold; and Fiedler annex, a mostly-below-ground bunker that served as home to the student union, a makeshift food court whose stock-in-trade was super-sized sodas and the ever-popular "disco fries," a cramped performance space that hosted poetry readings in front of an exposed brick wall and the occasional experimental theatre production, and the campus bookstore.

"Good morning, Shyla," Padget said to the work-study student behind the reception desk in the Humanities department, where the English Department was housed. "How are your classes going?"

"Gotta paper due later today that I'm still working on," she said, more casually than he would have expected, given the proximity of her deadline. "Maybe you can ask Dr. Moravian to give me an extension?"

"I'll talk to her — but I'd keep writing if I were you." He smiled at her and then pulled a few inter-office envelopes out of a cubbyhole, absent-mindedly sifting them for importance as he headed to his office down the hall.

"You've got a student waiting for you," Shyla shouted after him. "She's been here for about 20 minutes. I told her you were in class, but she wanted to wait."

"Ok. Good luck on your paper."

Hopefully, the student is only here to get a signature, he thought, leaping ahead in his mind to his imminent date with the food truck. As he approached his office, he saw her — and then stopped abruptly.

"Is that a ghost I see?"

"Hi Dr. Padget!" she said joyfully, stepping forward to give him a hug, which he awkwardly accepted.

"Sorry, got my hands full," he said. "Goodness, Monique, what has it been — almost five years?"

"Yeah, but this place hasn't changed at all since I graduated."

"It hasn't changed since I got hired 20 years ago," he replied, wresting the key out of his pocket and opening the creaky wooden door of his office. "Come in. How's the podcast?"

"Going great. I've got more than a thousand subscribers."

Padget nodded, not sure if that was an impressive number in the world of podcasting. He'd heard a few audio samples — early broadcasts — that Monique had emailed him shortly after she graduated. Her show was called "Nique's Peeks," a weekly, chatty roundup of movies, TV shows, music, and pop culture in general.

He thought she seemed a bit too casual and jokey — he was more of a sober traditionalist when it came to media — but he sent her some positive comments. They hadn't corresponded since, though he still remembered her fondly as one of his best and most conscientious students. That's how it was with almost all his former students, even the ones who seemed to really like his courses: once they moved on, communication ceased. It used to bother him until he came to realize it was not only common but probably necessary. New attachments, new directions. Still, he was happy to see her — even if she was interrupting his lunch hour.

"So I can't imagine what I can do for you — especially since you're famous."

"I've got something... um, do you mind if I close the door?"

"No — please, feel free," he said, a bit surprised. If she were there just to ask for a letter of recommendation, there'd be no need for such privacy.

She paused to collect herself. "I've got something important to ask you — but it's going to sound a little weird."

He figured he'd heard it all in this claustrophobic, book-crammed office over the past couple of decades. Genuine weirdness would be a welcome break, so he indulged her.

"You've got my attention."

***

Forty-five minutes later, Professor Russell Padget was still in a bit of a daze as he handed over a few crumpled dollars and grabbed the white paper bag containing his lunch.

"Hey, Russ! Wanna join me?"

Camile Danforth was the kind of professor students gravitated towards: a free spirit, blunt, endearingly eccentric, but totally devoted to her work. Padget had always wondered why she hadn't gone further in academia. He was always wondering about his colleagues — how did they get stuck here? But Camile seemed to love it, the challenge of working with students from "non-traditional" backgrounds, those under-prepared learners who had not yet caught intellectual fire. She had the enthusiasm of a first-year teacher, although she had been there almost as long as he had been. And she always seemed to be of good cheer — yet she was a *math* professor, a fact Padget (who *hated* math) couldn't reconcile with even a modicum of joyful feeling. Oh well, a friendly face — and a sympathetic ear to bend — was exactly what he needed at this moment.

"Hi, Camile. I'd love to," he said, sliding onto one of the metal lattice work bench-and-table combos planted around the food trucks in kind of an informal al fresco diners' mall. "You won't believe what I just heard."

"Oooh. A new rumor! Do tell. Is it about the curriculum committee? I hear they're cutting the Western civ requirement next year."

Padget paid as little attention to academic politics as possible for a man in his position. Committee work bored him, though all professors were expected to take their turns on the various entities that academic bureaucracies seemed to spawn like bacteria in the bio department's laboratory. But he had mastered the fine art of deferring. "Would love to, but I have an article coming out in next month's journal and really need to focus. Sorry — next time." There was no journal, just as there would be no "next time." Surprisingly, it kept working — so he kept using it.

"Camile, I just met with a student, and what she told me was, well, pretty shocking." He looked at his over-stuffed veggie wrap, turned it this way and that, finding the best angle of attack, then he chomped into it, careful not to let the tahini sauce trickle from the underside of his hands onto his cuffs.

"I'd think nothing would shock you by now," she said, probably *not* meaning to make him seem like someone serving a long-term sentence. "You talk. I'll eat."

Camile Danforth, Ph.D., tore into her bacon cheeseburger with the unselfconscious ferocity of a cave woman.

"If the plant managers saw you now, they'd petition to have your tenure revoked." The "plant managers" was the name of the college's vegan club. She smiled chewingly, the back of her hand squeegeeing her mouth, a smear of mayo striping her chin.

"They're good kids, really. They just can't think clearly," she said between bites. "Not enough protein in their diet for proper cognitive function."

After another quick hit of his veggie wrap, Padget swallowed, sipped his green tea, and laid it all out for his carnivore colleague.

"Do you remember a student named Monique Tyson? Graduated three years ago?"

"C-."

"Really? You remember her grade?"

"That's all there is to remember about her. She hated math. Told me so the first day. A for honesty. For algebra, not so much."

"Yes, that's Monique. She was more of a word person. She did well in my class. In fact, I always had a sort of soft spot for her. I worked with her closely on her honor's thesis on literary modernism. Anyway, she came to see me this morning."

"Grad school application?"

"That's what I thought. But it turns out she had a different reason for coming. She has this friend — well, I gather it's a former romantic partner — who came to her in some distress. This fellow was in a Ph.D. program, done with all his classes, finishing up his dissertation, and he suddenly got kicked out."

"Geez, that's rough. You're finally at the threshold, and they boot you. What the hell did he do? Plagiarize some academic paper?"

"Nope. That's not why he was black-balled."

"What is he, a flat-earther? Some conspiracy theory nut? Or did he sleep with his dissertation advisor?"

Academia was not above tawdry dalliances and vindictive payback, Padget knew.

"Well, according to Monique, this fellow has discovered a lost literary work."

"Bully for him. That's usually academic gold. So why the death penalty?"

"Camile, this isn't some unknown writer the kid's uncovered. Supposedly, he's located a lost work by… you'd never guess."

"Russ, remember who you're talking to. I haven't read a novel since my last sabbatical, and that one had a half-naked pirate princess on the cover."

"You've heard of *this* writer, believe me. He's one of the biggest names in literature. And he wrote maybe the most important book of the twentieth century. An unknown work by this guy would be the literary equivalent of the discovery of Fermat's last theorem. If it's true."

That got her attention. She put down the remnants of her cheeseburger and cocked her head slightly.

"Is this all a joke, Russ?"

"I don't think so. Or at least, Monique doesn't think so. She asked me to meet with this scholar friend of hers and hear the story from him firsthand. She thinks maybe I can give him some advice, maybe help him get into another program, help him out. I don't think there's any chance he really did find the work he's claiming. Actually, it's impossible. And I'm not sure why they axed him, unless they thought he was making it up."

"Enough of the mystery! Solve for X already — who's the writer?"

Padget leaned forward and whispered the name like he was imparting the secret code of some clandestine society, an emissary from one world with knowledge of the other.

"*James Joyce?*" Danforth's jaw dropped, discrete flecks of lettuce and bacon bits annotating her now gaping mouth, her eyes as wide as onion rings.

"James Joyce."

"No shit?" She resumed chewing. "Well, you're right — I have definitely heard of him. Who hasn't?"

Padget nodded robustly. "Of course. He's arguably the most important writer in English since Shakespeare. But," he said, his bearing suddenly becoming professorial, "that also means he is one of the most thoroughly scoured writers ever. Dozens of full-length biographical studies, thousands of scholarly articles, subsets of English department faculties in Europe and the United States actively explicating his work, and new Joyce acolytes joining the feeding frenzy every year." He shook his head, stole one of her French fries and used it as a sort of pointer, biting and then indicating. "And among them all, precious little agreement about what his works actually mean. There is universal agreement, however, about what those works *are*. The Joyce `canon' has long ago codified into a handful of significant works. Joyce himself tirelessly promoted his own work, and there is simply no record, no mention at all, by Joyce or anyone else of a `lost' work. It's beyond credible, beyond even conceivable. It's lunacy."

"So you told her that?"

"Well, no. I was being, you know… polite. I told her I'd meet this friend of hers. He's dropping by to see me after my composition class this afternoon. Purely a formality."

"Let him down gently," she said, finishing off her cheeseburger. "Uh oh… you feel that?"

Since they had been talking, the cloud-clotted sky thickened and now threatened. A light rain was beginning to fall, and their fellow diners began an exodus from the outdoor tables toward the student union building.

"It droppeth as the gentle rain from heaven upon the place beneath," Padget said, rising, stuffing the remains of his veggie wrap into its foil sleeve and jamming it into his pocket.

"That sounds familiar. Joyce?"

"Shakespeare." He gathered up the detritus of their dine and walked over to the garbage can with a smiley face painted across the top. "Thanks for letting me vent."

"Thanks for the wild tale. Remember: be gentle with this guy. You were a grad student once too, and you probably thought you knew everything."

"Yeah. You're right, I did." *I think that even more now*, he might have admitted to himself as he loped back to the classroom building and a new batch of somnambulant students.

***

As the limpid drops of rain splashed and then dissolved against the grime-encrusted windows of Professor Padget's office, he stood there staring down at the concrete campus, thinking of oxen. Like most bookish types, he was not immune to romanticizing nature, and he remembered a poem from graduate school that he'd written a paper about Henry Wadsworth Longfellow's "Rain in Summer," a celebration of the cleansing, revivifying act of rainfall, as "across the window-pane it pours and pours." One particular image from the poem had always stuck with him:

In the furrowed land
The toilsome and patient oxen stand;

Lifting the yoke encumbered head,
With their dilated nostrils spread,
They silently inhale
The clover-scented gale,
And the vapors that arise
From the well-watered and smoking soil.
For this rest in the furrow after toil
Their large and lustrous eyes
Seem to thank the Lord,
More than man's spoken word.

The delight these beasts of burden feel amid the rain, however brief, always touched him when he thought about it but also made him a little sad — and even shamed him as he ran to his car in the faculty parking lot or after class when he got caught in a downpour without an umbrella. In moments given to poetic repose, comfortable and dry, he imagined himself the kind of free spirit who would raise his arms to the sky and greet the rainfall as a blessing from the heavens. He felt diminished that he saw it as a nuisance when he was actually in it. Anyway, romanticizing rain-drenched oxen was, he knew by training, a prime example of what literary critics call the "pathetic fallacy," attributing human qualities to animals or nature. A harsh phrase, and one he was not above applying to other aspects of his life in his more morose or cynical moments. A terse knocking on the door corrupted his reverie.

"Your roster assessment is late. I need it. Like, *now*!"

The door swung open, and there stood the department chairperson, Angelo DePonne, a humorless (so far as Padget could tell) bureaucrat whose sole purpose in life seemed to be the orderly transmission of paperwork from faculty to chairperson to dean to God-knows-where after that. Padget had neglected again — he was *always* neglecting — DePonne's emails.

"Sorry, Angelo. I'll turn it around right away."

"Too late for that," he said curtly. "'Right away' was last week, when you got my final reminder."

"Right-o. Sorry. Must have overlooked it amid the rush of pre-semester emails."

"Rush?" he said, his voice rising an octave in indignation. "Yeah, right. Try my job," he said, now fully stepping into Padget's office, his inflamed cheeks and furrowed brow betraying a lifetime of pre-emptive anxiety. "More like Rush-more."

Frequently sad are these attempts at witty wordplay by Chairperson DePonne. And in this case, a bit perplexing as well. He might have been making some sort of comment about having to "rush *more*" than the faculty to ensure the proper functioning of the department. Or perhaps he thought he deserved enshrinement on a stone monument. Given the egos of most academics, you couldn't really tell.

"Rushmore?"

"Don't change the subject. Get me those rosters, *ilicet!*"

When in doubt in academia, just throw around some Latin.

"*Vita brevis est,*" Padget said, bowing slightly. "I shall get to it at my earliest convenience."

DePonne glared at Padget, hiding none of his disdain for the professor's practiced disregard for protocol.

"I'm no fool, Russ."

"Well then, I'll disregard the rumors. Was there anything else?"

DePonne might have erupted right there in Padget's office had someone not interrupted them.

"Doctor Padget? Oh, I'm sorry, I didn't mean to intrude."

Padget looked at DePonne and then back at the visitor. "That's all right. Chairperson DePonne is on his way out. Oops — another rumor," he said, with faux sheepishness.

DePonne scrunched up his face sourly and then brusquely navigated his way past the visitor, undisguised contempt flashing from his eyes, his body shaking mildly with thwarted bureaucratic zeal.

The visitor took this in somewhat sheepishly, hands jammed deep into the pockets of his rumpled corduroy sport coat. He waited for Padget to invite him all the way in.

"Please," the professor finally said, gesturing toward the chair facing his desk. "You must be Monique's friend."

"Augustine Hiatt," he said, extending his hand, fingers lightly splotched in a patchwork of indigo. "Call me Augie."

Padget held his visitor's hand, looked at it quizzically, turning it 45 degrees.

"*Diamine Majestic?*"

Hiatt shook his head.

"*Waterman's Serenity Blue.*"

"Ah."

Padget eased into his ergonomic Naugahyde desk chair.

"Nothing like a good fountain pen ink," he said buoyantly. "You can always tell a fellow enthusiast by the stains on their fingers. It's like a secret signal we flash to other members of the cult."

"I was just re-filling mine this morning." Hiatt flicked his fingers before him like a magician having just made a dove disappear. "Of course, refilling your pen on the bus is not the smartest strategy either."

"Well, I could talk to you all day about fountain pen ink. But I believe there's something more pressing we need to address."

Hiatt bit his lower lip and nodded.

"Paper! So, what do *you* like to write on?"

Hiatt didn't miss a beat.

"Rhodia classic orange. Superb quality, fair price. Their paper has that famous smoothness Rhodia is known for, and that bright orange cover stands out, so you're not likely to forget it and leave it behind you in some coffee shop."

"Hmm. I'm partial to the Clairefontaine Triomphe notepad. Highly absorbent but hardly any show-through. Texture like silk. Glorious."

"That's a bit beyond a grad student's budget," Hiatt said self-consciously. "Well, when I *used to be* a grad student, I mean," he emended.

"Ah, yes. Monique mentioned something about that. I was a little intrigued by some of what she told me."

"I think when you hear the rest, you'll be more than a *little* intrigued," he said, a definite note of indignation coloring his formerly respectful, even shy, conversational manner.

"Well, let's not jump to conclusions."

Hiatt hung his head slightly and mumbled almost to himself. "Yes, yes, of course. Sorry."

"Mr. Hiatt, no need to—"

"Augie."

"Right. Augie, there's no need to apologize. From what Monique told me, you have a right to feel sort of, well…"

"Betrayed?"

"I can see why you might feel that way. But why don't you fill me in, kind of bring me up to speed, and maybe then we can talk about, um, your next move."

Next move? Padget knew he was in no position to help this fellow out, even if he bought into his story. What could he do, anyway? But he had gotten so used to telling students that he could help them — what they usually needed was just someone to untangle a minor bureaucratic snafu — that he might have overplayed his hand here. Ah, what the hell. *Maybe, for a change, I might actually be able to make a difference.* Keep an open mind. Hear him out.

"As I understand it, you were part of a Ph.D. program, and after you completed all of your course work, with only the dissertation left, you were asked to leave."

Hiatt sat cross-legged, fidgeting with his cuffs. Without looking up, he offered an amendment to Padget's narrative.

"Kicked out."

"Excuse me?"

"You said they asked me to leave. That's not the case. They didn't ask. They told me to get out."

"I see."

Muttering as much to himself as in response to Professor Padget, he continued: "Years of research — *really* important research — all for nothing."

"Yes, well, Monique was a bit vague regarding the circumstances of your, well, departure, shall we say." Padget was fibbing. He wanted to hear it for himself.

"It's simple," Hiatt said, perking up. "Jealousy. They were jealous of my work."

Padget nodded, trying to seem neutral, open-minded. He knew well that jealousy fueled a great deal of academic locomotion, and — if he was being honest with himself — it played a role in his own career. Some of his early scholarly output (back when he considered himself to be a productive member of the academy) was the by-product of his resentment of his more successful fellow graduate students. He felt publicly overshadowed by many of the people he had gone through school with, though he secretly continued to feel smarter than they were. Was that so bad? Doesn't a desire to be taken more seriously fuel most intellectual progress? Padget liked to imagine that E=MC2 was Einstein's "fuck you" to some overachieving Type A post-doc fellow, spouting off in the faculty lounge.

But jealousy of a Ph.D. student by a committee of tenured graduate school professors? It just didn't make sense.

"I can appreciate why you might see it that way, but —"

"Professor Padget," Hiatt interrupted, now looking at him directly in the eye, his gaze confident and fixed. "I'm not some naïve, or bitter, grad school washout. What I discovered in my research was real. It was groundbreaking. In fact, it would have been *revolutionary.* And my dissertation advisor couldn't handle that because he had built his reputation on asserting that what I uncovered could not, has not, ever existed."

How to play this? Hiatt asked himself. *Should I indulge the young man? Dismiss him politely? Dig deeper?* The prospect Monique had first brought to his attention was so tantalizing that Padget decided he had to keep going. He knew what this kid was claiming to have found, and that claim, if true, was a goldmine, a legitimate strike, precious pay dirt in a literary prairie turned into a dustbin by the churning and charring machinery of academia.

***

She was her father's daughter. He had always felt it was so. And when the darkness descended on her, James Joyce knew it for what it really was — and not for what the world said it was. He understood that sometimes to truly comprehend things, large things like relationships and war and death and small things like how to match your socks to your shoes or purposely mismatch your socks to your shoes, you sometimes had to go to a different place where a different way of seeing was available. And when you're in that place, the rules are different, so you need to act different or you just might not be granted a vision. But the vision is everything. He knew that, and had gone to such places himself even when the cost was personal loss or embarrassment or the end of a relationship. And when they tell you to behave or stop acting up and follow the rules, they are really telling you that you need to serve some larger purpose, a noble, larger purpose like ensuring the smooth operation of some grand and complex social structure, too complex to be comprehended by uninformed minds that won't collaborate in their own salvation. So when they tell you to serve whatever or whoever is demanding to be served, there is, of course, only one response possible: non serviam! Those might not have been her first words, but they were the first words he remembered telling her to never forget.

He remembered taking her to a café when she was six. They were all there, the four of them, the family raggedly together, listening to the conversations of the travelers and businesspeople and the local working girls and the artists and drunks marking time until happier hours, and the police and the lawbreakers breaking bread and dipping it in olive oil and laughing and sipping coal-black coffee from tiny white cups veined with the years of dark runoff; He remembered how a stranger politely tapped him on his shoulder and said he was a doctor, a local physician, and he couldn't help but notice how the little girl stared so blankly into the distance for so long, oblivious to all that was going on about her. "I'd have that looked into," he said quietly, patting her father on the shoulder. "Something isn't right." And so he worried a little about it because back then when he was broke and still unknown he worried a little about everything but when he got home and asked her what was she staring at she took a piece of foolscap paper from his writing desk and drew an exact replica of the pattern in the wallpaper of the café, wheels within wheels turning round and round, spokes splayed in a non-random repeating pattern that gave the gentle sensation of locomotion even if one was standing still. And as he stared at the drawing that she was making there in their cramped but comfortable home, he felt a stinging sense of remorse for having worried at all about that doctor and his asinine, unsolicited diagnosis.

***

The fluorescent lights overhead, their naked glare unshielded by any kind of plexiglass sheeting, buzzed lightly — though not loudly enough to be noticed by any of the veteran nightside detectives. Even when there wasn't the intermittent squawk of the police scanner, the radio on Mooch's desk perpetually belched a staticky talk radio station (an overnight show about conspiracy theories was his favorite, though he often referred to the show's callers as *sick fucking puppies*). The room was never what could be termed quiet, even in the so-called wee hours. The wooden desk chairs groaned and screeched when the detectives settled in, leaned back, or rolled themselves to the nearest open doughnut box. The frosted glass pane of the detectives' room door, with its 1940s film-noir patina, did little to insulate the space from the constant racket just outside of bellicose drunks, sobbing mothers, junkies freaking out, or media people shouting about their constitutional right to know. Even on its quietest night, the place was cacophonous. So when Sweater asked about Alana's informant at the Footsie, no one heard him. Or if they did, they paid no attention. As Mooch was fond of saying, "I got my own problems." But Sweater was feeling feisty tonight.

"Hey Mooch, the way you're tonguing that Boston Crème, you two should get a room. You want we should all step outside until you're finished?"

"Maybe if you practiced on one of these fucking donuts, you'd actually know what to do with a woman."

"I smell a sexual harassment suit unfolding," said Alana Stamos, stepping into the detectives' room from interrogation.

"Unfold this," Mooch fired back.

"Not tonight, boys, please. I've got a headache," Detective Stamos said, settling into her desk chair and leafing through her top drawer with a concerned look.

"Looking for this?" asked Sweater — technically Detective Fran Ferngull, which is maybe why he didn't mind people calling him by the nickname his penchant for always wearing cardigan sweaters had earned him. ("It's real simple," he explained to Alana her first week on the job when she asked about his moniker. "I need the pockets for my cigarettes. If you keep 'em in your pants pocket, they get crushed. Cigarettes in left pocket, see?" He patted the rectangular bulge reassuringly. *What's in the other pocket?* she had asked him. "Back-up," he said, pulling out another pack. "See? Always ready to go.")

"Yes, as a matter of fact, I am," she said tartly, grabbing the manila folder from him.

"Relax. I'm writing up the warrant request, and I just needed to check the phone records."

"Keep your hands off my stuff, Sweater."

"Phrases Sweater hears every weekend as he cruises the bars, for $200, Alex," Mooch lobbed from his side of the room.

"So, did your mole give a positive I.D.?" he asked.

Detective Stamos paused, bit her lip, and stared at her fellow detective like she really did have a headache.

"He flipped. I just got out of 3B. He changed his story."

"What the fuck? You said he was *money*!"

"He was. He should have been. Somebody got to him. What can I tell you?"

"You can tell me how the hell I'm supposed to get a warrant for Footsie without one fucking credible source to put before Judge Beal."

"Go in there on your knees," Mooch said. "I hear he likes his clerks to assume that position."

Sweater threw up his hands and shot her a perplexed… no, an *annoyed* look.

"No problem," Alana said, as much to herself as her partner on this case. "I've still got an insider. A sure thing. She'll come through. I just need twenty-four hours."

"She fucking *better*," he said, pointing a finger in Detective Stamos' face.

Amid the fairly noisy landscape of that night's Detective Room hustle and bustle, Sweater's stern ultimatum was heard clearly. Even Stanch, who colleagues called The Silent Knight because he never spoke when he didn't have to, chimed in. Well, he whistled.

"Hey, Sweater," Mooch bellowed, his mouth now fully vacant, although there was chocolate all over his fingertips, "this ain't fucking high school. And you ain't the fucking principal. Don't be pointing fingers in here unless you're prepared to lose them." But if Detective Alana Stamos was offended by her colleague's lack of professional etiquette and the affront to her self-esteem, she didn't show it. She got up slowly from her desk and headed for the door.

"Alana, let it slide. He's an ape," Mooch said. "Don't leave on his account."

"I'm going to meet my other Footsie contact," she said, matter-of-factly. "I don't want to be late." Then, glaring at Sweater, she added, "I don't want to get detention." She cupped her fingers in a bye-bye wave to Sweater but then turned her hand around, leaving only the middle finger upright.

"You see that Sweater?" said Mooch. "All that grief you give her, and she says you're still number one in her eyes."

***

"If you don't mind, I'm going to take a few notes." Padget grabbed the legal pad next to his keyboard, uncapped his Platinum Balance medium-nib fountain pen, and wrote at the top of the page, *A. Hiatt story*. "Why don't you give me the big picture, and then we'll go back and fill in any details, if necessary." The "if necessary" was purely a power move, but the young man sitting across from him either didn't notice or, more likely, had simply become inured to the subtle manifestations of superiority practiced daily by the high priests of the academy.

"Big picture? Ok… picture this: instead of holding in your hand a blank legal pad, you're holding an original, brilliant, and funny series of poems — an epic of sorts. About the world's oceans and the sea creatures who call this watery world home. A modernist *Finding Nemo*."

Padget nodded thoughtfully and wrote it all down, though he had no idea who Nemo was or why he needed to be found.

"Go on."

"And when you get to the end of this weird, wonderful work, you see written — in his own hand — the signature of the author. James Joyce."

So Monique wasn't making it up. This young man really *seems* to believe in a lost and totally unknown work by James Joyce.

"Well, um, Augie, that's quite a claim. I'm guessing that your dissertation provides evidence for this pretty incredible assertion?"

Augustine Hiatt held his head in his hands for several seconds and, speaking softly, said simply, "It would have."

The professor still didn't believe the outrageous claim, but he began to believe that this young man sitting before him believed it. It had been a long while since any of Padget's students exhibited this kind of emotional investment in their work. That was true for Padget as well. His frequent disappointment in his students kept him from thinking about his disappointment with his own scholarly work, which had all but ceased. *This kid might be a kook, but he really cares. Stay on this ride a little longer.*

Padget cleared his throat. "Have you anything with you that I could take a look at?"

"Well, just notes. I don't have the originals of the lost work. I never possessed the pages, in fact."

"You never possessed them? Then how do you—"

"I had to photocopy the work. But I saw it, held it in my hands briefly. I can show you the copies. I think I have them in here, somewhere. . . ." He began digging through his backpack, pulling out various file folders as well as a crumpled brown bag lunch, a water bottle, and a huge jangly key ring.

"Mr. Hiatt, don't worry. You don't—"

"Augie, remember?"

"Yes, I remember. You needn't upend all of your belongings. I was just curious."

"I must have left them at home. I'll bring them to you."

"Ok, that will be fine," Padget said, leaning back in his chair and making collapsible finger tents. "I'm wondering, Augie, if you can just share with me a little bit about the lost work."

"Sure," he said, beginning to cram all the items that had been spilled onto Padget's desk back into his rucksack. "And don't worry. It's not a lost work. I know right where it is. I have a place in my apartment, a kind of secret nook behind a bookcase where I keep a full set of the manuscript."

"This is beginning to sound like a mystery novel," Padget joked.

"Yeah — only I've solved the mystery. I know who the killer is: R. Lancaster Zale, my dissertation advisor. He killed my career."

Padget recognized the name. Anyone who ever studied modern literature seriously knew who Zale was. Once upon a time, Zale was one of the undisputed titans of Joyce scholarship, though Padget couldn't recall hearing or reading much from him lately.

"Monique told me you could help me," Hiatt continued, looking equal parts pathetic and endearing. "She said her Joyce class with you was the best class she ever had. If someone like you were to look at the material, maybe my dissertation committee—"

"Whoa, Mr. Hiatt. It's not likely I could do anything to change their mind, even if I... well..."

"Believed me?"

No use pretending.

"Yes. Even if I believed you."

Hiatt got up, grabbed his backpack, and opened the door.

"When I show you what I have, you *will.*"

As he stepped into the hallway to leave, a clap of thunder rattled Padget's office windows. *That's right — Joyce was afraid of thunder.* A definite sign, but as obscure in its meaning as anything Joyce himself ever wrote.

***

Footsie — which derived its name from the acronym for the London Stock Market (FTSE: *Financial Times Stock Exchange*) was a watering hole on the Jersey side of the Hudson River just across from Manhattan that catered to traders in the financial district whose shifts coincided with the European business day, which ended roughly around noon, stateside. Still wired, these masters of the universe often needed a place to unwind before heading home to log in and find out whether their brothers and sisters at the NYSE were extending FTSE's gains — or losses. The bar's happy hour was from noon until 1 p.m., and by 3 p.m., the place was deserted. The owner, a British expat, said he liked to keep "respectable English hours" and claimed he was home, asleep, by the height of the local rush hour.

About a month ago, Detective Alana Stamos, while working on another case, got a tip that the owner of Footsie's was catering to clients who traded more than stocks. The bar had allegedly become the focal point of a highly illegal (and nauseatingly immoral) sex-for-green-card operation. Asian women — some in their late teens — were coming to the New York area ostensibly to work as domestic help for the well-heeled in the bedroom communities surrounding Manhattan. In reality, the "clients" looking for nannies were phantoms. They didn't exist — except on paper. Actually, they *did* exist, but they never knew they were in the market for nannies. Brendan Cleese, Footsie's owner, pulled their names from the client lists of some of his stock-selling patrons (who were in on the scam). The operation was simple. Cleese contacted the Asian authorities on behalf of these phantom clients, filed the necessary paperwork to request a temporary work visa, arranged for the women's transportation here, but when they arrived, there were no domestic help jobs, just a cheap motel in Jersey where these newly imported, broke, and desperate women became sex workers, restoring the flaccid spirits of Footsies stressed-out clientele. Living in "safe houses" that were little more than squalid brothels, they could spend months, or years, waiting for their green cards to come through. Many of the women did manage to escape, though none had yet filed police reports for fear of deportation or arrest. Caught between a rock and hard time, they remained silent and either went along with Cleese's grisly ultimatum or drifted into the landscape of the city's lost and downtrodden shadow people.

Alana Stamos thought she had convinced an insider, a stock trader named Les Greider, who provided his client list for the scheme, to testify against Cleese. She'd charmed and persuaded Greider — or so she thought — over the last several weeks to testify against Cleese in exchange for immunity from prosecution. She also assured him he'd be able to keep his Series 7 license and remain in the stock trading business. And just when he was set to give his deposition, he got cold feet, clammed up, and said he didn't know anything about any green card operation.

Stamos' other "sure thing"– a woman who escaped from the "safe house" and was willing to testify — also failed to keep her appointment that night. So the detective found herself at 2 a.m. at an all-night diner called the Steampot with little appetite and nothing to bring back to the squad room — like, say, a witness who might help make the case. Rather than face Sweater's wrath, she ordered a cup of tea (which she used to wash down three aspirin), took out the tattered paperback she always kept in her purse (*Patti Smith: The Complete Lyrics*) and decided not to return for the rest of her shift. Maybe tomorrow, something would happen to turn the case around. Fated to mere hope, she swirled a teaspoon of honey in the warm amber liquid, her tea cup a vortex of sweet deliverance.

Well, the case turned around the next day. Alana would hear about it almost as soon as she clocked in at the precinct the following night. But that was still an hour away. Working the night shift for the last several years had given her a different perspective on daily human activity. She'd finally made the transition to what long-time night-shift workers call "shadowing," the innate and certain sense that the nighttime represents normalcy, the daytime a fierce and brightly lit interruption to our normal state of being. At some point, she simply stopped thinking of the typical 9-5 workday as the workday at all, but rather a prelude to the dusky charms of the nocturnal world. "You gotta think like a cockroach," Mooch had once told her. "Scurry when you see the light. Embrace the darkness." Wasn't there a Ramones song about living like a cockroach? Or was that the Sex Pistols? Well, she'd crack that mystery when she got back into her car (The Sex Pistols were in heavy rotation in her CD player). Her thoughts drifted from vermin and punk bands ("No difference between them that I can see," she imagined Mooch saying in her head, bringing a smile to her lips) to focusing on the task at hand: picking up a cranberry and walnut batard at Swirls, a local bakery and bistro run by a lesbian couple that Alana met after they had been beaten up by a couple of inebriated heterosexuals out for a night of drinking and skull-bashing. Ever since she had worked the case, she felt compelled to support them somehow, so even though it was out of her way, she had become a regular customer there, and besides, the batard was *so* worth the trip. Unfortunately, she got there just at 6 p.m. as the place was closing, and although they always let her in — the owners were forever grateful for her assistance in tracking down the Neanderthals that had tried to divorce them from their fully-functioning skeletal system and never seemed to blame her for the D.A.'s decision to dismiss the case due to lack of corroborating evidence — the batards were long gone. She had to settle for a half-dozen boysenberry scones and a chai latte (or what Mooch called, in one of his less enlightened moments, "fag coffee.") Still, she left there feeling pretty good, heading to her car as the waning shafts of sunlight pierced the industrial spew of northern New Jersey, a painterly sky filled with purple and burnt orange and dusty rose, the smoldering atmospheric backwash of the Garden State's smokestack plumage.

She got to the precinct just in time to see a couple of uniforms struggling to escort a shirtless, overweight man, late 30s, she estimated, with what appeared to be bloodstains on his jeans and a neck wrapped with a cobra tattoo. "Fucking slut!" he yelled as he saw her, the two young cops wrestling with him on the way to a police cruiser no doubt headed to the municipal lockup. Before she could take his comment personally, he screamed more epithets as he wheedled and wended his way towards his one-way ride downtown. "Goddamned cunt!" he screamed. "You think I'm finished with her? She's gonna fucking *pay*." He didn't seem to be too concerned about that part of the Miranda warning about how what you say can be used against you in a court of law. And that's when it hit her: *Kafka!* She couldn't remember the name of the story about the cockroach, but she remembered it was a Franz Kafka story, not a Sex Pistols song. Thoughts of cockroaches were still in her head when she got to her desk and found a one-word Post-It note on her phone: "Millner."

She laughed to herself in a "Could this night possibly get off to a worse start?" sort of way and then headed down the hall to Captain Tate Millner's office. None of the other nightside detectives seemed to have checked in, or if they did, they were already dispatched to their respective urban night-time horror shows. She saw that Mooch's desktop calendar was smeared with what looked like mustard, or perhaps he'd killed a bug and left its smeared remains there as a warning to other impertinent insects. *Why am I thinking about bugs tonight?* she wondered.

Captain Millner's office was a grim place — not just because Millner himself seemed more often like a prisoner than someone who sends people to prison. It was an old story with Millner, and with lots of cops who made their way up the ranks from beat cop to detective to precinct captain — and then no further. What once was a burning desire to make the world safer, better, was replaced over the countless long nights on stakeout, endless trials made more so by defense attorneys piling on time-wasting motion after motion, and the paperwork hydra of duty rosters, monthly reports, requisitions, and personnel transfer requests. After a while, it all seemed part of some unfolding, improvised Samuel Beckett play — *Waiting for Justice* — while the broader world smiled daggers and went about its daily grind at the whetstone of perpetual motion. Nothing to be done.

No, what made the Captain's office so dreary-seeming was more literal: dozens of framed pictures that covered the walls, each of them a still image captured from the famous Zapruder film, the first-hand video account of President John F. Kennedy's assassination. Millner's grandfather was one of the secret service men assigned that day to protect the president, and according to several of the Captain's former drinking buddies (though he quit drinking just before getting assigned to his current position at the precinct, never so much as setting foot in a bar since his reformation, all praise to God in the mercy he shows to drunks — though Alana thought the guy always looked like he could really use a drink) his grandfather *swore* there was a second shooter. Millner kept the images on his wall in the hope that maybe he'd see something that might finally crack the case. They were also grim reminders that no matter how well a cop did his or her job, sometimes mayhem wins. And at this stage in his career, Millner seemed resigned to managing the mayhem rather than trying to combat it.

When Detective Alana Stamos knocked on his door, she felt only an abstract leaden compulsion, not any particular, localized dread. Millner often summoned cops to his office, sometimes seeming to forget why he had called them there in the first place, often telling them stories about his days at the academy, or maybe talking about how the country began going to hell, more or less beginning its descent November 22, 1963. She certainly didn't see what was coming — what Mooch would later call "the old switcheroo."

"Captain Millner?"

He waved her in while cradling the phone under his fleshy cheek, gesturing toward the chair facing his desk. All the furniture in the room looked like it had come from a raid on a rowdy Amish roadhouse, plain wood, well-made and simple in design but beaten up, scuffed, scarred in the way that angry drunks regularly disfigure once-fine things.

Millner grunted once or twice into the phone and then hung up. He looked at her, tilting his head as if trying to figure something out, and then he leaned back and opened his top desk drawer.

"I've been looking at Ferngull's report on the Footsie investigation," he began, using the name no one else used for Sweater.

"I'm intending to go back there tomorrow, when it's open, to do a bit more digging," she said, cutting off what she sensed was a coming re-hash of her failure to secure reliable testimony.

"No need," he said, throwing the file on his desk. "It's over."

"The investigation? You're shutting it down?"

"No, Stamos. The bar. It's over. Closed down. We sent a black-and-white over earlier today, and the place is cleaned out. Not so much as a shot glass left. An empty room, no forwarding address, no sign on the door. They must have gotten nervous with all the attention we were giving their patrons. Cleese might be halfway to Mexico by now. If that was his real name."

Stamos was stunned. Months of work setting up traps, and now the rabbit has run away.

"It's not entirely your fault," he said, in a failed attempt to assuage her disappointment. "We probably should have put the place under surveillance. Then again, without a warrant, it would have been a little ticklish."

Ticklish. Detective Alana Stamos thought of all the young women forced into sexual servitude, women whose stories she hoped to tell as a first step toward getting their lives restored. Now, they're on their own. *If Sweater so much as raises his eyebrow at me for any of this, I swear to God I'm going to unload on him.* Such petty after-the-fact bickering would do nothing to improve a truly rotten turn of events. But if Detective Alana Stamos thought the collapse of her case against Footsie was going to be the low point of her night, she was as wrong as those who believe Lee Harvey Oswald acted alone.

***

"Hi, Augie. This is Reyna at Tongue-in-Cheek. We need additional rewrites. I emailed you the pages. Please get them back by the end of the week. Devlin said to tell you he's shooting Monday — either the movie or the writer. He said he didn't care which. Better hurry on those pages."

Augustine Hiatt's urgent voice mail message from his employer barely seemed to register as he continued smearing peanut butter on his rye toast in what appeared to be a leisurely, almost random way, though he was actually making little swirls, like Vincent Van Gogh's famous painting *Starry Night*. In fact, Augie was thinking of the first time he ever saw that painting, on a field trip to New York in junior high, shortly before he decided to become a writer. Whenever he felt himself being pulled off the path, he thought of Van Gogh and the struggles he went through to remain true to his artistic vision. Poverty, self-doubt, madness — he'd faced it all but remained committed to his art. *Let them scoff*, he thought, but I'm staying true to *my* vision. And it's true: he *was* a writer — something he hadn't been able to say since he'd stopped work on his dissertation. And the fact that he was now writing scripts for X-rated films was beside the point. The porn industry might be sordid and debauched, but it paid decently, and Augie was surprised how easily a writer with a genuine facility for words (and a strong stomach) could move up in the adult movie business. He had already been given his first solo assignment, a 12-minute cock raiser (in the legitimate theatre, they call them "curtain raisers") titled *Pants De Leon and the Fountain of Youth*, a costume drama (well, for the first couple of minutes) about a swashbuckling explorer (really just a hunky gardener) and his well-heeled employer's 19-year-old heiress daughter (a buxom blonde addicted to nude sunbathing.) Twelve minutes of shooting meant six pages of dialogue, something he could dash off with little thought. But Augie put more than a little thought into his scripts. He figured he might as well raise a few IQs as well as a few, um, curtains. And now, he was also re-writing other writers' scripts — or what was called in the porn trade "straddling." Bobby Devlin, the executive producer for Tongue-in-Cheek, might not have professed a great deal of love for writers, but the first two checks cleared and the work kept coming, so Augie was grateful. It didn't take the sting out of what happened with his dissertation committee, but it gave him something to grab onto. He badly needed a distraction, and he found that thrusting himself into his new job helped him deal with his lingering anger. And who knows? Maybe this Padget guy would actually help him fix his academic career.

He finished his sandwich and guzzled a warm can of ginger ale from his backpack. He logged onto his laptop and downloaded the pages Reyna had sent, a short scene leading up to a gang-bang in a film about an aspiring actress who finally makes her long-awaited debut, titled *Rhonda's Big Opening*. There were a few other pages from a few other works-in-progress. Run-of-the-mill stuff. Nothing spectacular. Not yet, anyway — but Augie would work his magic. His fingers hovered over his laptop's backlit keyboard.

"Porn lovers, prepare to be blown away!" he said, typing away like someone in the throes of an all-consuming passion. But only a few miles away, someone was also typing with vehemence — a letter Augie would find waiting for him the next time he showed up at Tongue-in-Cheek.

***

It was an odd place to prepare for the rapture. From the outside, the century-old building retained its utilitarian spirit, a former tool and die factory that had been converted into loft and office space about five years ago. Its industrial, blue-collar character conveyed the history of the town, a once-upon-a-time lunch-bucket suburb of New York City on the Hudson River, home now to an increasingly affluent corps of well-dressed and well-spoken renovators and speculators, a gaggle of genteel gentrifiers scouring the prized empty spaces that once resounded with the steady hammering of the drill press and keypunch. On the third floor (Todd and Beth Lawson both understood that three *is* a magic number), just at the end of the hallway with its creaky floorboards and its unforgiving fluorescence, the smell of sawdust and silica grease still lingering in the air ducts, was an office with no identification on the door, just a simple cross charred into the fabric of the mahogany door with a homemade word-burning kit. It looked at first glance more like a flaw in the woodgrain than a deliberate, secret signal to pilgrims seeking salvation. Yet those who worked behind the door knew — they just *did* — that the same guiding hand of providence that brought seekers to the building would usher them along to the smear of burnt cross emblazoned on the door, a silent clarion call to the good and the just. Although (God forgive them!) Todd and Beth would likely not have heard someone knocking upon the door that particular morning, absorbed as they were in the serious work before them, the repetition of a monthly ritual that demanded Solomonic concentration.

Todd was sitting behind a computer desk. His sister Beth was on a small Persian rug on the floor, sorting through a pile of newspapers, press releases, handwritten letters sent in by their followers, movie posters, and weekly news and celebrity magazines. Each of these items had already been gone through by at least one of the board members of Friend to Man in the past 30 days, which explained the many annotations, underlines, circles, and multi-colored highlights which decorated many of the pages.

"Let the separation begin," Todd said, cracking his knuckles, fingers perched above the keyboard like a concert pianist awaiting the conductor's downbeat.

"Ok, let's see who's going to hell this month," his sister said.

And so began the monthly updating of their "Lost and Found-Out" list, a "who's who" of sinners and soul-corrupters in the public sphere, people who were actively working to undermine the righteousness of the Lord. Friend to Man scoured these written records for evidence of resistance to the Good News; people who had lost their way and, like Satan in the Garden of Eden, were now tempting others to abandon the straight and narrow path. These included politicians who sponsored or supported anti-God legislation on topics like abortion or gay marriage, criminals who had been sentenced for crimes like child molestation or prostitution, celebrities who appeared in movies that mocked fundamentalism, businesses that advertised in publications that included photographs of people in little or no clothing (sometimes not even wearing fig leaves!), and publishing companies that were bringing out books that might undermine all manner of public decency. It was quite an exhausting task, and, second only to their regular filming schedule for their online video channel, they believed it was one of their most important functions. After making these monthly lists, Todd would choose a handful of malefactors and write letters to them, telling him they were on to him and urging the sinner to repent. These weren't threats, exactly — merely revelations of the threat that awaited the unrepentant. Purely coincidentally, Friend to Man would say (and *had* said, through the law firm they kept on retainer) that they had nothing at all to do with the untimely death of a few of the recipients of their private shaming campaign.

"People who believe in ultimate judgment don't need to hasten death in this realm," Todd had said to investigators during one of his interrogations. His sister put it slightly more enigmatically during her interview with authorities: "God kills."

There they sat, sifting through the monthly cultural discourse for clues to the next anti-Christ — or at least some serial cheaters, blasphemers, and onanists. That was how they originally came across Augustine Hiatt. One of the devoted eyes and ears of Friend to Man had copied out the credits for the latest Tongue-in-Cheek release and mailed it in, and Beth had plucked it from the pile. Todd didn't recognize the name as a repeat offender, so he fired off one of his usual scare-em-straight letters (they believed first-time offenders were more susceptible to the saving grace of Jesus than the hardened reprobate). All of this sifting and letter writing happened amid a near-deafening wave of evangelical rock blasting from a boom box on top of Friend to Man's filing cabinets, something that got their adrenaline flowing and their righteous indignation firing. As the music played, Beth's hands danced through the heaps of newspapers, magazines, letters, photocopies, and printed material while Todd resembled a bobble-headed toy dog on the dashboard of some van speeding down the turnpike, nodding and typing in time with the pulsating music. Today's musical rapture was being provided by a far-right Christian band called The Pierced Hand, a group of former drug addicts who met in a rehab program run by a fervent evangelical named Rubin Claudel, a Haitian immigrant who found Jesus after almost dying of mercury poisoning after getting shanked in a prison bathroom by a Nazi with a sharpened rectal thermometer.

Beth does the scouring, Todd the intimidating. There is no vetting to see if the information Beth is relying on to single out malefactors is accurate. There is no time; souls are at stake. The music blasts, Beth reads, scowls, shakes her head, and elevates offending candidates to Todd's desk. He grabs the document and begins pounding out his cease-and-desist letter according to a format he's refined over the many months of threatening by mail: keep it short, keep it vague, keep it Christian. Don't name call, don't directly threaten, and don't explain. Instead, make an impression and let the Lord work on the hearts of the recipient. This goes on most of the afternoon, and after a few hours, both Beth and Todd are exhausted. Saving souls is *such hard work!* Once the letters are written, addressed, and stamped, brother and sister move on to the second phase of their session's work: strengthening their own resolve.

Beth and Todd realize that being a Christian warrior requires no less a commitment today than it did when the work was done on horseback or in the dungeon. And they are *committed.* So what happens next might seem shocking only to those who did not fully appreciate the depth of their devotion to Christ.

Beth usually starts. She turns off the Christian rock and flips over to a smooth jazz station on the radio. She dims the lights, then removes her blouse, ankle-length skirt, slip, bra, and panties. And then Todd follows, un-suiting: he removes his jacket, tie, shirt, pants, and underwear. They face each other naked, a modern Adam and Eve, devout and unashamed. What happens next varies from month to month, but the point is always to drive each other as deeply into physical temptation as it's possible to go and still be able to resist. And, well, *sometimes it's pretty hard.* But what they do — what they tell themselves they're doing — is create a safe, supportive space in which to experience the limits of human lust. Weak-willed people give in *so easily* to the pleasures of the flesh. Beth and Todd do not. At least, they haven't yet.

Some rules: touching is allowed. In fact, it's usually necessary. How else to drive one to the absolute limits of carnal frenzy? Remember: *they do this to each other because they love the Lord.* So, for instance, today's session: Beth walks over to Todd's desk and opens the bottom drawer, pulling out a bottle of baby lotion. She squirts a squib on her palm and then walks slowly toward her brother. He stands there, expectant but flaccid. She traces a finger from the middle of his chest down to his stomach, and then slowly and deliberately lower, into the nether regions, an area they both call "Satan's playground," culminating at the junction of his lower torso and his penile shaft, which has now begin to swell just a wee bit. Rubbing up against him teasingly, her breasts forcefully grazing his upper body, she grabs his penis firmly and begins moving her hand back and forth, slowly at first, and then with more intention. The *Bible* speaks of all manner of temptation — hunger, greed, sexual appetite. Jesus himself survived 40 days in the desert, the victim of the devil's cruelly clever attempts to cleave him from his heavenly father. But Jesus didn't bite. Beth, however, does. She takes her brother's earlobe in her teeth and bites just a bit harder than either of them expected. Continuing to stroke him like some piston-operated fabricating machine that operated in this same office space almost a century ago, she whispers seductively, "You know you want to come. Do it. *DO IT!*" Her grip tightens, her pace quickens, and she begins moaning, "Yes! Yes! *YES!*" Well, no matter what you think of Todd's spiritual leanings, you've got to really admire his resolve. He's gone just about as far as someone in his position can go, and just when he's about to achieve salvation from his desire, he screams out, "NO!" And pulls her hand away from his throbbing member. This is not what he really wants to do, it should be noted, but it's what he *needs* to do to understand human weakness. It will make him a better person, a better Christian, and a stronger vehicle to carry forth their battle. He stands there now, panting, hands curled so tightly into fists that his fingernails are cutting into the skin of his palms, the stigmata of sexual denial, the half-moon indentations a fleshy sign of his resolve. His sister wipes her hand off on a paper towel and begins dressing wordlessly, her demeanor all business, only the slightest hint of a smile deforming her stoical countenance, a barely-visible acknowledgment of the good she's doing to advance the salvation of all mankind, one aborted hand job at a time.

***

Dear Heathen,

Because He is a merciful Lord, this is a warning. If you do not repent of your wickedness, thou shall be smitten with the flaming sword of the Lord's wrath. Do not tarry in your expiation, for the end may well be nigh. The filth you spew is an abomination to Almighty God, and it will not abide. The demon is deft, but the Kingdom of God is awesome. Fear thou its awesomeness.

Friend to Man

***

"So, what is this, a joke?" Augie asked Reyna when he dropped off the rewrites. She grabbed the letter, knuckled up her reading classes from the end of her nose, and shook her head.

"Nothing funny about those people. They're scary, hon. You better be careful."

"What are you talking about. Who is this 'Friend to Man'?"

"Maybe Bobby should tell you."

"Tell me what?"

"It's just he knows them better. He had a... well, an encounter with them once."

"Them?"

Reyna took off her glasses and scooched her chair forward, placing her hand on Augie's knee in a motherly sort of way.

"It's a Christian cult. They're crazy. They think they've been appointed to weed out the un-righteous in preparation for the rapture. They've even got a social media channel which they use to help spread the word. It's got all these amateur videos, some kind of surreal Christian Punch and Judy stuff, costumes, puppets, silly songs. But don't let the kiddie-show vibe fool you. They're dealing in some pretty dark imagery, and they're psychotic enough to do something dangerous."

"Dangerous... like, what? Plant a bomb or something?" he said, laughing nervously.

Reyna nodded.

"You're kidding."

She shook her head.

"How did they get my name?"

"Probably from the new release — *Good Vibrations*. You're listed as the writer. They must have got your name from the credits."

"What kind of evangelical nut watches porn?" Augie asked. *And what kind of porn viewer watches the credits?*

"These people do. They're one of our biggest customers." Bobby's got a drawer full of letters from them. So do most of the talent we use. The thing is, four or five of our actors and crew have disappeared or died under mysterious circumstances in the last few years. Personally, I think it's these nut jobs and their flaming sword that's responsible. But the police have never been able to pin it on them. But still, better watch yourself."

"Christ Almighty."

Reyna nodded again; her head slightly cocked. "Exactly."

***

Diary extract: Dr. Charles Hastings, consulting physician, St. Elizabeth's Hospital. Northampton, UK:

...and yet I can't help but feel the pangs of remorse at the consequence of my decision to concur. The patient, Lucia Joyce, has been recommended for involuntary commitment by no less than the eminent Dr. Jung, as well as Staffordshire and [name blotted out], but my own examination revealed a self-aware, if troubled, woman. Her tendency toward violence, and the reported instability of her moods, are compelling but not, I would argue, conclusive. After the formal examination, during which she gave mostly rote answers to questions she seemed bored by, I put down my pad and spoke to her. And for those moments, she seemed as lucid as anyone, impassioned even. I asked her about dancing (under "occupation," in her admittance form, someone had written "dancer"), and but for my protestations, I believe she would have spun about right there and then. Maybe I should have let her. I can't help but wonder what effect this incarceration might have on her creative impulses. I sincerely hope her stay will be brief, though I fear she's now likely to be the guest of Dr. Staffordshire & Co. for some time....

***

The subject of today's lecture was Ezra Pound, and the class seemed even more bored than usual.

No one reads Ezra Pound anymore, Padget realized — in fact, almost nobody read Ezra Pound even when he was *alive.* He'd become a footnote to literary history, long ago washed away by the tidal surge of contemporary pop culture. But Ezra Pound was *important* — at least to Russell Padget, who was never as bothered as other readers by Pound's fascism and antisemitism. *It's the art that matters,* he told himself. He knew such a view was sharply at odds with the current intellectual climate, but if he let contemporary realities intrude in his classroom, he'd have almost nothing to talk about. Many years ago, during a particularly grueling semester, he could feel something happening, something inside the classroom and something inside himself. He knew that his awareness of current pop culture, the flotsam and jetsam that washed across the beachhead of millennial knowledge, was growing as unfathomable as a fading lighthouse beacon to a storm-tossed ship at sea. He knew he was fated to understand less and less of their world, and they were just as likely to know — or care — less and less about the things of his world, the things he cared deeply about. This is not a new revelation, this passing of the generations heading in different directions. It's the story of wisdom taking form across time. But it was new to Russell Padget, and rather than simply accept with a shrug the inevitability of these generational ice floes drifting past each other, he convinced himself that the knowledge he possessed was better, more important, and thus more *necessary* than the knowledge his young charges brought into the classroom. So like a French language teacher who bans all traces of English so as to force their students to live completely in a Francophilic world (at least for a little while), he stopped explaining and translating all of his allusions to the classical literature, painting, music, and history that meant so much to him and instead he required his students to write down every reference he made to every thinker or historical moment that predated his class's sphere of knowledge.

"If you wish to pass this course, you must keep an accurate record of the names and events I refer to in my lectures. Failure to be comprehensive will result in a comprehensive failure of the course."

So for that one semester, he required his students to come to his office once a week and recite the names of all the cultural allusions he had dropped in the course of his previous week's lectures. Students hated it, and many simply chose not to do so, but a handful tried to keep up faithfully. Padget would occasionally interrupt his recitation of these arcane allusions and ask the students to say something *about* the thing they had written down. If they couldn't, he'd assign a one-page essay on the subject (*"Two hundred and fifty words on Charlie Chaplin, due on Monday morning."*). It was maddening for the students, a never-ending always-shifting lexicon of western civilization that was too random to be meaningful. But Padget became convinced that students really needed this information, that it would benefit them in ways tangible and intangible. In the course of this somewhat unorthodox approach to the teaching of English literature (or what some of his colleagues would have simply and rightly called it: *showing off*), what was really happening was a paradigm shift in the way he saw his students. No longer were he and they mutual "questers after truth," as he used to tell his students at the beginning of his teaching career, but rather they had become warden and prisoners. He alone held the keys to their freedom, he believed, and he wasn't about to allow them a lifetime of incarceration in the confining world of their cell phones. He saw his efforts as holding forth the path of intellectual freedom and power. The word got around that Padget was being a first-class prick, and as a result, his enrollments declined the next semester, enough to get even his attention. So he abandoned the requirement, but he never gave up on the belief, and as a result of this mid-career epiphany, he continued to hold his students in modest contempt for their ignorance and their unwillingness to eradicate it. *Look at all the things they are missing!* One student, who had seemed promising and kept the weekly appointment in Padget's office for the first six weeks, accidentally left her notebook of allusions in his office. Padget thought he'd give the student the notebook back when he next saw her in class, but she never returned. He kept it in the top drawer of his desk and occasionally leafed through it to remind himself of how much his students didn't know. These were the entries just for Week Six (the week that apparently pushed the student off the metaphorical ledge):

Bela Lugosi
The Trail of Tears
Cicero
The Pieta

Miles Davis
The Rape of the Lock
Fanny Burney
German Expressionism
Iago
Frida Kahlo
Seabiscuit
The Great Vowel Shift
Cincinnatus
Jim Thorpe
Martha Graham
Topo Gigio

He was leafing through the list when Augie Hiatt knocked on his door. This time, he didn't wait to be invited in. Instead, he stuck his head in confidently and asked, "Anybody wanna read a brand-new work by James Joyce?"

Padget sat there like a student, but unlike *his* students, he was absolutely captivated by the story he was hearing, though he tried not to show it. And Hiatt unfurled his story like the professor he wanted to be.

"As you know, Joyce once told a friend of his, after the grueling seventeen years of working on *Finnegans Wake*, he wanted to write something simple. And he said it would be about the sea." Padget remembered reading that somewhere, and he nodded as if he could recall it clearly. "True to his word, he did. It's called *Archimedes at the Gear Fair*, and it's a poetic mini-epic about the development of life in the sea, right up to the time the first sea creature walked up onto the land."

"Archimedes — as in the ancient Greek mathematician?"

"Yep — the inventor of cogwheel gears. Except in Joyce's story, he's a catfish."

"A catfish."

"Yes. The story is playful and quite simple — as befits simple creatures. *Archimedes at the Gear Fair* is entirely in rhyme, full of Joycean wordplay and lots of silly and wondrous adventures."

"What about the title? That doesn't seem so simple. It's rather a mouthful."

"The 'gear fair' is Joyce's term for the carnival of life that was evolving in the sea, in essence creating the gears that would drive human existence. And 'gear fair' is an anagram for 'farraige.'"

Padget cocked his head.

"'Farraige' is the ancient Irish word for 'sea.' *Finnegans Wake* ends with the sea. So it was the next logical place to explore. And with Joyce's eye problems, he wished to move from an inventory of the visible world to a fantasia on a hidden, unseen world."

Padget was intrigued, but his practiced sense of academic resistance to any idea not his own still kicked in.

"Let's assume, Mr. Hiatt, that you are correct. How is it that this work has escaped detection for eighty years?"

"Scholars have been looking closely at Joyce's work and the places he lived for decades. But where he really lived for the last few years of his life wasn't in Trieste or Zurich, where scholars have focused their research."

"Actually, it was."

"No. Where Joyce lived during those final, turbulent years was in the clinics and sanatoriums where his daughter Lucia was institutionalized. Not physically, no, but he spent his days thinking about her, worrying about what would happen next, contacting doctors, and writing her letters. *That's* where he lived," he said, pulling out a sheaf of papers filled with tiny scrawls in a hand that Padget recognized from his work many years ago in graduate school. "And that's where I found *this.*"

***

"It's my responsibility to make sure our resources are allocated properly," Captain Millner said to Detective Alana Stamos, the unseen weight of obligation bearing down on his words like a compression brace on a misaligned vertebrate. *This is one of those times when he looks like he could really use a drink,* she thought.

"Yes, of course," she said, a thin knife blade of uncertainty jabbing at her stomach. Am I about to be fired? Fired for one fuck-up? She glanced up and noticed again all of the framed stills from the Zapruder film, circling her in dizzying inescapability. Whoever allowed JFK to ride in that convertible through Dealey Plaza really fucked up. She wondered if that person was fired for his or her lapse in judgment.

"Let me cut to the chase. You've done a fine job in general investigations, but the administration thinks you should be re-assigned to HCU. So that's where you'll be going, starting next week."

Hate Crimes Unit. It wasn't a firing or even a demotion, but the knife blade twisted and turned just the same. It had taken her most of the past couple of years to get over some of what she encountered during her last stint on the hate crimes unit. Her time on the HCU was mentally exhausting, a daily encounter with the worst of humanity's intentions. General Investigations, her current assignment, was depleting in its own way, but it had a greater variety of cases and even the occasional happy ending. HCU was psychic darkness. And to make matters worse, it was a daylight assignment: 9-5. Ugh.

"Sir, I've finally gotten used to working nights. Maybe if you asked one of the other nightside detectives..."

"Those guys? Who are you thinking of? You want foul-mouthed Mooch to hold the hand of some transgender teen who just got beat up to within an inch of his life? You think the emotionally volatile Sweater is the guy to comfort an Indian mother whose son was just shot at for target practice by some white supremacist? Or how about Stanch — he never says the wrong thing. In fact, *he never says a fucking word*. His monk act would be a big hit at the press conference after a gay bar firebombing. Truth is, Stamos, I got no one else to send, and the mayor is busting my balls to beef up the HCU. Those are the cases that get the most attention, and they need someone who knows the terrain. That's you. You do empathy better than anybody else around here."

He talked about empathy like it was a foreign language, a skill to be employed only by trained specialists under specific operating parameters. And clearly, Captain Millner was incapable of empathizing with *her*. She was going to renew her protests, but he quickly changed the subject back to the JFK assassination — a sure sign that further dialogue was unnecessary and unwelcome. "You know, speaking of hate crimes, Oswald must have really hated Kennedy, doncha think? I mean, to shoot a guy *that* handsome..." He shook his head, and his voice trailed off, his eyes darting around the room, blinking back sadness and a little bit of awe.

***

If someone was wholly unfamiliar with this particular strain of performance-based Christian zealotry, what was happening on the video monitor — and would soon be available for consumption throughout the world on a popular video-sharing website — might seem incoherent, even twisted. But, God be praised; it was all for *His* glorification! The whole point was to *disorient*, to expose reality as a mere facade, to present symbols and images that spoke to a deeper and more profound truth. So here's the scene: it's the middle of a workday, and in a nondescript coffee shop sit an array of people dressed mostly in business attire. But look more closely. Something's a little bit... off. *Exhibit A*: that businessman sitting there by himself: he's not texting, see? He's furiously turning the knobs of an old-school creative toy known as an Etch-a-Sketch and laughing to himself, mouthing the words, "Hall of Fame, baby!" over and over. *Exhibit B*: The woman with the horn-rimmed reading glasses and the faux-leather satchel with a yellow legal pad jutting out one of its pockets isn't scrolling through her email. No, she's stirring a bowl of flour and water with her hands. Soon she'll be tearing bacon-shaped strips of newsprint from her copy of the *Wall Street Journal* and submersing them in the mixture, squeezing out the excess between her fingers and applying them directly to her waiter, standing patiently at her table. She'll cover him in paper mache strips as the glutinous solution trickles down gloopily from the tip of his manicured bangs onto his gold lame bullfighter's outfit. *Exhibit C*: Just barely visible in the corner of the frame is a tow-headed toddler, likely no more than three years old, in a tuxedo and lasagna-noodle cummerbund feeding tapioca pudding with a fork to an elderly woman dressed in a leopard-skin loincloth, her wrinkled and liver-spotted flesh spilling injudiciously over the taut seams. Music is playing in the background: an all-banjo ensemble's rendition of Richard Wagner's "Ride of The Valkyries."

Now things get a little weird: Entering from the ladies' restroom, riding a tricycle, is a middle-aged man, mustachioed, wearing a head-to-toe white fleece Easter bunny outfit. He churns the pedals furiously, and awkwardly rams into the table of the woman paper mache-ing her waiter, and then the man contorting the knobs of the Etch-a-Sketch, and then finally into a couple that's sipping tea from two crude wooden chalices, the tea tags hanging limply from the tea bags steeping in the brew as they gaze into each other's eyes and each blink out "Love *is*" in Morse code. As he, the tricyclist, backs up, a 20-something woman in a checkered shirt, cowboy hat, suede chaps, and lizard skin boots races into the coffee shop from outside. She shouts, "Apospasi! Apospasi!" ("Distraction" in Greek). She pulls from beneath her fringed skirt a gleaming butcher knife and dashes toward the Easter bunny on the tricycle. He pedals and pedals futilely, accidentally running into the toddler feeding the elderly woman, upending the tapioca bowl. The cowgirl-samurai lunges at him and buries the butcher knife between his clavicles, rivulets of pink blood now streaming down his fleecy second skin.

"Ex nihilo!" the expiring bunny gurgles in a falsetto voice, a dying fall splaying his rabbit-ish self on the fade-resistant wood laminate flooring, his coursing blood now turning the white bunny outfit a blazing crimson. As he falls over, the front wheel of his tricycle spins like a pinwheel, whirring gently. The other customers in the coffee shop pay no heed to what has happened. The assassin cowgirl kneels near his body and spits on his twitching corpse. A waitress on roller skates glides up to her and says, in a heavy Brooklyn accent, "The special today is redemption, with a side order of glory ever after. What'll it be?"

Fade to black, just for a few seconds, until a white-gloved hand holding a bright magenta lipstick reaches out in the blackness and writes on a mirror: "The Easter Bunny isn't real. He's a deceiver. Jesus is real. *Don't you be deceived*," underlining the last sentence. The hand withdraws and behind the writing on the mirror appears the face of a middle-aged man named Jeffery Kincaid; the proprietor of a local kiddie-themed pizzeria named Mousie's. "Hiya folks! Mousie's Pizza-the-Action is proud to support the *Incarnate* program. Remind us that Jesus loves you when you call and get ten percent off your next take-out order!" A blinding white light engulfs the mirror, and a toy guitar plays a pizzicato "How Great Thou Art" as the credits roll.

"Cut!"

Beth and Todd Lawson walk solemnly but hurriedly onto the set (which in this instance was a real-life coffee shop, a donor's establishment made available after business hours to help spread The Word), clasp hands, and kneel down. Completing the circle were the actors from the scene, including the Easter Bunny, Howie Mumford (even as the mix of canola oil and sriracha sauce that passed for blood on camera continued to congeal on his skin), and the cowgirl Christian warrior-princess, Abby Lopes, as well as the rest of the production crew, who knew the drill so well they could execute it in their sleep.

"Dear Lord, we ask that You bless our efforts to spread Your word among the heathens," Beth said, eyes tightly closed, head bowed. "Grant us the courage to face down our enemies with the flaming sword of Your wrath." Amens all around from the actors and crew, who then wasted little time getting all that gooey fake blood and real tapioca off the floor before it started to harden.

***

She sat in her car, hoping again to get lost in the music. When she was a teenager, Alana Stamos discovered punk rock and suddenly felt less alone in the world. Or maybe she was still alone but with lots of others, who were also alone. A community of ones, all of them satellites circling the planet Normal, hoping someday for a consolation prize, like acceptance, or understanding, or in the words of the singer Toni Neighborhood, the front woman of a punk band called Migraine, "a feeling of forgetting how very fucked we are." And that's how Alana now felt: totally fucked. By Millner. By the department. By life.

HCU. Those three letters beat in her brain like the double bass drum on the Migraine song "Liver Die," a rousing six-minute sonic explosion about an alcoholic stockbroker who hates his life and decides to kill himself by jumping off the George Washington Bridge but not before secretly transferring millions of dollars from his investment-banker employer to a cat sanctuary in rural Pennsylvania.

License to steal
Don't never squeal
I can make it all okay
Nine lives minus one today.

She mouthed the words, the crunchy power chords and screeching guitar licks knocking her back into adolescence. In her mind, she was sitting on the edge of her bed, holding the album cover, rubbing her fingers gently over the artsy, blurred-image cover of a cocktail party at some Gatsby-like mansion where all of the well-dressed, well-heeled guests were drinking from bottles of furniture polish, insecticide, antifreeze and Tab. She was thirteen and still a couple of years away from the tragedy that would change her life. But not her taste in music.

Swiss bank shuffle
Bosses muffle
any voice that tries to speak.
Fuck your conscience, feline freak.

At the end of the song, the stockbroker loses his nerve, and, steadying himself with the guide wires that run along the bridge's ledge, he climbs back to the safety of the walkway. Remembering that he left his car idling in the roadway, he straddles the guard rail, un-pockets his keys, and climbs back onto the pavement. As he's walking to his car, he is struck by an ice cream truck and killed instantly. The driver of the ice cream truck neither swerved to miss him nor stopped after striking him, the singer notes, adding the coda:

Life's a fucking ice cream sandwich
Some are squished and others melt.
Very few know what he felt
But I know. And you do too.

HCU. Alana Stamos had been dealing with the consequences of hate since she was fifteen years old. She knew what the stockbroker felt. But shortly, she was going to experience an emotion so unfamiliar it could only be defined as the opposite of hatred.

***

Dear Papli,

Your last letter made me so very sad. ALL your letters make me sad even though I know you write them to make me feel happy. Still, they all remind me of how much fun we always have when we go to the cafes and the clubs where [name blotted out] dances to the wild jungle music with her feathers and capes and sequined dresses or with the fringe and tassels and yes I think about the tarts and the creampuffs and the Turkish coffee with the waiters who flash that frozen smile like they're sneaking something into your demitasse that'll make you sleep or forget who you are or why you're there except to dance and sing to the band with their jumpy jazzy music all trembly and goose-pimply. How divine those nights — and how awful to hear from you telling of those custards at Mondard's with the curlicue of brown sugar that tastes like Christmas. Shame, Papli! Shame for bringing the memory of them into this place, knowing that they (the blank men who patrol the halls here) won't let us have sweets. Nothing sweet here gets by the blank men!

Oh, but you'd be proud of me if you had seen me last weekend, was it? At the walk they take us on, once around the grounds because Dr. Rochester (the one with the squint that makes him look like a sort of fox or better a pig who senses a truffle trove might be buried nearby, and he KNOWS how yummy they'll taste even if he's never had one before — oh Papli, they ARE yummy, aren't they?) "Ladies, chins up, nice rounded breaths, keep moving," he'd say to us, clicking his heels on the pavement like a flamenco dancer, and all of us strung along the path like we were playing follow-the-leader or swans-a-courting. I couldn't help myself, out in the sunshine and bracing cool of the morning with the lilacs perfuming the air, so I started to dance, the wind rustling the hospital gown like an invisible puppeteer, and so I swayed and gamboled along the glistening cinder path until one of the blank men dashed over to me and hit me with those straps I told you about in my last letter, and after that, he took me off the path and away from the glorious sunshine and locked me back in my room and said I wouldn't be walking outside again until I learned to not be "such a disruptive influence" on the others! Doesn't that make you laugh? I wasn't the one being disruptive. I was the one BEING disrupted! THEY were being disruptive — the flowers and the trees and the sun and the breeze and the birds and the sky and the squirrels and the brook. THEY were disrupting the blank men as they tried to keep us from noticing or hearing or smelling or touching the life all around us. Papli, I felt so free as I danced there for an audience of sparrows and meadowlarks. Disruptive? The very existence of the world outside these dry, bitter, and silent walls is disruptive to everything they try to do to us in here.

Please, Papli, no more talk about creampuffs!

Lu

***

Russell Padget's philosophy of teaching could be stated simply: students should shut up and listen. But it wasn't as heartless as it sounds. Rather, he believed, it was simply the best and most efficient way to communicate the important, even life-altering, lessons of the greats. And despite the narcissism that he felt had infected college-aged people everywhere because of their addiction to short-term gratification and their mania for self-esteem boosting, he didn't think any of them had ever done anything that could be termed "great." *Not even close.* He knew what it took to be great, how likely one was to fall short, and how painful the reminders of genuine greatness can sometimes be to those who have been unable to achieve it. And sometimes, he wished the students before him knew what real greatness felt like so they would understand just how far they were from any semblance of it. But instead, they simply persisted, those dopey, hypnotic grins on their programmed faces and their ignorance and unearned confidence that comes from spending your days in a social media circle jerk. What would Alexander Pope have to say about this lost and deluded generation? *A little learning is a dangerous thing.* Padget used to love preparing his lectures on writers like Pope and his eighteenth-century counterparts and would imagine himself spouting heroic couplets as if he was strolling through Pope's famed grotto. Now, the thought of his poetic recitations wasted on this cohort of twits made him queasy.

To keep him from ruminating on the abiding deficiencies of today's generation of pseudo-scholars, he retreated to the past. Ever since Augustine Hiatt had shared with him the still ridiculous-seeming notion of a lost Joyce work, Padget had begun burrowing back into the world of Joyce's Paris in the 1920s, sifting his memory — and a half-dozen books he had checked out of the college's library — for any sign that maybe Joyce *had* been working on some secret, undisclosed work. But all the evidence pointed in the other direction. In fact, the more he researched, the more confident he felt that Hiatt was delusional — or perhaps he had been hoodwinked. A young man like Hiatt, over-eager to join the sainted cabal of the professoriate, had leaped before he looked closely at the material. A little learning is a dangerous thing, indeed.

The collection of books about modern literature in the college's library was impressive — due almost exclusively to Padget's frequent entreaties to the library's director, Nance Baldwin, a former professor who had been denied tenure after the requisite five years and who then promptly threatened to sue the university for discrimination. As a consolation prize (and to avoid bad publicity), she was offered the assistant directorship of the library, which got her to drop her lawsuit. Three weeks later, the library's director, a young and vibrant librarian named Hoyt Weller, dropped dead. The rumors of Baldwin's involvement began swirling before Weller's body had completely cooled. Of course, it seemed preposterous to most of the faculty that someone would kill just for a promotion. But there were whispers about the college having initiated an investigation — though nothing was ever confirmed. Within weeks of Weller's passing, Baldwin was named "acting" director, and shortly after that, at some point nobody remembers, she simply became "Director." There was no official announcement, and the campus community blithely accepted this transition, content to believe the official story that Weller died from "Undetermined natural causes" — the kind of phrase that would have driven Padget crazy if it had shown up in a student essay. And while many faculty members felt it best to keep an arms-length relationship with Nance Baldwin, Padget always felt a connection to her, someone whose love of bound books bordered on the obsessive and whose distaste for academic bureaucracy matched his own. When he called her and told her the library needed to acquire such-and-such a volume, she didn't give him the requisite administrative sob story about resources being limited. Because Padget was well-known as a rabid bibliophile, Baldwin never questioned the necessity of the acquisitions, and his orders went right through. This was not always true with other members of the faculty, as Padget had heard over the years. Baldwin seemed to secretly resent those faculty members who promoted new technology over standard pulp-and-ink and was said to even sabotage certain requisitions for databases placed by the more tech-tickled faculty members. Baldwin would have made a great Medieval monk, Padget thought.

One of the books Padget checked out in his recent sweep was titled, *Homebodies in Motion: Domesticity and Displacement in Modern Literature*, a book that explored the idea of "home" as it was portrayed in the works of a handful of writers in the 1920s who were always on the move: Ernest Hemingway, Marcel Proust, Djuna Barnes, Ezra Pound, Amy Lowell, and James Joyce. The book flap made him think it might shed some light on Augie Hiatt's quixotic notions. It read: *The idea of "home" has been central to Western Literature since Homer sent his hero back to Ithaca. However, the notions of "stability," "comfort," and "family," which are integral to the idea of home, take on new meaning when refracted through the works of writers for whom "home" was a far more elusive concept. For writers in the 1920s and 1930s, such as Ernest Hemingway or James Joyce, who relocated every few months (sometimes because work called, sometimes because the landlord called), the idea of a stable, central location as a permanent comfort in one's life no longer obtained. And yet, the writers mentioned above (and many others) continued to create plots and characters for who "home" was elemental. This groundbreaking study explores the domestic life of this lost generation and the place "home" occupied in their work and in their imagination as they found themselves in often peripatetic circumstances.*

Padget loved reading book jackets and often imagined the words that would appear on his own book flap. Writing a book was something he planned to do once he could clear his desk of all that bothersome student writing. In the meantime, he contented himself with other people's writing. In *Homebodies in Motion*, he found several passages that seemed to provide support for the idea that Joyce was simply too overwhelmed with managing the stresses of his tumultuous domestic life — as well as producing masterpieces of modern literature — to write any "secret" work. Especially in the 1930s, when Hiatt claims the undiscovered work was written, Joyce was preoccupied with health problems (debilitating ulcers and near blindness), writing woes (*Finnegans Wake* had become a decades-long labyrinth which he nonetheless continued to revise through the fog that surrounded his head), the growing threat of European war (soon to cause further anxious relocations) and most especially, his daughter Lucia's mental breakdowns and subsequent confinement in a mental hospital. As *Homebodies* put it: "Joyce was somehow able to ignore almost all the demands on his time and intellect in his pursuit of the perfection of his art. Money problems, fights with his wife, Nora, the demands of a shifting social circle with their own ulterior motives, and the declining health that often reduced him to an immobile and prostrate patient in his own home weren't enough to keep him from his work. But the one thing that seemed to stop his creativity in its tracks was his worry about his daughter, Lucia. Her mental deterioration seemed to engender a parallel condition in him."

Padget made a mental note to share that paragraph with Augie Hiatt. If Joyce was so worried about his daughter, how could he have possibly started a new work?

***

It was thoughts of the physical, not the mental, that preoccupied Hiatt at the moment. He was on the set of Tongue-in-Cheek's latest video shoot, a script called *Angie in Arrears,* about a woman who falls behind in her rent and offers her landlord a non-traditional payment plan. It was his first time on a movie set. Until a couple of weeks ago, Hiatt had never even *seen* a pornographic film, let alone see one being filmed. The idea of watching naked people cavort had never really appealed to him, and when his friends in college would head off for a frivolous evening of liquor and porn, he'd head instead to the library. Now here he was, holding a clipboard with a script clamped to it, trying to look nonchalant but sticking out like an erection at a nunnery.

"Hard, right?"

Hiatt had been so focused on himself that he hadn't even noticed the woman who sidled up to him between the camera and the director's chair.

"Excuse me?"

"Hard to watch. You have the same expression I used to have during shooting — and they haven't even started yet. You might want to think twice about staying," she said, reaching across and grabbing a ham salad sandwich from the cut-rate craft services table.

"It's alright. I can handle it. In fact," he said, with a rush of perverse pride, "I wrote it." He lifted the clipboard and pointed to his name on the title page.

"Oh, a writer," she said, with mock adulation. "How proud you must be to have your name scroll over the gang bang that ends the film."

"Well, I did the re-writes. Somebody else came up with the, um, you know…"

"The gang bang."

"Right."

She gave him a sideways looked and laughed lightly but not derisively. "A porn writer who can't say `gang bang' without blushing. You're a curiosity."

"Well," he said, leaning in to whisper, though no one in the cast or crew would have heard — or cared — what he was about to say. "I'm not really a porn writer — it's just a job to, you know, pay the bills."

"And then?"

"And then... well... I'm not sure."

"I see. Maybe you should work out your story before writing other people's happy endings," she said between bites of her sandwich but still playfully enough to pique his attention. She was probably in her early twenties, Hiatt guessed, though she still looked very much a teenager: hot pink cat glasses framing cool emerald eyes, her raven-colored hair pulled back, terminating in a ponytail. She wore a Nirvana tee shirt and cobalt-blue jeans, strategically torn in descending rectangles like fleshy windows.

"My life is a work in progress," he said, immediately regretting the banality of his lame riposte. And then, with not much more verve, "What about you? What do you do here?"

This time, there *was* a derisive edge to her laugh. "*I don't work here,*" she said. "I'm just here to support my mom. That's her," she said, nodding to a woman off-stage who was just starting to disrobe. "These gang bangs scenes are always rough on her. She's gonna need all the support she can get." The young woman flashed her mother the thumbs-up sign, grabbed a pastry off the food table, and took a seat behind the camera, preparing to watch her mother get gang banged on film.

There's a lot about this business I'm just never going to get, Hiatt thought, suddenly feeling more like a voyeur than a writer, an undutiful son who, even in his capacious imagination, could simply not imagine cheering on his mother through a gang bang, even one he scripted.

***

Alana Stamos's first day back with the Hate Crimes Unit was filled with flashbacks to her work with that division three years ago. In many ways, she felt like she was stepping into a comfortable pair of broken-in jeans and well-worn sneakers. She was surprised at how familiar things seemed. "Hiya, Poison," said Captain Dan Felton, the same supervisor she had when she requested her transfer. "Missed us, huh?"

"Like the flu," she said, but then she smiled. She had always liked Felton and marveled at his ability to stay so good-humored in his position, a front-row seat for the grim and gruesome pageant of humanity's dark impulses.

"Good to have you back. Desi will catch you up," he said, gesturing with a manila folder to a young man in his twenties sitting across the office.

"Hmmm. Suspenders, French cuffs, tie clip, Bruno Magli shoes… the pay must be better here than it used to be."

"Yeah, he's a real dandy. But he's a good cop. And I see you haven't lost your eye for the telling detail. I'm surprised those rocket scientists over at general let you go."

There was always a lot of mostly good-natured jabbing among the various detective bureaus: General Investigations, HCU, Vice, Homicide, Internal Affairs. It wasn't uncommon for some detectives to have spent a little time with each, so everybody pretty much knew someone in one of the other divisions. For example, Stamos began in Vice, then moved to HCU, then to General, and now back to HCU.

"Well, I asked for more money, and they sent me here. I presume my new position comes with a sizable raise?"

"Are you kidding? I had to call in a few favors just to find you a desk," Felton said. And he probably wasn't kidding, Stamos realized. "There it is — welcome home. Hey, Arroyo!" He shouted across the office, "Put down your GQ and get over here."

Detective Desi Arroyo looked even younger up close. How the hell did a kid like this make it to detective grade?

"Detective Arroyo, this is Detective Stamos. She's new. Show her the ropes, will ya?"

"Most certainly," he said, sizing her up with the practiced gaze of a trained detective.

"He gives you any trouble, Poison, just pull that move that you used to use."

"Whoa, Captain — I'm a lover, not a fighter," Detective Arroyo said. He smiled at her and winked. "Though I do my best work undercover."

"Charming," she said, rolling her eyes and carrying the small box of personal belongings she had with her over to her desk.

"If you don't mind my prying into your personal life, why do they call you Poison?"

"I don't mind. There are no secrets in the HCU, if I remember."

"That's pretty much true. I can tell you how many times a week Landon over there sneaks into the John to jerk off and how many cigarettes Phillipa smokes in the evidence room, even though she's told everyone she quit two years ago. Now, as for me..."

She cut him off.

"That's quite all right. Don't need to know everything on my first day back."

"Back? You been here before?"

"Two years, hard time. I just got transferred back from General."

"No shit? What's it like? I thought maybe of requesting a transfer there. Or Homicide. But Captain Felton says no transfer requests will be processed while we're still short-handed. I guess that's why you're here."

"Yep."

"So you never answered my question. Why 'Poison'?"

How much did she want to tell him? How eager was she to open the door into a part of her life that had been closed off for years? It was inevitable that most of her secrets would be discovered, as sure as Landon's me-time appointments in stall #3 and Phillipa's smoke-and-mirrors routine had become common knowledge. Captain Felton would probably spill most of her beans anyway — not because he was a gossip (he wasn't) or vindictive (ditto) but because the only way to survive the daily grind down here in the muck was to trust each other. And secrets were corrosive to trust.

"'Poison' was a nickname I brought over here from vice. Felton is one of the few who even remembers it. Nobody calls me that anymore. You can call me Alana. What should I call you?"

Detective Arroyo laughed lightly and nodded.

"Well played, Alana. That's a veteran interrogator's move. Classic misdirection. But you still didn't answer my question. *Why* did they call you Poison?"

"You didn't answer mine either."

"Fair enough. Call me Desi."

"OK, Desi. Nice to meet you."

He nodded, and sensing he'd gotten as much from her as she was prepared to reveal, he decided to drop his interrogation. He turned to go back to his desk, but she didn't want to build walls on the first day, so she relented.

"When I was in vice, I was assigned to a narcotics unit operating in the clubs downtown. There was a ton of candy coming in through the ports and getting sold after hours in the dance clubs along the waterfront. Every time vice got close, some snitch turned us out, and we kept coming up empty. So Captain Krueger — have you met him? — decided we needed a better approach. He knew I had a musical background and used to be in a band, so he came up with this plan to have me pose as the lead singer of a punk group called Chromium Dreams. He gave me the stage name "Poison," and we actually put together a band made up of cops.

"No shit?"

"Well, actually pretty shitty. The guys who made up the band — most of them even younger than you, could barely play. But it's punk music, so whatever."

Arroyo looked confused.

"You don't know punk music? It's like three chords. You don't have to be much of a musician to play it. You just have to play loud and fast and jump around and scream. You know… like the Ramones?"

His blank stare stunned Alana.

"Jesus, you really are young. Anyway, we actually started making a little noise in the club scene, writing songs, even getting a following. After a couple of months, the club owners all knew us, hung out with us after the clubs closed, even did drugs with us."

"Isn't that against the rules, detective?"

"Technically, yes. But we had to fit in. And we did. So much so that they used to talk about the drug shipments right in front of us. Well, after about six months, we had the names of all the major suppliers, the local dealers, even the boat pilots and dirty dock workers who unloaded the stuff for their cut. It was a pretty big operation, and the bust went down like clockwork. A lot of those guys are still in prison. But of course, once it happened, my rock star days were over. I came to

HCU to cool off, but after a couple years, there was an opening in general, and so I transferred."

"How's it feel to be back?"

Alana paused, unable to formulate an answer.

"I'll let you know," she said distractedly. In her mind, she was back in the clubs doing her bad girl act, courting the dark side, the oily smell of waterfront dives filling her head, the crunch of her guitar and the raspy screech of her vocals bouncing off the rising swell of the city's vampires, filling the acrid and claustrophobic dawn with non-lethal doses of Poison.

***

As Russell Padget's passed through the department on his way to his office, a representative of a textbook company with a suitcase full of next season's must-have teaching resources, over-eager to meet anyone who might want to take a business card and talk about "tech support for grammatically challenged students," ambushed him.

"Professor…. um, professor…?" She was waiting for him to say his last name, but Padget was an artful dodger of such solicitors. He just nodded at her and said "Yes," and then tried to get to his office unmolested. But she followed him.

"You teach English? We have some very popular texts, and I'd be happy to—"

"Thank you, no," he said, turning to face her. "I'm very happy with the books I use. I'm not looking to change."

"But you haven't seen what we have to offer. If I can just have a minute of your—"

"Sorry, but I'm running late myself. Good luck," he said in a way that made clear he didn't really care whether her luck turned out to be good or bad. He turned away brusquely and headed down the hall to the cocoon of his office. When he heard the knock a few minutes later, he grimaced and prepared to refuse her textual entreaties once again. But it was actually Augie Hiatt, and he was carrying a text with him that Russell Padget wanted to review very much indeed.

***

"How then to be the child of a genius? Hmm? And not just any run-of-the-mill genius, but the daughter of the man who changed modern literature? What a crushing weight, how crippling that could be for anyone in that position. And a creative child looking to make her way in the world of arts? The expectation, the presumptions... gentlemen, I tell you, this young woman was doomed from the start. But I think, with a bit of time — and a bit of distance — she can finally find herself. I think she can be helped. I'm not sure, however..." He paused and cleared his throat. "I'm not sure that she can get what she needs here. In fact, I believe that in the long-term, keeping her confined here and removing her from a like-minded creative community might make things worse. Perhaps much worse."

Dr. Hastings, a consulting psychiatrist with admitting privileges at St. Andrew's, pocketed his notecards and sat back down at the conference table, a half-dozen board members of the hospital gathered around, exchanging glances and making notes of their own. The hospital's director, Morgan Staffordshire, had called the meeting after receiving a letter from James Joyce himself, inquiring after his daughter. The letter seemed as much a confession as a request, with Joyce blaming himself "for her Bohemian upbringing" and her "disdain of convention." Well, yes — Lucia certainly manifested those qualities. But it was other qualities that her mother, Nora, had articulated upon her daughter's admittance: a tendency towards violent outbursts, incoherent speech, lack of social skills, obsession with dancing at all moments of the day or night, even pyromania. So her mother signed the papers alleging her daughter was "an immediate danger to herself and others" and left Lucia in a psychiatric hospital (without even saying goodbye, Staffordshire noted at the time). After two months, the patient continued to manifest some of the behaviors her mother had complained about. There was another side to Lucia's story, however — a side Dr. Hastings had noticed in his frequent visits with her — that suggested perhaps she wasn't a candidate for involuntary commitment. After an initial, somewhat chilly reception, she seemed to have warmed to his visits, taking almost a clinician's interest in his line of questioning, often asking him follow-up questions about her condition and his opinion of her that suggested clear-headedness and even a quick wit.

Stately, plump Dr. Staffordshire rose to address the board. "We thank you for your evaluation, Hastings. Now, if you'll excuse us, we must deliberate on this matter further." Staffordshire had no intention of allowing a genuine deliberation. The daughter of one of the most famous men on the planet was a patient in his hospital. Not in London, not in Paris, not even in Manchester. But here in Northampton at St. Andrew's — a facility Lucia Joyce was helping to put on the psychiatric map. He'd already fielded press inquiries from New York, Dublin, and Zurich. As long as Lucia was there, people in the psychiatric community would be forced to acknowledge the existence of St. Andrew's. And as beneficial as the profile-raising was, the prospective fundraising was even more promising. Lucia Joyce was a gold strike.

The official record of the board meeting that afternoon concluded with the following statement: The patient in question, having been determined to be a continuing and imminent threat to herself and others, is hereby denied release and designated a candidate for long-term care, pursuant to the periodic review of the appropriate authorities.

***

"After Joyce died, the academic bloodhounds chased his ghost to all the places he lived, but they never thought of chasing *Lucia*," Augie said, handing over a sheaf of papers to Professor Padget. "But everything Joyce sent his daughter was an original, and this work — *Archimedes at the Gear Factory* — was actually written as part of the letters themselves, dozens of letters, like monthly installments. Joyce didn't make any copies of these or even show them to anybody, so naturally, none of the biographers found evidence of it. So they concluded — wrongly, as I've proved — that he left no new work after his death."

"But surely someone must have gone to the mental hospital to talk to Lucia or ask her if she had any papers from her father, or letters, or anything from him."

"There's no way they could have. They would have needed written permission from the family. Even if they had somehow snuck in, all of the correspondence Lucia received would have been filed away by the psychiatric staff — strictly off-limits until her death. And after she died, the attendants boxed up her clothes, her books, everything in her room that was to be dispersed to her remaining family members, but they never thought to go through the psychiatric files and pull her letters. But the director at the time had been putting all her correspondence in her medical file after Lucia was given a chance to read it. That was standard procedure for all patients. It was considered part of the patient's psychiatric history. So when her family received her belongings, they assumed that was all there was. Her file — which was confidential — was marked "inactive" upon her death and put in storage with hundreds of other files. No one knew Joyce had written this work, no one knew Lucia had received all these letters, and once she was dead and her other belongings were returned to her remaining heir, a nephew, people had no reason to keep looking at the hospital."

"So, how did you come upon them?"

"I went to St. Andrew's to do some research for a novel I was going to write about Lucia Joyce — as Monique might have told you, I used to be a creative writing student. In fact, I was doing an MFA and had no real interest in Joyce himself. I was interested in Lucia, having come across a footnote in a book about Paris in the 1920s that said Lucia had gone crazy or something, and I thought that might make a good story. You know, the dark side of the jazz age, or whatever. So I'm working on this novel, and it's not really going anywhere, and I felt like I needed a break from it. But I had a second cousin in England who invited me to stay with him on spring break, so I decided while I was there to do some research for the novel, maybe jump-start the book. I went to the hospital where she was confined for decades. That's when I came across this dusty box in the hospital's basement. It had the year written on it when she died — 1982 — and inside was an envelope with all of these original letters from Joyce. Well, to tell you the truth, my MFA advisor wasn't being too helpful to me, and I didn't have high hopes that she'd help shape my novel into a best-seller, so when I realized what that box held, I decided to change from creative writing to Lit and turn this treasure trove into my dissertation."

Padget nodded periodically while Augie Hiatt told the tale of how he had come across this literary bonanza, trying to seem thoughtful and judicious. But inside, he was secretly cringing, berating himself because he had never thought of doing what Hiatt did. Padget spent the better part of graduate school trying to think of things to say that no one else had said about works that had been written about for decades, or sometimes centuries. But this MFA washout who sat before him had found the golden goose and didn't have to worry about trying to say something original. Instead, he had *discovered* something original — the photocopies of which Padget held now in his hand.

"Any chance these could be forgeries?" Padget asked, trying to retain his intellectual bona fides.

"No chance at all," Hiatt shot back. "Look at the writing yourself. That's Joyce's hand." He was standing now, excited, maybe a little defensive. "When I pulled those letters out of that box, I was only like the third or fourth person ever to read them. You can even see small checkmarks or, in some instances, underlines. I'm not sure if that was Lucia's work or one of the doctors'. Probably a doctor."

Padget nodded, quickly thumbing through the pages, not reading them so much as reveling in them. He might have been fated to spend his intellectual capital at an academic backwater, but he recognized what he was now holding and its truly extraordinary nature.

"They wouldn't let me take the originals with me, but it had nothing to do with how valuable they are. They don't allow *any* originals of what they call their 'archival' material outside the hospital. After I made copies, I gave the originals back to the attendant. But I noticed he didn't put them back in the box where they came from. He just held on to them, told me he'd re-file them sometime later. I have reason to believe he never replaced them."

"You mean he kept them?"

"I can't say. He might have put them into the wrong box or forgotten about them and just stuck them in some drawer. Or he could have kept them himself. All I know is my dissertation advisor…"

"Zale, if I recall correctly?"

"Yes, Dr. Zale. When I shared my discovery with him, he called the hospital, but they said there was no record of any such correspondence and that the box marked 1982 didn't have any Joyce letters. So naturally, he didn't believe me. In fact, he called me delusional. But maybe that attendant figured out these letters were valuable, and he hung on to them. Now that I'm not going to be publishing a dissertation, there's a risk that he — or whoever he gave them to — will beat me to it. That's why I need your help. We've got to get this work out there before anybody else does. If I can get these published, the committee will have to reinstate me and give me the doctorate. Now that you've seen the letters, will you help me?"

Padget recalled another poem he had read once as an undergraduate, a Robert Frost poem about a road less traveled. He felt like he was now standing at a fork in the road, contemplating his future, the ghosts of his past nudging him, whispering in his ear that this was his chance.

"I'll have to think about it," he said. "Let's stay in touch."

Hiatt re-collected the photocopies, stuffed them in a file folder and put them in his shoulder bag.

"Less than a handful of people have seen these, and I seem to be the only one bothered by that fact," he said a little angrily, shaking his head. "Jesus, what does it take to get an academic's attention?"

Hiatt needn't have worried — he had Padget's full attention. Behind his aloof exterior, the professor was already making plans to make sure Augie would get his wish that the world sees this work.

***

You wouldn't know it from its nickname — *Hellhouse* — but the place was actually pretty small. In fact, it was just a room, located one floor above the squad room for the Hate Crimes Unit. It's where all of the case files were kept on microfilm. Detective Alana Stamos unlocked the door and flipped on the lights, holding a list of numbers and scanning the cabinet drawers to determine which one held the microfilms for the dozen or so cases she intended to review. As part of getting up to speed in her new position, Alana was going to spend the afternoon unspooling the "highlights" of current open cases for the HCU, a deep dive back into the sea of hostility where Alana made her first splash. She glanced down at the numbers, leaned down and pulled open a drawer, and then lifted a handful of small plastic cylinders that contained individual microfilms. She silently congratulated herself that she remembered how to thread the reader, and pulling up a chair, made herself comfortable for what would prove to be an uncomfortable couple of hours.

"Let's see how all you boys and girls have been behaving while the teacher has been out of the room," she said to herself, flicking the switch for the reading device's bulb and slowly turning the thumbwheel that controlled the parade of images and text. Suddenly the bigotry and prejudice that percolates just beneath the surface in an over-stuffed urban melting pot leaped into gory, illuminated glory on the view screen. The first case Alana reviewed was one of the more recent, and one which Alana had actually worked for a brief time on, involving an attack on a gay computer graphics designer who was abducted on his way out to a tapas bar and grill and taken to a still-unidentified railroad-style apartment where he was videotaped being sodomized by multiple tormenters using, among other things, a fireplace poker, a travel umbrella, and a deep-sea diver G-I-Joe. Welcome back, Detective Stamos.

Alana knew well the occasional horrors that investigators in the HCU would encounter. It was the same with all of the detective bureaus: vice, narcotics, homicide, special investigations, general. No one was bringing them fresh-cut flowers and bonbons every day. They had chosen to traffic in the darker regions of the soul, and the price they paid was a kind of hardening of the heart. It was simply impossible to look upon the coldness and cruelty that humanity descended into under just the right set of wrong circumstances and still retain a naive faith in the inherent goodness of people. Alana Stamos understood the equation that some bad people doing bad things meant some good people would have to try to stop them. You couldn't stop them if you weren't willing to get a little muck on your penny loafers or sometimes a little blood on your hands. When she was barely a teenager, she had witnessed up-close the consequences of bad people doing a bad thing — and that time, there was no one around to stop it. She carried that with her, using it like a kind of armored vest she would slip on when the muck was being flung at her. But there was something about hate crimes that penetrated the shields of even the most veteran detectives. Crimes of passion, crimes of greed, acts of violence intended to silence others who might ruin one's reputation or send one to jail, these all seemed, in their twisted ways, understandable. A jealous mistress threatens to expose the doctor she's having an affair with unless he finally leaves his wife, so the good doctor takes a little chloroform along on the next assignation. Suddenly the UPS man starts piling packages up at the door because the corpse inside can't sign for the exercycle and yoga pants she ordered last month. But hate crimes unfolded according to a different logic, a calculus that defied the usual, "There but for the grace of God go I" rationalization that allowed a least a tiny shaft of sunlight into the stultifying darkness. Hate brings different weapons to the human brawl, a gleeful destructiveness that Alana found physically chilling. As she watched the video of the victim of the sodomy fest being forcibly held down, writhing as he absorbed the deep-sea plunge of a child's toy until just the weighted boots were visible, Alana shivered.

Each of the microfilms contained as complete a record of a particular incident as possible: case file, photographs of the victims and the crime scene, video testimony, investigators' notes, even press accounts. There were hundreds of these microfilms in the cabinets in Hellhouse but a quick, if queasy, review of these files revealed they tended to be grouped into just a handful of classifications based on intent: racial, sexual/gender, political, and religious/supernatural. Other file cabinets in the room were filled with documents: court transcripts, psychologists' reports, letters, diaries. They were filed according to month and year and cross-filed according to intent.

Alana flipped off the bulb of the microfilm reader, rolled her chair over to a nearby cabinet, and pulled open a file drawer containing the most recent unsolved cases. Her finger tripped lightly along the tabs of the loosely stacked manila envelopes. Many of the names struck a familiar nerve, but there was one file — stuffed with copies of typewritten letters — whose label was unfamiliar to her.

"Hmmm. 'Friend to Man,'" she said, pulling out the file and wheeling her chair over to a plain blonde-wood carrel. She opened the file and pulled a handful of letters out. They were neatly typewritten, brief, and addressed to a variety of recipients, including a U.S. Senator, a reference librarian, and even a high-school drama teacher.

"The flaming sword of the Lord's wrath," she said softly, shaking her head and putting the letters back into the file. "Lovely." Alana Stamos was raised in a religious household and was familiar with such apocalyptic language. She knew that many phrases that came from sacred texts often featured hyperbole, but she also knew many believers didn't see it that way. For them, the spiritual call to purification was a mandate, not a metaphor. "Friend to Man," she said, laughing lightly to herself as she replaced the file and closed the cabinet door.

She rolled herself back to the microfilm reader, rewound and removed the sodomy case spool, and cued up the next microfilm, which bore the label "Aryan Turpentine Attack." *Great name for a punk rock band*, she thought, the easy cynicism taking hold of her again like some snug, protective body armor.

***

Beth Lawson was a pragmatist. She understood, in the way her idealistic brother Todd (who regularly lost himself in foggy rumination about the "bigger picture" issues of sin, redemption, and the disposition of the soul for eternity) did not, that math — and not metaphysics — was the proper focus of anyone looking to make a mark in *this* world. Friend of Man had finally achieved a certain prominence in the apocalyptic Christian community, not because of the zeal of Todd's righteousness but because of a clearly defined strategy to boost *numbers*: subscribers to their videos on social media, readers of their monthly newsletter, contributors who stuff checks into envelopes every month, and mentions in the media during discussion of cultural issues. Behind the prayerful mien, Beth Lawson was calculating. It was she who decided early on that Friend to Man move out of their trailer park in Warsaw, Indiana and head east. "Belly of the Beast," she'd regularly intone as she and Todd made their way to Hoboken, New Jersey in their wheezing Dodge Dart. "In the shadow of Sodom and Gomorrah," she said to herself when the skyline of New York City first came into view. A more business-minded partner than her brother might have raised legitimate objections to the relocation: sky-high rents, loss of daily contact with a cohort of evangelicals, even hostility toward them from the people they'd now be forced to share space with. There were lots of good reasons to oppose the move. Beth and Todd's family all hailed from the Midwest, and most of their support had come from pastors whose roots ran deep into the dirt sanctified in unadorned church graveyards and fertile farmland, generations of holy harvests and dearly departed whose spirits swirled around Beth and Todd like a blinding dustbowl haze. Hoboken, New Jersey, to many of their friends and family, was either a punchline or a punishment.

But Beth understood that to grow a business, one needed access to capital, media outlets, and an audience. The internet gave them the global reach they needed, but a northeastern headquarters address projected the credibility and confidence of a serious player in the new media world. And that's what Friend to Man sought to be and what Beth *knew* it could be. She recognized in her brother the authentic anointing of prophecy and felt that with the proper exposure, he could be their generation's Bishop Sheen, Jimmy Swaggart, or Joel Osteen. And they would do it with a mix of traditional fire-and-brimstone theology and a street artist's gift for self-promotion. The videos they had been shooting were getting a lot of attention, as much for their surrealism as their Christian content. What started out as an idea to do a kiddie-show with faith-based messages quickly turned into a melding of Crusades-era piety with a Pee-Wee's Playhouse goofiness, aimed as much at adults as a younger audience; a mix of spiritual zeal conveying a martial Christian commitment and a Martian zaniness.

Over a half-million subscribers to a video channel means something, Beth knew. Their work had begun to get the attention of advertisers, and many unaffiliated evangelical churches had begun linking to their site. Friend to Man was becoming a friend to those who thought the world was rapidly rotting and that God's wrath at America's spiritual stupor was not to be stayed. But something else had been happening that Beth, the savvy Christian pragmatist, understood could bring it all toppling down if they weren't careful. Friend to Man had begun to attract some folks who were downright *unfriendly* to man, a tiny but toxic cohort of kooks who had begun to make manifest the metaphor of God's wrathful sword. Still under the radar, an apparently unconnected series of recent violent incidents involving "sinners" — gays, pornographers, abortionists — waved a red flag to Beth. Friend to Man was not implicated in any of these incidents, nor even mentioned, as far as Beth could tell. Still, some of the quotes uttered by these perpetrators after their arrests raised questions in Beth's mind, the echo of things said by the perpetrators startlingly similar to what was said in some of Friend's videos and newsletters.

It might have been logical, then, to suspend the monthly roll call of shame, the poison-pen letter campaign aimed at the public miscreants, but Beth was playing the odds on this one. Her calculations were simple: the more that Friend to Man resorted to personal correspondence as a means to address deviant behavior, the less likely they'd be seen as venturing into actual violence. A terrorist group planning to attack seldom broadcasts its targets in advance. Beth also knew that no publicity is bad publicity, and if groups like Friend to Man became linked to a sub-set of anti-Christian warriors striking at the heart of moral decay, *the donations would pour in.* Her experience with the community of evangelicals was that they were always quick to denounce violence against sinners publicly, but privately they were all for it. She knew that any public linking of Friend to Man and private acts of vengeance against transgressors could lead to a financial bonanza. So why not let the media — or even law enforcement — make the link? The belly of the beast needs to be stuffed, and if well-intentioned Christian survivalists wanted to finance the high-priced rent at their formerly-gritty-but-now-hip Hoboken headquarters, well, the Lord works in mysterious ways. These are thoughts she had not, *would* not share with Todd (who always seemed bored by these types of business-related details). Beth felt confident that she could continue to steer this ark safely, no matter the flood of innuendo that might be coming their way. And even if things got out of hand, well, she knew that God protects His people. And who was more deserving of His protection than a true and devout Friend to Man?

She logged on to her computer, heading to the site that hosted their videos. Beth regularly checked Friend to Man's metrics, and this week, the news was good again. More than 3,500 new subscribers to their site in just the last week, many of whom also clicked on the link to subscribe to the newsletter. They were creating a lot of buzz — and building a base that could propel them from a social media platform to, perhaps, a television network. Once that happened, once you got on a few cable systems, then it was just a matter of time, a slow and steady crawl from the grave of obscurity to their rightful ascension in the pantheon of Christian broadcasters. Friend to Man had a potent message, a necessary message, and if a few nay-sayers wanted to dismiss them as loons — or, more specifically, *dangerous* loons — then they simply didn't understand the Word. Or maybe they understood but chose not to believe. No matter. God would take care of them: Deuteronomy 32:35 states, "It is mine to avenge; I will repay. In due time their foot will slip; their day of disaster is near and their doom rushes upon them." Doom was always good for business, Beth knew. But tempered with a clown costume, a man in a bear suit, or a cowgirl in leather chaps, it seemed to work even better. People wanted their salvation served with a side order of entertainment and mystery, and Friend to Man was only too happy to oblige. Their next video (which some critics would label "shocking" and "disturbing" and which would put them on the mainstream media's radar screen) was scheduled to be shot in just a couple of days. It wasn't doom that was rushing upon them — it was the usual production deadlines, as Friend to Man needed to construct a full-sized crucifix, preparing for a spectacle that would top anything they'd ever filmed before, and all that self-denial Todd had been practicing would finally be put to good use.

***

"Package!"

Edwina Torrance flew into the front room of the small, garden-level apartment she shared with her boyfriend like she was shot from the barrel of a gun. He playfully held the package aloft with his right hand, momentarily stopping her charge and holding her at arm's length with his left.

"Hmmm. Maybe we shouldn't be so quick to open it. What if it's a bomb? You know, there's crazy people in the world, and I wouldn't put it past—"

"F U!" she yelled at him, leaping at the package and almost knocking poor Augie down in the process. "I pray to God it's *not* a bomb," she said, grabbing the package and ripping open the taped brown paper flaps. "In fact, just the opposite. I hope it's a big, big *hit.*"

"Me too," Augie said sincerely. He knew what this moment meant to her, meant to any writer. To hold in your hand the first copy of your first book, well, that's a pretty special moment. Edwina had been working on this novel ever since they met in the MFA program. They both knew that most first novels never find a publisher and are destined to live out their anonymous lives in the dark of seldom-opened desk drawers and overstuffed milk crates that preserve the detritus of a grad students' intellectual scavenger hunt, tucked under the eaves or jammed in the back of a closet, taken out only after a little too much Scotch one night, a silent sentinel attesting to one's unappreciated genius, a moment frozen in time when all things seemed possible.

"Look!" she said, her eyes glistening with unalloyed glee. "I *did* this, Teddy Bear!"

"You sure did, Baby Doll!"

After several weeks of dating, when it was clear they saw a future together, Edwina had a 'writerly' idea. She suggested they pick out the most cloying and gag-inducing pet names they could think of for each other and to use them in public as a kind of private joke at their revulsion for such sentimental inanity. After all, both Augie and Edwina were accomplished enough in their writing to understand how weak and wounding a blatantly cliched expression could be to genuine originality, and so they both avoided clichés like the plague. At first, once they chose these names from a list of candidates like "stud muffin," "honey bun," and "snookums," they could barely keep from laughing when they called each other by their dopey new designations. But then, weirdly, the names actually seemed to feel, well, *appropriate*. And in the wake of unwrapping her first book, Edwina was too high to feel anything other than the kind of dopamine-rush that makes such nicknames feel organic. It was a moment out of time. But there was more euphoria to come.

But also a reversal — one profound enough to cast a pall over the gauzy delight they experienced that day two months ago as Edwina tore open her first book and embraced its heft like the weight of a lover. Augie thought about that moment, as he regularly still did, whenever there was a package in his mailbox, as there was this afternoon. He took it out of the mailbox and keyed his way into the empty apartment.

He knew he shouldn't have said anything at all, knew that there were areas in relationships that people just shouldn't go to, psychic locales cordoned off by mental yellow tape like the kind police use at crime scenes. He wasn't trying to hurt her or belittle her achievement. At least, that's what he told himself. He had been very complimentary of her work, and he took pains to make sure she would catch him reading her book because he knew how happy that would make her. So he really didn't mean anything by his idle remark as he was lying in bed one night, reading her book next to her. He looked up from the page he was reading and had a mildly quizzical look on his face.

"What's wrong?" she asked, putting down the book she was reading, a collection of first-hand accounts of people who had survived near-fatal run-ins with wild animals called *Close Encounters of the Ferocious Kind.* It was a gift from her agent, who had inscribed on the title page "...and you thought literary agents were tough to deal with!", a book written by a client of his that he was trying to create some buzz for, not a bad book but really, when you've read the story of one animal attack, you've pretty much read them all.

"Nothing. It's just—" And that is precisely where he should have stopped. *Just let it go, say nothing, bury it deeply.* Because that is where everything turned, and once he started down that path, there was no way to retrace his steps. It was as foolhardy a course of action as trying to outrun a grizzly bear, swim away from a crocodile, or dodge a cobra in mid-strike, a close encounter of the most ferocious kind.

"What is it? Something wrong?"

"I'm just having a moment of déjà vu here. I guess I'm just remembering this part from what you read to me when you were working on it."

She leaned over and looked at the page he was reading.

"I don't think I ever read that part to you. I only read you the beginning and ending."

The puma crouched silently in the bush. The cobra coiled just beyond the victim's line of sight. Nearly motionless, the crocodile glided through the dark water towards its prey.

"Hmm. It just sounds familiar. You probably told me about it, that's all."

"I don't think so," she said, leaning forward now, a look of mild concern creasing her brow.

"Well, no matter. It's very good, by the way."

"But *familiar,* in some way? Are you saying that I... what? That it's *not* original?"

"No, No. It's really good. I'm just, it... it reminds me, you know, of something."

"Something you read? Something you saw, like, in a movie? Or what, exactly?"

The wild boar snorts. The moose shakes its antlers. The piranha swirl about.

"I can't really... maybe something I read," he said unconvincingly. "Maybe a previous work you shared with our writers' group? Or maybe, I don't know, something somebody in the group might have—"

"You think I stole from somebody else? From our writers' group?"

Edwina was working herself up into a pretty good froth. The one unpardonable sin for a writer is the thievery of another's work. The more familiar word writers use comes from the Latin word *plagiary,* to steal.

"Oh, come on, baby doll. Forget I said anything. Slide in here next to me."

"You wouldn't want to share a bed with a plagiarist!"

"Edwina, please. I'm sure you didn't *mean* to —"

That was it. That was the moment. The condor swooped in and plucked the shivering vole with its sharpened talons. The jaguar tore into the gazelle's flesh. The boyfriend accused his writer girlfriend of being a plagiarist.

In fact, he had remembered, and with great clarity, a short story written by one of their MFA friends named Franklin Jelenik, a quiet guy, weirdly quiet, but whose writing career also recently had taken off, that contained a situation identical to the one he had just read on page 97 of Edwina Torrance's debut novel.

In time, the anger she felt toward Augie would be replaced with anger at herself for having indeed borrowed a major plot point for her novel from a fellow writer. She told herself all the usual things in an attempt to justify the act — all writers borrow, no one can copyright an idea, imitating a fellow writer is a form of flattery. But in the end, she knew. A novelist climbs lots of foothills on the way to the summit, and in some cases, if the trek is arduous and the hiker exhausted, one is sometimes seduced to follow the well-worn footpaths of those who have found a way through the thicket. That's all she did. When she faced this particularly thorny patch in her story, she must have seized on Franklin's idea, forgetting quite honestly that it wasn't self-generated and plodded ahead. Now there it was, in a book that was not only published but getting some good early reviews. If Franklin Jelenik reads this work — as he probably might — he's certain to notice Edwina's unauthorized borrowing. And if the critics discover she plagiarized a part of it, they'll slaughter her, and her book-writing career will be over before it ever really gets going. She'd have to live with this, she knew, but she also knew — probably from that night that Augie paused at page 97 — that she couldn't live with him any longer. Artists can be weirdly sensitive, and her feeling that she had let him down as well as herself set off an unhealthy cycle of recrimination that kept Baby Doll at arm's length from Teddy Bear. She became silent, moody. She couldn't write when he was around. And he clumsily offered words of encouragement that seemed patronizing, like she really was a baby doll. They couldn't sustain the artificial conviviality that had subsumed their relationship. She decided that she had to move out. She didn't say goodbye in person but, after a week of mostly mopey silence, left him a note, stripped of all the cliched phrases. It said simply: "I need this book. Please don't tell anyone ever what I've done. The consequences would be horrific," with "horrific" underlined twice. Premonitions of ferocious close encounters clouded his imagination as tears filled his eyes.

***

Padget's close encounter with Joyce's unknown work — if it really was that — reinvigorated his own scholarly impulses. Over the years, he'd begun and abandoned several reviews, articles, and books, only to revisit them months or years later, dust them off, tinker a bit, maybe add a few paragraphs, and then, convinced he had finally found the right project, congratulate himself. After another couple of days' reflection followed by a struggle to regain momentum, he'd wonder why he'd even gotten his hopes up, and the whole cycle would start over again: Abandon. Recover. Restart. Relent. It was a kind of madness — but wasn't the creative impulse madness as well? Wasn't Augustine Hiatt a madman for claiming he'd found a lost Joyce work? Wasn't Joyce himself absolutely mad, having spent his life creating obscure word orgies that only a few readers seemed willing to puzzle out? His daughter, Lucia, was surely mad — or at least that's what the historical record seemed to indicate. And yet, from his reading, he had discovered that she was a dazzling creative artist in her own right. So madness and creativity, unlike parallel lines, do meet, but they meet in the dark corners of the world where happy, well-adjusted souls seldom wander except by mistake. But that was only how things appeared. Joyce knew better. As he once wrote, "A man of genius makes no mistakes. His errors are volitional and are the portals of discovery." Padget took comfort in that, as he often indulged in the fanciful notion that he, too, was a genius and that the muted arc of his career wasn't a mistake but rather the prelude to something grander, something that would arrest the attention of the scholarly world. He understood the anger and resentment Augustine Hiatt felt, being denied a seat at the table after having dutifully served as a water boy at academia's intellectual feast. He dared to imagine, as surely Hiatt must have so many times before, the indignant reception Joyce's unknown work would engender if unearthed by this rather forgettable and undistinguished Ph.D. washout and the lusty last laugh Hiatt would enjoy when the work was authenticated. Padget would laugh too. He decided right then, as he sat there in his expensive but still rather drab one-bedroom apartment overlooking the Hudson River, with a notepad in hand, decorated with a half-dozen book titles he'd come up with over the last hour or so, that he'd become the lost work's advocate. He'd have to take a closer look at the pages Hiatt had photocopied, of course, but if they seemed upon keener inspection to bear out his first impression, then Padget wanted in. Maybe this turn of the wheel would be the one that finally hit — the black ball — not a polite form rejection by some scholarly journal or publisher but one that finds its way into a numbered slot that corresponds to a felt square where Padget had stacked his chips. He'd call Hiatt and ask to review the pages, and then he'd help him plan his next move. He took a sip of port wine, closed his eyes, and heard in his mind the small wooden ball roll around the rail of the spinning roulette wheel, about to take a rare, lucky bounce.

***

Augie Hiatt wasn't home to get Professor Padget's call the following day. He was on the set of a new film. Well, he liked to call them "films." They were really just X-rated romps. But he took his position very seriously. After the humiliating experience of being booted by a group whose approval he so desperately sought, it was gratifying to discover that among the riding crops, leather harnesses and baby oil, he felt like he really fit in.

In fact, in the short time he had been there, he had aroused a good deal of attention from Tongue-in-Cheek's executive producer Bobby Devlin, a fairly vile human being by most standard measures but a kind of savant when it came to spotting genuine talent. Devlin would be the first to admit that everything he did was about him and for him, so when he recognized and promoted anyone within the production company, it wasn't to boost their ego or make them feel validated. It was because they could help Devlin make more money. Augie appreciated that kind of unvarnished sincerity. Academia was filled with lots of self-important blowhards who lamely tried to assure their students and their colleagues that they were all about the "higher values" and that the joy of communicating timeless truths was the only reward they really cared about. Augie learned pretty quickly what bullshit that was. Most tenured professors were only interested in protecting their precious sinecures. Bobby Devlin had a word for people who pretended they cared more about the world than themselves: Merkins.

"You're all set to zoom in for a beaver shot, you know, a nice tight closeup, and you'll discover the girl's got something going on down there. You know, eczema, stubble, a rash, all kind of goddamn things you wouldn't believe. So you need a pubic wig, which is called a merkin," he told Augie over lunch one day during a break in the filming of *Cherry Poppins*, the story of a British nanny who gets sodomized by a chimney sweep. "That's what most people are. Merkins. They present a false front to the world instead of being honest about who they are, what they want. That's the irony of the porn business, chief: we pretend to be about the surface, but we're really about the deepest issues people face: the need for love, hidden desire, longing, satisfaction, exposure, acceptance. All that deep-seated shit."

Augie always took a lot of notes when he was around Devlin. He had never thought about porn as anything other than a rather unseemly genre that catered to the lonely and the perverse. But after a few lunches with Bobby Devlin, Augie came to wonder if *everyone* wasn't lonely and perverse. So Augie tried to capture some of that pathos in his scripts, and although Devlin scratched out or re-wrote lots of Augie's lines, he also left a lot in. And once, during the shooting of a scene involving an Australian tourist whose car broke down in front of a Nevada brothel in a movie called *Cockadile Dundee*, Augie saw Devlin chuckle to himself at a line of dialogue Augie wrote. Of course, he took that as a compliment. The Madame was asking Cockadile Dundee what he looked for in a woman:

C.D.

I like my women just like I like my alligators.

MADAME

[Laughing] With a big mouth that snaps shut?

C.D.

With a thick skin.

That was Bobby Devlin. You needed a thick skin to survive in the movie business; and to survive in the porn business, you needed fucking tarpaper. Devlin expected the people around him to be just as tough, and Augie didn't think he'd be able to hold his own among this grizzled and darkly experienced gang in which he'd suddenly found himself, somewhat adrift but paddling like mad. Yet here he was now, with the formal title of "Script Supervisor" (which, in truth, meant little more than the person who copies the scripts and distributes them to the actors and crew in advance of the next day's shooting). Yet the amount of writing he was doing had increased from mere re-writes to original scripts, and he had become a fixture on the set during shoots. He was surprised to discover that watching porn being shot was the least sexually exciting experience he'd ever had. The amount of time spent trying to artificially sustain erections, frame vaginas for close-ups, lighten areolas, and simulate looks of genuine ecstasy, take after take, hour after hour, was depleting. Porn movie sets were about as sexy as high school hygiene lectures from a Catholic nun.

He stood there, watching the gaffer snake a trunk line behind the set and up into the light rigging as the makeup woman applied a thin layer of pancake to the buttocks of the star of this particular film, *Don't Ass, Don't Tell.* This was not one of Augie's scripts. It was written by Bobby Devlin's long-time girlfriend, a former actress who hit it big doing voice work for cartoons. Her best-known character was Lolly, the talking Lollipop in the animated show *Candy and Gumdrop*, about a sweet shop deep in the forest that only kids knew about. When she wasn't giving voice to the tart-tongued six-year-old with the owl glasses and the lavender ringlets, she was writing scripts about sucking dicks and getting fucked in the ass. "Broad's got range," said Bobby Devlin, for whom linguistic appropriateness stopped evolving in the early 1970s.

Augie had his usual notepad on his knee and was sketching the scene for future reference when Reyna, the office secretary, came up to him and handed him a letter. He had never seen her on the set before, and his surprise at seeing her, coupled with the letter, gave him a bad feeling. If it was important enough to deliver in person, then it must be bad news. But he noticed the letter had no return address. Just a cross where the return address should be. He relaxed. He wasn't being fired — the letter couldn't possibly be from Tongue-in-Cheek productions. Bobby Devlin hadn't made a sign of the cross since his dark masterpiece of nearly a decade ago, *The Sexorcist*, a raunchy parody that featured Devlin as a priest who performs exorcisms on young demon-possessed females by sprinkling not holy water on them but rather standing over their naked, prostrate bodies and coming on their breasts. The movie achieved a kind of cult popularity when the actress playing the demon-possessed heroine was killed by a crazy person who pushed her in front of a subway train. Under questioning from the police, it was revealed that the psycho who pushed her was a petty thief and drifter who had previously seen the movie at a New York City adult movie house and, whacked out on crystal meth, recognized the actress one night as she stood on the subway platform. Thinking she was still possessed and that he was doing the world a favor by dispatching the devil, he shoved her in front of the Brooklyn-bound Number 2 train, killing her instantly. "The worst thing that could possibly have happened to her," Devlin once confided to Augie, "was the *best* thing that could possibly have happened to us."

***

The learning curve wasn't steep for Detective Alana Stamos. The contours of hate had not changed much since her last stint with the HCU. But still, there were things to absorb. Probably the most under-rated aspect of police work — and the one they teach you nothing about at the Academy — is how to work with other cops, especially your partner. As Alana discovered early in her career, the relationship with your partner can be one of the most important relationships in your life. If all goes well, if that elusive chemistry occurs, then the job becomes, if not a pleasure, then at least bearable — and perhaps even satisfying. Sometimes, however, the needle never finds the groove, but the record still spins, emitting a scratchy static that over time becomes almost unbearable. So despite Desi Arroyo's somewhat off-putting first impression, when he seemed more interested in dissolving her resolve than in solving cases, she agreed to meet him for lunch at a local restaurant called Antoinne's, a downscale restaurant with a fancy-sounding French name that cops liked because the owner, an ex-con everyone called Butcher, offered lots of freebies to those who were "on the job," the phrase cops use for police work. So, for instance, a cop trying to shake off a bad day on the beat might find his martini glass refilled numerous times even though no martini ever appears on the check. Ditto dessert. And a party of six might get a bill for, say, a party of only three. Theoretically, these kinds of gifts were forbidden by the department, but no one was interested in making a federal case about it. Instead, cops got a little pat on the back, and Antoinne's earned a reputation as cop-friendly, meaning there was almost always a police officer there during its round-the-clock operation. Robbers got the word, too. Antoinne's had not had a stick-up on or near the premises in the last five years, an extraordinary record for a neighborhood "in transition" where most bar and restaurant owners had the cops on speed dial.

Desi was greeted with practiced familiarity by the hostess.

"Nice to see you, detective," she said, ignoring Alana. "It's been a few weeks. You haven't been cheating on me, have you?"

"I only cheat on my wife," he said, a crass and easy line that knocked him down a few pegs in Alana's estimation, though she chuckled out of politeness. She knew that cops used a sort of crude lingua franca in their professional lives, the by-product of being around so much pain every day. Cynicism was as common among cops as falsified timesheets, but still, Alana didn't like it. Joking about cheating on one's spouse might give one street cred in the sour provinces of the world, but Alana was always reaching for the sweetener. *We're partners,* she reminded herself. *Try to keep an open mind. We need to make this work.*

"So, what got you interested in police work?"

She felt stupid asking the question, which struck her ear like something you might blurt out if you were speed dating. She remembered her mother once telling her when she was thirteen (it would be one of her last memories of her mother) that she should always act interested in what the boy had to say when on a date. "Laugh at all his jokes if you want him to like you," she said, plowing up the same ground that had buried generations of female originality. And it took years to get past that mentality, that need to seem worthy of male attention. Yet here she was, acting like a school girl out on a date with the captain of the baseball team. But it was a reasonable question to ask one's partner, right? *Don't over-think this.*

Desi took a long sip of water, pushed his Buddy Holly eyeglasses back up the bridge of his nose, and breathed deeply. This was not shaping up like a speed-date reply.

"My family was like this really strict, super-religious family living in Queens, you know? My parents were Cuban exiles who escaped with the help of the Catholic underground in Cuba. Very simple people, very devout, like something out of a Bing Crosby movie from the 1940s. It was them, me, and my twin brother." His demeanor softened just a bit. "I suppose when you hear "twin," you probably think we were pretty similar to each other."

“Well, that not always the case,” Alana volunteered. Desi nodded and took another sip of water.

“That certainly wasn’t the case with us; you’re right. When we were fourteen, my brother told me he was gay. I guess I always sensed that, but we didn’t spend a lot of time talking about sexuality at home, you know? So anyway, he tells me this, and he tells me he doesn’t know what to do.”

“Did your parents know?

“Unh-uh. No way. Absolutely not.”

“So, what did he do?”

“Nothing. He tried to act like it was no big deal or like he was joking and wanted to take back what he said to me. But I could tell how much pain he was in. Maybe because we were twins, there was a special kind of bond, a feeling between us. I don’t know. Anyway, it hurt me to see him in pain, so I figured I should do *something*. I didn’t know what to do; I was only trying to help him, Alana. I swear.”

She could see how troubled he was telling this story. Alana had asked a much deeper question than she intended.

“What did you do?”

He uttered a light, nervous laugh. “What every good Catholic schoolboy is told to do when you’re facing a crisis. I went to the parish priest to ask him what I should do, what I should tell my brother, you know? I thought maybe he might let Abie off the hook with a few Hail Marys or something.”

“Abie?”

“Alberto. I called him Abie. So I went to the priest during lunch hour one day and just sort of told him what Abie said and then asked him what I should do. He didn't seem like he was shocked or anything when I told him, so I figured he was just going to pray for him or something. That's what he told *me* to do."

"But he did something else, didn't he?" Alana's instincts picked up a pattern.

"He sure did." Another long sip. He looked right at Alana with tears now welling in his eyes, and his tone became slightly bitter, his words articulated more slowly and with greater force. "He told my father. I couldn't believe it. I thought priests were obligated to keep that kind of stuff to themselves."

"Your father didn't take it well, I'm guessing?"

"He threw him out of the house. At fucking *fourteen.* Packed up his stuff while we were at school. We walked back one day — it was a Friday, I remember —and there was all Abie's stuff, right there on the front lawn in a couple of moving boxes."

"So what happened to him?"

"Abie was a fragile kid, but he also had a tough side. Our neighbors had a son in college who was home for the weekend, and his family had a van. So Abie asked him to drive him and his stuff to Brooklyn, where we have an aunt, my mom's sister. He figured he'd finish out the school year taking the subway back and forth— it was May, we just had another month — and then, maybe over the summer, my father would cool down and let him back home. But that did not happen."

Alana had conducted enough interrogations, heard enough confessions to sense that the story was about to get worse.

"Abie tried to keep things cool at school, you know — telling people my aunt was sickly and just needed someone to help her out, and that's why he was living there. But somehow, the real story got out, about my father throwing him out — and *why* he threw him out. And remember, this is like a really conservative, homophobic Catholic school. And so one day, after track practice — Abie was on the team, he was a really good runner, fast, you know? — a group of upperclassmen grabbed him while he was changing and dragged him from the locker room to the football field, which is where the track team practiced. They stripped him, wrapped a bunch of duct tape around him, tying him to the goal post. Kid couldn't move, you know? He would have cried out for help, but they stuck a sweaty gym sock in his mouth and told him to "suck on that." Then they put a jockstrap over this head and left him there.

"Later that night, when he didn't come home, my mom called the school and got the custodian. About twenty minutes later, he found Abie."

"Was he—what had happened?"

"Well, we're not completely sure. The guys who dragged him out there could have been the ones who grabbed his head and slammed it against the goal post — though they deny it. The police said it was more likely that Abie did it himself. They couldn't say whether he was trying to get free or if he was doing it to, you know, hurt himself. The police report said the contusions were self-inflicted. I believe it. I think he was just so ashamed that he wanted to die right then and there. But he didn't. He died the next day at the hospital as a result of some bleeding in his brain that the doctors couldn't stop. But he never regained consciousness."

Now Alana had tears in her eyes too.

"The worse part — if you can imagine anything worse — is that my dad never talked about it. Ever. It's like Abie didn't exist. My Mom was broken up for weeks afterward, couldn't even get out of bed, but my dad just got up the next day and went to work like nothing happened."

"Jesus, how awful."

"And the school did nothing," he said, his voice filled with the controlled anger of someone who's rehearsed this recitation before. "They held an assembly on bullying, for God's sake, and the kids who were involved got a Saturday detention. That was it. My mother tried to get the police involved. She wanted the mutants who did this to get arrested, but the investigators declared it a `boyish prank' and didn't pursue charges. The school went on the record telling the police that Abie was a `troubled' soul with suicidal tendencies. Can you imagine?"

"No, I can't. What about the priest?"

"The only thing he ever said to me about it came about a month later, at the end-of-the-year school picnic, which they called "Field Day." I was moping around, mostly just sitting on the metal bleachers — how the hell could I run around that track with the same guys who did that to my brother? Anyway, he came up to me and put an arm around me, and said he was sorry something so tragic happened to my brother, and he sincerely hoped it wouldn't hurt my faith. I couldn't say anything to him. I was still numb. It wasn't until months later that I realized the "tragedy" he mentioned wasn't my brother getting killed by those monsters who tied him up. No, the tragedy in his mind was that my brother was gay. After that hit me, the fact that the very people who are supposed to protect you and look out for you are the ones who sometimes make things so much worse, I knew what I had to do with my life. That's why I requested HCU. I keep Abie's picture on my desk, and I look at it every day before I start the job."

The waitress arrived to take their order. Desi took off his glasses and rubbed his eyes.

"Just a cup of coffee," Alana said, reaching out and empathetically squeezing her partner's hand. "I've lost my appetite."

Desi lifted his eyes and gazed at her, a hint of a grateful smile tugging at the corners of his rueful countenance.

"Sorry for ruining lunch."

"No problem," she said. "I'll ruin the next one."

There wasn't a hint of cynicism in his laughter.

***

Russell Padget was surprised to see so many nice homes. Always in his mind was an image of where students lived that comported with his sense of the intellectual separation between them. Padget equated the good things in life with the good *people* in life — that is, the *smart* people. But as he pulled up to the house Augie Hiatt was renting, he was surprised to see so many people on the street who appeared to be so presentable. Nice cars on the street, well-dressed women pushing strollers, and even a wine store named *I need a Medoc*. Padget loved the pun — though he felt superior knowing that Medoc, a French varietal wine, was *not* pronounced like the English "Medic." Still, it showed a little flair. More than he expected in a neighborhood populated with mostly 20-something residents, many of whom likely split their time between school and jobs decidedly unintellectual.

There was a note with Padget's name folded and taped to the screen door. "Be back by 2 — key's under the frog. Let yourself in. A." Augie was supposed to meet Padget at 1 p.m. to go through the Joyce manuscript. He told the professor he no longer felt comfortable carrying the copies back and forth to campus. Last week, Hiatt had been mugged in the wee hours waiting for the train by a man-and-woman tandem after a late-night session at Tongue-in-Cheek. The perpetrators were able to wrest from Augie $7, his iPhone, and the shooting script for *Cum as You Are*, a "Dinner party fantasy where *everyone* is on the menu." Augie was handling the re-writes. As he rode the train home after the mugging, Augie imagined that the depraved duo that mugged him would probably consider the script and not the iPhone, the true prize of their night's work.

Padget puzzled for a moment over the reference to the frog until he looked around and saw a green-bronze statuette of a frog, about six inches high. The frog was holding out a top hat, and its lips were parted to reveal a row of what must have been at one time gleaming bronze teeth. But now, after years of welcoming visitors to the scraggly patch of weeds that nudged the walkway, the teeth had acquired a mossy green patina. Padget thought it was the most hideous lawn decoration he'd ever seen. But under the divot created by one of the frog's legs was indeed a shiny piece of metal that Padget dug out with his index finger. The front door key. *If this is his idea of safety precautions, no wonder he gets mugged,* Padget thought to himself before letting himself in to Augie's place.

The first surprise was how neat everything seemed. There were lots of books and papers around, but all in curated little piles. Augie once made a joke about how you can't spell "doctorate" without OCD, and Padget thought now that maybe he wasn't kidding. The second surprise was finding a young woman sitting on a Papasan chair in the living room, eating a plate of spring rolls with a pair of chopsticks and singing Joni Mitchell's "*Chelsea Morning,*" swaying lightly, the cords of her headphones curled against the edge of her plate. She was dressed in a Trader Joe's Hawaiian shirt and a pair of bicycle messenger shorts. She was in her mid-twenties, Padget guessed. It made sense — Augie couldn't afford this place on his own on just a pornographer's salary. The third surprise — which shouldn't have been a surprise at all — was the pervasive scent of marijuana that hung in the room like so much mind-softening smog.

"Excuse me… hello there? Miss?" Padget walked slowly toward her, hands in a "don't shoot" position. She looked up at him, picked up one of the spring rolls by the chopsticks, and held it out. "No thanks," he waved her off. She didn't even ask who he was, what he was doing here. Was she that trusting? Was she that stoned? Or did she just not care?

Padget decided to engage.

"I'm here to meet Augie. This is his house, yes?"

She nodded, though it seemed to be as much in keeping time with the music she was listening to as an acknowledgment of his question.

"He left this note for me on the door," he said, holding it forth like a search warrant. "I'm going to just wait for him if you don't mind. He has some papers I need to look through."

More nodding.

"I got the key from the frog. I didn't know anyone was home, or I would have, you know, knocked first." He stood looking at her for several seconds, but she had tuned him out. "I'm going to get started with those papers. Don't let me disturb you." She paid him so little heed she might as well have been one of his students.

Padget found Augie's desk without any problem. There was a stack of screenplays with "Tongue-in-Cheek" ink-stamped on the cover pages, as well as an empty and rinsed-out jelly jar that held three or four fountain pens. He opened the top drawer of the desk and saw a large envelope, similar to the kind Padget was always getting in inter-office mail, large enough to hold a medium-size manuscript. On the outside of the envelope was a Post-It note with one word, PADGET, written on it, so he didn't feel like he was committing an indiscretion by opening it.

Not Doctor Padget? Just "Padget"? That's kind of rude. He turned up the skinny metal collar points of the clasp and gently pulled out a sheaf of papers, his heart starting to beat a bit faster. He held in his hands what he sensed was the entire set of Joyce's lost work, a collection of photocopies that, for all he knew, was the only remaining proof that the work existed. Here was history, a literary legacy that (if authentic; *if*) could be one of those discoveries that changes the way scholars would forever view Joyce. He felt light-headed — *could it be the haze I'm inhaling?* — and he sat down on the metal folding chair tucked under the writing desk. Joni Mitchell's doppelgänger was totally lost to the music, and as Padget switched on the gooseneck desk lamp, he took a deep breath and felt himself getting a wee bit high — but not from the weed. He was about to enter a portal of discovery that Lucia Joyce leaped through before she slipped away forever, a magical world of words mysterious in meaning, mesmerizing in beauty and depth, an ocean of possibility.

***

"Those certainly are, well, interesting pictures. Did you draw them?" The volunteer at St. Andrews, a war widow named Agnes Simmons, still dealing with the loss of her husband — technically, he was lost, as no record of the Worcestershire fighter pilot's body being retrieved in the half-decade since the war ended ever surfaced — had been advised by a neighbor who was a retired ophthalmologist that the best way to deal with her lingering depression was to volunteer to help other people in distress as well. Misery loves company, that sort of thing. (The neighbor had facilitated many group sessions involving veterans who were blinded, or nearly blinded, during combat, and he believed that the veterans benefitted from being part of a larger and blinder world than the one they stumbled through in isolation every day). And as Agnes was new on the ward and hadn't yet met Lucia, she had gone in with the hopes of finding a redemptive path forward for herself through the pain and loss of those with whom she'd be interacting. She met Lucia on her first day volunteering on the ward.

"Or did someone send them to you"? Agnes asked this because the drawings that were hanging throughout the room exuded a juvenile, undisciplined quality, something that a room full of schoolchildren might produce after a field trip to an aquarium. There were all kinds of colorful sea creatures — fish, mostly — but also what looked like lobsters, clams, shrimp, and jellyfish. There were other creatures, too, abstract shapes and half-formed visions settling into the cool and dark of the sea. The vivid colors in the sketches were in stark contrast to the drab, prescribed decor of the room — and the ward itself. The thinking behind such a scheme was not very original nor scientific: a lackluster environment was thought to dispel feelings of emotional intensity,

the uneasy management of which had brought many of the patients to St. Andrew's in the first place. "Perhaps a niece or nephew?"

Lucia, who was drawing in a notebook at the time, didn't even look up at Agnes or acknowledge her in any way. She was absorbed in her sketching. Agnes paused in front of one particular picture, which was draped over a lampshade, tied there with a small bit of string run through two makeshift holes in the corner of the drawing paper and looped around the antique brass finial at the top of the lamp. Lying against the shade when the bulb was lit gave the picture an oddly luminescent quality, the colored, wavy lines of the fish a joyous and surreal presence, causing Agnes to exhort "Oh my, how lovely!" when she came across it.

"That's Archie," Lucia said softly.

"Hmm? What did you say?"

But just as quickly, Lucia was lost again to the present task, her face contorted in scrutiny of her current sketch, which Agnes could not see but which absorbed the patient in room 218 so fully that the well-meaning but still grieving volunteer felt her continued presence would be pointless. There was no healing to be had here. If Agnes were going to get over her depression, she'd have to find a different conduit than the mute, scribbling woman with the visually vivacious love of all things aquatic.

***

When Monique asked Augie to be a guest on her podcast, *'Nique's Peek*, he immediately said yes. It seemed to him like a win-win: he'd have a chance to start building a "platform," a first step at re-establishing his academic legitimacy, of bolstering his moribund reputation, and she'd get some premium click-bait for her podcast: a bona fide porn film writer who could share some of the sordid secrets of the industry that he'd witnessed firsthand. This kind of interview could help elevate *'Nique's Peeks* above the thousands of competing internet blab fests — and maybe even give her own stagnant career a boost.

But Augie, who'd already run afoul of the academic overlords, was about to become an unwitting victim yet again. He had underestimated the reach of his friend and former lover Monique's modest little podcast. He had never imagined that anything he'd told her would reach any of the people he worked with — they really didn't seem like the kind of people who spent much time thinking about the culture at large. Their attention spans seemed to mirror the duration of the typical hard-on. So imagine his surprise when he was called into Bobby Devlin's office and presented with a printout (12 pages!) of Monique's interview with him.

Although the interview didn't achieve the viral popularity she'd been hoping for (apparently, "Porn Writer Tells All!" did not have the cachet she naively expected in the filth-besotted cybersphere), the conversation with Augie *was* heard by an assistant editor at VoiceBox productions, the company that handled all the audio work for Tongue in Cheek (and run by Bobby Devlin's step-brother, Crawford). Using voice transcription software, Crawford sent Bobby Devlin a transcript of the interview. What Augustine Hiatt took to be disarming frankness about the porn industry Bobby Devin saw as a stab in the back. The portion of the interview that had most enraged Devlin had to do with Augie's view of the typical audience for porn. He hadn't meant to sound so contemptuous of the clientele for Tongue-in-Cheek, but boy, that's sure how he came off:

Monique: So why did someone so educated, so eloquent —

Augie: Thank you.

Monique: Well, it's true. A Ph.D. in English —

Augie: Almost.

Monique: And here you are writing porn scripts? How did that happen?

Augie: Well, you're right. Most of the writers of porn films aren't highly educated. But they know their audience.

Monique: Meaning?

Augie: Well, your listener can probably picture the typical guy who watches a porn movie. Generally, the audience isn't looking for Shakespeare. They are expecting a type of visceral experience, and for them, the words don't really matter.

Monique: You're saying they're not too bright.

Augie: Monique, porn doesn't aim for the head.

Monique: And you didn't feel this type of work was beneath you?

Augie: Just because someone isn't smart doesn't mean we shouldn't try to accommodate them. And that's what I try to do in my scripts: accommodate the viewer. I know the people watching these movies aren't going to go to the public library to check out *The Decameron.* They probably don't even have a library card. Or even know where the nearest library is. So I figure, let's give them a little culture *within* the movie.

Monique: You mean trick them into learning something?

Augie: Exactly. Trick them into culture, into language, into beauty, into metaphor. Everyone's lives should be filled with the sublimity of great art. And if you are the kind of guy who never would watch an art film, why not put some of that art into the cheap world you're already living in? The Jesuits have a saying that's emblazoned over the entrance to many of their schools: "*In through your door, out through ours.*"

That was the line that Bobby Devlin used when he fired Augie. It came at the end of an uncomfortable (though brief) meeting a few days after the interview with Monique was broadcast.

"Chief wants to see you," Reyna said. "He didn't sound happy."

"How would you even know if he was?" Augie had shot back, feeling increasingly confident and comfortable in the world of Tongue-in-Cheek. "Probably needs to fire somebody and wants me to step in and pick up the slack. I'm getting used to it," he said. In the few weeks he'd been working there, Augie had really come to think of Tongue-in-Cheek as a sort of home-away-from-academia. Having moved up so quickly — from itinerant script doctor to credited writer to many things that he knew fell under the purview of assistant producer — Augie felt his star was firmly hitched to the knock-kneed wagon that was the porn industry. Last week a raise, then the interview with Monique, now — what? — a promotion? He knocked on Devlin's door and walked in without waiting for a reply.

"Hiya Bobby. How's it hangin'?"

"Shut the fucking door!"

Reyna couldn't make out the exact words, but she knew when her boss was in a genuine lather. It wasn't long before Augie walked out of the office, decidedly different from his entrance just a few moments earlier, with Bobby Devlin's stinging rebuke still ringing in his ears.

"WHAT THE FUCK IS WRONG WITH YOU?" Devlin began in his trademark subtle fashion. "You call our customers *morons* and *degenerates,* and you hold yourself up like you're some kind of St. Augustine, here to absolve us of our sins?"

"Funny you say that, Bobby. I was named after him, and I used to think–"

"Fuck you *and* St. Augustine!" Devlin bellowed. "Do you know how much damage you've done to this company? Our customers might not go to the library, but they do use the internet rather frequently, and with the shit you said about our company coming up in every web search for Tongue-in-Cheek, you've made us look like manipulative and elitist assholes. *You're fired!* Get the fuck out before I decide to sue you for breach of contract and defamation!"

"Bobby… is this… are you really firing me?"

"In through your door, out through ours, *asshole.*"

Augustine Hiatt, no saint, meekly rose from the chair and, trying to process what had just happened, slowly made his way out of Bobby Devlin's office, suppressing the tears which would only have further enraged his now former boss. And that was how Augustine Hiatt's career as a writer of porn films ended, not with a bang but a whimper.

***

What kind of person uses a letter for his first name? Padget had never had cause to cross paths with R. Lancaster Zale, the eminent critic and professor, contributor of countless scholarly articles to countless academic journals. He first became aware of Zale's work in graduate school. It kept coming up, in the footnotes and bibliographies of the work Padget always meant to complete, the scholarly works that somehow never panned out, the learned papers and critical essays that never escaped the cozy confinement of Padget's oak desk drawers. Zale was a bona fide brain, Padget, a perpetual aspirant. Their paths never crossed because their orbits occupied distinctly different quadrants in the academic cosmos, he knew: Zale a comet streaking across the sky, Padget a piece of space junk, forever hurtling earthward.

"Dr. Zale's office. Please hold."

Of course, he doesn't answer his own phone. Which was just as well because Padget still wasn't sure what he was going to say. His encounter with the folio full of Joyce's letters in the envelope in Augie's desk left him convinced that the kid was onto something. Was it really Joyce's work? The handwriting looked authentic, Padget thought. The letters to Lucia that Augie copied contained a mini-epic by Joyce, the father to his daughter Lucia, a playful and poetic creation that — if authentic — deserved a wide audience. Zale, who apparently knew both Joyce's work *and* Augustine Hiatt well, would surely extend Padget the professional courtesy to answer some questions about both. The music emanating from the telephone receiver was classical, maybe a string quartet. *(R. would probably know which one.)* As Padget waited for the distinguished professor to pick up the phone, he rehearsed in his mind what he intended to say, though it was still mostly a spontaneous jumble. There was a time when Padget would have been genuinely thrilled to talk to Zale. Just now, however, he felt a surge of resentment — perhaps the right frame of mind to prosecute Augie Hiatt's case. He needed an edge, something to bring to the table in case Zale tried to roll him over. Or worse, dismiss him as insignificant. Which is what, unfortunately, happened.

"Zale here. And who is this who wishes to converse with me?"

Pizzicato yielded to sprezzatura.

"Good day, Doctor Zale. My name is Doctor Russell Padget, and I'm calling to talk to you about Augustine Hiatt."

No string quartet adagio filled the sustained silence, so Padget continued.

"I've been sort of, well, counseling him, and it seems to me—"

"Look, Doctor… whoever you are. You've obviously let yourself be conned by this embittered and troubled young man. My advice is to avoid any further contact. Now, if you'll excuse me."

"Yes, of course, but you see, I've *seen* the Joyce letters. To his daughter. The work seems like it could be—"

"It's not. And if Hiatt doesn't quit this campaign of harassment, he's going to lose more than his reputation. I've had it with his — and your — wasting my time. You don't know what you are dealing with."

And then, after a breathy pause, a dismissive click.

Padget, trying to process what Zale had just told him, cradled the phone in his fist for a moment and then gently returned it to its base.

"Haydn's Sunrise Quartet, Opus 76," he said aloud. "You're not the only one who knows things, R."

Professor Russell Padget determined at that moment not to give R. Lancaster Zale the last word.

***

The #10 bus lurched along the crowded street Monday morning like a fullback dragging tacklers. The four-lane roadway was littered with all sorts of impediments to progress: double-parked delivery vans establishing impromptu unloading zones; daredevil bicyclists weaving through the street in crazy-quilt routes that redefined forward progress; headphone-wearing pedestrians unselfconsciously singing along with their private soundtracks, oblivious to traffic lights; horns honking; the rude and frequent gestures of a mobile and impatient populace imprisoned on the roadway, and the occasional, inevitable accident investigation, lit up like a blue-and-red backlit flashmob. Northern New Jersey at rush hour: no good options. For decades, municipality after municipality crammed more and more people into their confines to reap that lucrative property tax revenue, but the roads never seemed to change, only getting more crowded, more dilapidated. Some days, it was an act of pure madness (or, more generously, extreme naiveté) to climb behind the wheel and try to motor along from Point A to Point B because the whole exercise could well prove pointless.

Such was the scene as Monique Lawson rode the #10 toward Hackett County Community College to see her former professor. All around her on the bus were steely-eyed commuters, mostly immune to the daily bump and grind. Some slept, but most stared hypnotically at their cell phones. Others looked blankly out the window like the world unspooling outside the bus was an urban-wide reality show. Monique was the only person on the bus crying.

She was still distraught as she waited outside Professor Padget's office 45 minutes later.

"Goodness, Monique — we've got to stop meeting like this," Padget glibly tossed off as soon as he saw her. However, he immediately felt foolish for his inane remark when he got close enough to see her face. "Oh my, what's wrong?"

She didn't speak but instead erupted again in tears, biting her lower lip, her hands visibly trembling.

"Ok, Ok," Padget said, placing one arm around her as he fumbled with his keys and opened his office door, escorting her inside.

"Whatever it is, I'm sure it's not that bad. Here," he said, handing her a box of tissues he kept for other occasionally weepy students. "Take a deep breath, and then just—"

"He's dead!" she said, falling into a paroxysm of more tears.

"He?"

Padget waiting anxiously for confirmation.

"Augie!" she said. "They found him in his apartment this morning."

"Oh my," Padget said, putting his prayer-clasped hands against the tip of his nose. "I'm so sorry. Do they know how he died?"

She lifted her head and, with tears streaming down both cheeks, unconsciously summoned her authoritative podcaster's voice.

"He was murdered!"

Padget raised an eyebrow and then nodded solemnly. He reached for the phone, pressed a couple of numbers, and after a moment, said, "This is Dr. Padget. Please cancel the rest of my classes today."

As Monique Lawson tried to catch her breath, Professor of English Russell Padget shook his head mechanically. Blocks away, traffic ground along like clogged clockwork, frustrated drivers checking their watches to see just how late they'd be. But inside his office, time seemed to be moving backward, Monique seeing in her mind's eye her friend and ex-lover, recalled perhaps at some tender moment while Padget's head filled with visions of scribbles hidden in a dead man's desk.

Monique shook her head, banged her fist against her thigh.

"I cannot believe they got him."

"They?"

"Yeah. What Augie called the 'Academic cabal.'"

"Whoa, whoa… Monique, you're not seriously suggesting—"

"Augie told me they'd never let him publish his findings. *Never.* Too many reputations at stake."

"But honestly, Monique—"

"You've got to find the guy who did this."

"I don't really see how I can do anything here."

"I know his name. Zale. He destroyed Augie's career. And then when Augie wouldn't take it lying down…" She glared at Padget.

"Oh, wait a minute. Just because I made a few calls?"

"They knew… Zale knew you were on to him. He knew you were going to help find a way to get the Joyce work into print. That would have made a laughing stock of Zale. And guys like him *never* allow themselves to be laughed at."

"But murder?"

"And theft."

It was Padget's turn to glare at Monique.

"The manuscript?"

"Gone. I told you, these folks don't play!"

Had Padget's well-intentioned fact-finding led to Augie's murder? That was a preposterous notion — although he remembered feeling that way when he first heard the story about the secret manuscript. Still, the idea Augie was killed for the Joyce manuscript seemed like something more out of a novel than the realm of reality.

"Get this bastard," Monique muttered. "He's guilty. Don't let him get away with this. *Please.*"

Monique was in real pain, and Padget was still in shock. But now, it was his turn to shock Monique with the vehemence of his response.

"I will."

Her eyes, still moistened with tears, brightened as Padget simply nodded and repeated, "I will," the wavy lines of Joyce's handwriting dancing in his mind like so many sea creatures swimming against the tide.

Part Two

Fearless, and Therefore Powerful

[CODE TWO-FOUR-SIX, DOA, ROBLES STREET, NUMBER NINE, SOCO REQUESTS FORENSICS. ALL UNITS BOLO ARMED PERP OVER]

"Another one bites the dust," Mooch said, turning down the squawking police scanner on the cabinet near his desk. "Come on, Sweater. You'll have to finish your crossword later."

"Keep up your impudence, and you'll hear quite a few cross words," Sweater replied, grabbing his notepad and heading out the door.

"Maybe the murder weapon was your razor-sharp wit," Mooch shot back. "*Oh, help me, I've been mortally wounded!*" Mooch said, staggering out the door like he'd just been gunned down.

Sweater shook his head in disdain and blindly followed.

Alana Stamos would have shaken her head as well at such juvenile and unprofessional behavior, but she'd been transferred and wasn't around the squad room anymore to chastise her colleagues. Tonight's "Code 246" at Augustine Hiatt's place was all theirs.

***

"Are you registered?"

The polite, 20-something woman behind the table half-stood up, preparing to lean over and grab the appropriate plastic-coated I.D. sleeve from the columns of name tags identifying attendees by title, school, and discipline (thus facilitating the inevitable punch-bowl meet-ups that followed every session: *"Oh, I see you're a medievalist. So tell me, do you feel Boethius has ever received his proper due?"*).

"No, I'm more of what you might call a walk-in," Dr. Russel Padget said. "I was told I could still attend the sessions."

"Oh yes, of course," she said, sitting back down. He couldn't help but notice her copy of Rimbaud's *Illuminations* lying tented at her elbow. *Remember those days? Reading Rimbaud so you could tell everyone you were reading Rimbaud? Or maybe she really liked him.* "But there's a fee per session for non-registrants. Did you know what panel you want to attend?"

Right, *panel* — it was all coming back to him. It had been years — no, decades — since he'd attended an academic conference. Sensing his momentary confusion, she handed him a program of the afternoon's panels. He scanned it quickly, looking for one particular name — but he didn't see it.

"Um, I suppose… ah, how about this one?" He pointed to a session that was underway: "Pop goes the Moment: The Consequences of Cultural Lapse in 1960's Utopic Fiction."

"That will be $20, please," she said, tearing off a perforated "Hello, my name is _____" from a long roll of the sticky, one-sided I.D. badges. She picked up a Sharpie. "Can I have your name and affiliation?"

"Well, if you don't mind, I'd like to just kind of stay anonymous," he said, winking. He handed over a $20 bill. She looked perplexed. Why would an academic even come to these things if not to boost their name recognition? She shrugged and took his money.

"Room 108, just down the corridor and to the left — but I should tell you the session is almost over."

"That's fine," he said.

The final presentation was underway when he entered the lecture hall. There were four people — the *panel* — at the front of the room on an elevated stage, and someone who appeared to be a moderator just a few feet away from the table, which featured the dutiful array of microphones and water glasses — one for each presenter. One of the academics appeared to be midway through his presentation. Padget took a seat in the back row, stretched out, and began catching up with what he'd been missing. The room had about 20 people in it, Padget estimated.

"In this particular case, the consequence of failure was societal, and its cultural reverberations redounded far beyond the tiny fictional island, beyond McLuhan's 'islands of isolation,' and even beyond the 'sceptered islands' receiving the transmission."

In the darkness, Padget couldn't read the program to see exactly what this talk was supposed to be about, so he took out his phone and shone a light on the tiny print in the program. Each presenter's speech had a title followed by a brief abstract. Judging from what he had just heard — and the lateness of the hour — Padget guessed he was listening to Dr. Bradley Stokes, an American Studies professor from Garton College in Eastern Iowa, presenting "Shipwrecked by Silence — Sherwood Schwartz and the Failure of White Imagining." The abstract said the paper was about "how very different American social history would have been if the Professor on *Gilligan's Island* had been black."

How about that? And I thought this was going to be a waste of time. The sneaky and warming realization that he was part of a Ponzi scheme called academia made him chuckle guiltily. He leaned forward and listened intently for the remainder of the presentation, absolutely rapt. When it was over, and the lights were turned on, he approached Dr. Bradley Stokes as the participants were gathering their papers and heading out the door for the punch bowl in the common corridor.

"Great presentation, Dr. Stokes. May I ask you a follow-up question?"

"Yes, of course." Tell an academic he or she is great, and they'll always let you ask a follow-up question.

"Would the consequences have been the same if, say, Ginger, or Mr. Howell, had been black?"

Dr. Bradley Stokes uttered that dismissive laugh that comes only after years of discovering how far superior one is to almost everyone else.

"No indeed. You see, the professor is the *thinker*. He's the one who solves most of their problems, yes? He's the *smart* one. Just imagine if a generation of mid-60s families had gathered around their televisions once a week to see a black man solving technical and scientific problems for a group of hapless white people. Can you imagine how much further along race relations would be today? Don't you see what that would have meant to a young black boy or girl watching that? The message that would have sent to black America? To White America? It staggers the mind."

"Even for such a silly show?"

"Silly show? Sherwood Schwartz, the creator of *Gilligan's Island*, pitched the show as a 'social microcosm.' His words, not mine. But an all-white group of castaways is hardly a social microcosm. Yet if he had created a *genuine* microcosm, I believe we could have avoided decades of incalculable racial turmoil."

"Hmm. You should write a book about that."

"I'm writing one," he said, turning his back on Padget and heading out the door. *Guy didn't even ask me my name.*

"See ya, little buddy!" Padget shouted, hoping Stokes would find the *Gilligan's Island* reference amusing. But he ignored it or at least didn't acknowledge it. Padget turned to what he took to be the moderator. "Excuse me, I wonder if you can tell me. Have you heard of a Professor named Zale? He's supposed to be giving a paper on—"

"Are you kidding me? *Everybody's* heard of Zale. That's why half the attendees are here. He's giving the keynote address tonight."

"Right. Thanks."

Padget already knew this — it was the message he got when he called Zale last week after he'd gotten the news about Augie Hiatt's death. Well, he'd gotten the message from Zale's secretary. Zale himself couldn't be bothered. His secretary said Zale was working on his keynote address and that if Padget really wanted to speak with him, he should go to the conference and try to talk to him there.

"No guarantees," she added. "He's a very popular speaker, and there are always a lot of people who want to talk to him. But I'll give him your name. Who shall I say called?"

"Archimedes."

Padget smiled grimly to himself at his little 'in' joke as he made a note on his calendar to confront Zale at the academic conference, knowing their encounter was likely to be far less smile-inducing.

***

The memo stated simply, "Production Meeting, usual time— Full Crew, MANDATORY." Most of the time, these meetings were not of great value. Todd or Beth — or both — would gather the crew together pretty informally and simply remind everyone what the script required: props, costumes, special lighting. But

Todd and Beth likely had already worked out the details. For most of the production staff, there wasn't anything new or critical during these quick recaps. In fact, sometimes, it was *only* Todd and Beth at these pre-shoot meetings. So "mandatory" was a bit of an attention-getter, as was "full crew" (usually, it was just whoever happened to be hanging around at the time and could help out), who now milled about a bit nervously, wondering what was happening. But when Beth arrived, it dawned on those assembled that the upcoming shoot was going to be different. She entered the studio space they sometimes rented on the first floor of the former industrial building where their offices were located dressed as the Virgin Mary. Ok, no sweat — many of the Friend to Man videos were costume dramas of a sort. But when she spoke — in character, it seemed — the assembled members of the production crew sensed something about this shot was different.

"My brothers and sisters in Christ, I ask you for your prayers and your strength. What we are about to do will not be easy. Let us clasp hands and pray together for the strength my son will need." Which they then did. Normally, the hand holding was done *after* the shoot because prior to the shoot, everyone was holding a script, which each performer or crew member had marked up according to their specific job. But for this shoot, no script had been distributed. So hands were free to hold other hands.

"God in Heaven, we humbly beseech you: grant us the faith and endurance to convey our great and abiding love to all your children. No matter what. Amen."

No matter what?

Beth/Mary resumed speaking in a quiet, calm manner.

"Today will be very special. Our strength will allow our followers to experience salvation *firsthand.* Brother John, will you come forward?"

Stepping from the fringe of the circle and carrying a small black leather bag was a serious-looking man in a dark suit, late 30s, just a touch of gray peppering his temples.

"Brother John — excuse me, *Doctor John* — is here in case of a medical emergency. He will be present at all times, so fear not."

The man nodded. "Hello, everyone. God be with you all." Then just as quickly, he retreated back to the fringes of the studio set. *So why is a doctor needed?*

"This is a big step for us today," Beth/Mary continued. "I hope you are all as excited as I am. Property master, would you and your crew please bring in the set-piece `Alpha'?"

Four of the production assistants stepped into an adjoining room. Beth/Mary remained silent, head bowed, eyes tightly closed. After a few moments, they returned carrying a heavy wooden cross about 12 feet in height. They heaved it past the assembled crew and set it upright into a rocky wooden base that had been fashioned and fitted last week in the carpentry workshop next door.

"Today, brothers and sisters, we will be witness to a crucifixion. Not a representation of a crucifixion but an *actual* crucifixion." She bowed and stepped back from the center of the assembled group, creating a gap. "Now, let us welcome our son and brother and share with him your love and strength as he prepares to sacrifice himself for our sins."

Walking onto the soundstage, in a simple woolen robe, was Todd Lawson. Or, as he would soon be known to all of mankind (or at least those with internet access), the crucified Christ.

***

Holdena Straithorne had it — that's what her boss, Jules Cirro, always told her. "Deena, you have *IT*," he'd say smilingly as he emerged from the weekly meeting with his boss, Lanny Sanders, president and publisher of Phalanx Publishing, and the rest of Phalanx's sales and marketing staff. In his time as acquisitions editor for Phalanx, Cirro had hired dozens of manuscript readers and watched them dutifully inscribe their deeply informed marginalia across the pages of the perpetually regenerative slush pile: "Promising — solicit additional chapters," or "Intriguing, but not for us," or some such conclusion, penciled in after pages and pages of annotations. But even the most savvy professional reader on staff seldom found that best-selling gem publishers dream about. At best, maybe one in ten manuscripts they published even turned a profit (ten percent was considered a pretty decent average at Phalanx). Holdena Straithorne's average was closer to eighty percent. As a result, she was treated as something of an oracle at Phalanx — and most definitely not held to the same standards as the rest of the submission editors. Holdena could more or less arrive and leave when she wanted to, take extended vacations (with little notice), and avoid attending weekly staff meetings. One might think this would cause a bit of resentment among her colleagues, but once they got to know Holdena, they realized she didn't bend the rules to accommodate her ego but her gift (remember, she had *IT*.) Holdena was convinced — and she convinced her bosses as well — that she could only function at her high rate of success under specific working conditions: No more than 90 minutes of work without a break of at least 45 minutes to follow, no emails or voice mails to respond to, no formal office wear (sweats and t-shirts for Holdena; standard business wear for everybody else in the office), and the same lunch of cold sesame noodles every day, delivered to her right at noon, after which she would retreat to the conference room and take a nap.

Holdena also had a gift for reading people as well as manuscripts. One of the other reasons no one resented her was because she was so accurate with her unsolicited assessments of people's individual problems. It was not uncommon for

Holdena to stealthily sidle up to a colleague in the lunchroom and whisper a verdict as brief but incisive as her literary commentary: "Dump him," "Move out of your mother's house," "Your contractor is ripping you off" or even "Don't abort." No piece of advice was too personal, and none was dismissed out of hand by her colleagues.

"It's like working with fucking Nostradamus," said a college student during his exit interview after an abbreviated summer as an intern at Phalanx. "My third week, she comes up to me and says, `Get tested for HIV.' Goddamn if she wasn't right."

Holdena didn't say these things to endear herself to her colleagues or even because she felt a strong inclination to help them right what was wrong with their lives. But, shy as she was, she simply couldn't help herself. The impulse that drove her to tell Reggie in accounting that he needed to start working out or Bev in direct marketing that earth tones would be more flattering on her than the bright colors she usually dressed in was like the unconscious reflex of an English major to correct grammatical errors on public billboards. It just happened.

Holdena was also, at heart, a genuinely nice person. Almost freakishly so. She frequently left little Post-it notes on colleagues' desks and office doorways with messages that might seem saccharine, or cloying, coming from other people: "I really like working with you," "The world is a nicer place because of you," or simply "You're SOOO cool!" Phalanx employees loved getting these notes - many of which were waiting for them in the morning when they arrived at work (Holdena often did her best work late at night or the early hours of the next day, and so she often had the office to herself and could leave these notes in the night like some kind of goodwill fairy.)

Her optimistic and overwhelmingly positive posture could easily be seen as ironic. She was, after all, named in honor of the hero of a well-known novel about an embittered teenager who was repulsed by the phoniness of the world (Holdena's parents met outside the home of J.D. Salinger, the reclusive author of the book, each on a sort of pilgrimage to the writer's house, and they memorialized that meeting in their child's name). But Holdena didn't see phoniness in the world — she saw glory: in the work that she did, in the people that she saw, in the books she loved. She rejected the pessimism of the modern world, choosing instead to revel in the goodness of simple pleasures: life as a tasty bowl of sesame noodles.

Yet she could also be harsh on the manuscripts she didn't like — literature was too precious, its power too transformative to waste in weak and watered-down prose. The dog-eared sheaf of papers that currently lay on her desk wasn't likely to make it to Jules Cirro. (Other readers had to submit their reviews and their manuscripts to Cirro for his final approval of their decisions, but he told Holdena not to even bother.) On the first page of a novella titled *Regret's Propulsion*, she had written "F&F," — her shorthand for "friends and family," meaning those were the only likely readers for that particular work of literature.

Having just awoken from her nap, Holdena still felt a little groggy, but she rubbed her eyes, stretched like a kitten in the sun, and reached into the slush pile, plucking out a fat rubber-banded manuscript called *The Fiendish Cats of Kosovo.* Only an optimist on the order of Holdena Straithorne could hope to find greatness there. She removed the rubber band, scrunched herself into her reading chair, and began sifting through the silt of American letters, searching as always for gemstones among the grit.

***

"Ladies and Gentlemen, our keynote presenter needs no introduction." But Professor Rosalind Deitz gave him one anyway — she wasn't going to miss her moment in the spotlight. She rattled off the usual litany: books published, chairs held, honors and awards, mentor to a generation of scholars, committed humanitarian, blah, blah, blah. Throughout her encomium, the subject of her laudatory praise sat on the stage in a leather wing chair, trying to appear humble. R. Lancaster Zale, distinguished professor of this, that, and the other thing crossed his arms, the tweed of his blazer's double-breasted lapels rumpling oh-so-slightly his silk monogrammed necktie, giving him the practiced appearance of someone who seems not to care how he looks despite the precise choreography required to pull off such nonchalance.

Professor Russell Padget, who had once again settled into his seat in the back of the auditorium, was surprised by the sustained — *thunderous*, even — applause when the introduction was finally concluded and Zale made his way to the lectern. *This guy is a rock star.* The printed program had simply identified the presentation as "Keynote Address," with no title or subject matter, so it would be up to the speaker himself to reveal precisely what he would be talking about. *We might not even know what his talk's about even after we hear it*, Padget thought, remembering when he was on the job market and had to attend these kinds of events to put in what his advisor called "face time." He remembered pretending to be interested in whatever the speaker was saying, always making it a point to go up to the presenters after they had delivered their papers and telling them how much he got out of their talks. It was a fraud, of course. Most of the papers were dull and incomprehensible. But it was what you were supposed to do, so he did it. And now here he was, expecting yet again to go up to the presenter after this particular talk — not to compliment him on his brilliance but to find out where he was on the night that Augustine Hiatt was murdered.

"Thank you so much for that wonderfully gracious introduction — and for not fact-checking any of that with my wife," the eminent Dr. Zale said to modest and polite laughter. "Tonight, I'd like to share with you some thoughts on a subject that has recently captured my fancy, and to which I've begun assembling notes for my next book, which I have tentatively titled: Guilty Pleasures: Immorality and the Intellectual Outlaw."

Guilt? Outlaw? *Something you'd like to confess, Dr. Zale?*

"My book will explore various instances throughout literary history of writers who have done something, well, unethical or immoral — all in service to their work. From Lord Byron's debauches to William Burroughs' drug abuse (which led him to shoot his wife in the head) to even the unassailable Shakespeare — who after all was a serial plagiarist — many revered writers have embraced a conception of themselves as outside the prevailing moral code because they felt their work, the end product, demanded it.

"To focus on one rather extreme example of the dozens I've been looking into, consider the case of Sir Thomas Mallory, who most of you know as the author of *Le Morte d'Arthur*, that most eminent collection of stories about King Arthur and the knights of the round table. Many of you here probably read it, perhaps even wrote papers about it in graduate school. Our very notions of Camelot, with its codes of chivalry, its damsels in distress, its questing knights, and its celebration of nobility and brotherhood, derive directly from that work. Mallory himself has come to represent a kind of high priest of the chivalric code. But how many of you know he wrote that work while he was in prison in London after being convicted of rape and murder? Of course, when you read *Le Morte d'Arthur* cognizant of its author's crimes, it's all there: murderous rage, sexual lust, the thrill of the kill. Our gilded age tends to sanitize literary history when, in fact, much of the body of western literature is, like Tennyson's famous assessment of nature, 'red in tooth and claw.'"

Feeling a little bit of the murderous rage yourself, are ya, Dr. Zale? Padget was locked into Zale's address in a way that he hadn't expected, and he was sorry he hadn't brought a notebook to write down these incriminating thoughts. Surely someone must be making a transcript of these remarks — just in case Zale refused to turn his address over to the authorities or refused to confess to the crime.

"These instances of the poète maudit are not limited, of course, to the literary patriarchy. One of my favorite stories — that is, one of the most revelatory — is that of the British crime writer Anne Perry, who at age fifteen joined her best friend in murdering her friend's mother, a fiendish task that required more than forty blows to the head with a brick wrapped in a stocking. Now, I want you to imagine that for a moment — a young girl, a teenager, bookish, genteel, resolving to murder a grown woman simply because they wanted her out of the way, and then, carrying it out in the most cold-blooded fashion. Because of her age, she was only sentenced to five years. For the rest of her career, she drew on those murderous impulses to create riveting, villainous characters. I'm ashamed to say she's one of my favorite writers. As I said, the title of the book I'm writing is *Guilty Pleasures.* I'm sure you all have yours, as well."

A light murmur of assent filtered through the audience.

"What are we to think of such transgressions of the social code? How are we to feel about works of literature born of blood? Is this just an extreme example of authors following that time-honored piece of advice, 'Write what you know'? And those of you who write, to what lengths would you go to acquire the knowledge necessary to fuel the fires of your own creative conflagrations?"

This was a surprisingly effective keynote address. Padget sat there, actually thinking about the questions Zale was raising. What lengths would he himself go to, how far outside the social norms he valued so greatly would he venture to achieve… what? Greatness? Fame? No, something less. Simple respect.

Padget immediately chastised himself for having gotten so caught up in Zale's address. *Stay focused — remember why you're here.* The goal, after all, is to get Zale to say something incriminating, or at the very least, have him provide something that points to Augustine Hiatt's murderer. He must know something. Zale was the king in this court, an academic Arthur ruling over his fawning squires. How far would he go?

"How far *would* you go?"

Padget surprised Zale a bit with that question, the first thing he said before even introducing himself.

"I'm sorry?"

"I was just wondering how far you would go? Bribery? Threats? Murder?"

Zale, who was still flush with satisfaction at having delivered an address that clearly resonated with the crowd, many of whom were still swarming about in hopes of catching his eye or ear, looked at Padget with bafflement. But then a glimmer of recognition flicked across his still sweaty brow.

"Oh, yes… we spoke on the phone. You're…?"

He knows my name but won't acknowledge me. Power play. I recognize it.

"Dr. Russell Padget." He didn't stick out his hand, nor did Zale.

"Yes, well, what is it you want?"

"I came here to ask you something. Nice speech, by the way. I wondered if you heard about Augustine Hiatt?"

"As I mentioned on the phone, I see no reason—"

"He's dead."

"What?"

"Murdered, actually. Last week."

"Goodness. I'm very sorry to hear."

"So you didn't know?"

"How could I know?" Zale asked, his annoyance undisguised.

"Maybe because you were there. Does the name `Archimedes' mean anything to you?"

"I have no idea what you are talking about."

"The Joyce manuscript? The one you denied existed and then stole after you had Augie murdered."

Well, there it was, all pouring out, with more passion and less restraint than Padget would have imagined. At that moment, he realized he completely believed Augie's story about the lost manuscript. Zale just happened to be there to absorb the brunt of Padget's epiphany.

"I hope you get the help you need," Zale said dismissively, turning aside to converse with a group of admirers who had made their way to the keynoter and were eager to share their insights while they had a place at this intellectual roundtable, however fleeting.

"The truth will come out!" Padget yelled, more like some angry college student protester than a mature and mannered college professor. The throng briefly acknowledged his outburst with a caesura of puzzlement and then returned almost immediately to bombarding R. Lancaster Zale with praise for his insights and gratitude for just a moment of his time, as they all wished to share their guilty pleasures with him. Almost everyone, it seemed to Padget, had something to feel guilty about.

***

"Told you."

It was a gentle reprimand from Alana Stamos to her partner Desi Arroyo. After their lunch together, Alana had thought a great deal about Desi's story about his brother. She often found herself staring over at him, watching him as he talked on the phone, or mindlessly filled out the reams of paperwork each case seemed to spawn. To her eye, there was something off-putting about his outward manner. He seemed to exude a kind of oily confidence, even a disdain for the world of substance. He could often be found glancing at the nearest reflective surfaces to reassure himself of his outward appeal. He frequently left high-end clothing catalogs on the lunchroom table, in the bathroom, or even folded outwardly in his blazer pockets, broadcasting his sartorial superiority like a peacock spreading his feathers. By all appearances, he seemed to be all appearances. But since that lunch — and in fleeting moments since — Alana, the detective detected moments when she glimpsed the real Desi, a sensitive man of deep conviction and an impassioned champion of human dignity. She was remembering an interview he did yesterday with an autistic young woman and her mother — the girl had been targeted by a group of bullies who stole her bus fare while she waited at the bus stop, and then emboldened by the easy mark they found decided to help themselves to her purse, phone, even her boots (knockoffs of a well-known and pricey designer from Australia). She saw Desi actually tear up while taking the report. His manner with the girl — Karina? Carolina? She couldn't remember — was more fatherly than prosecutorial. He had a natural gift for connecting with those people who had not won the genetic lottery, those that society had singled out as nerdish and needy. And when he was done taking her statement, and he escorted the young woman out of the squad room, she hugged him, and he hugged her back, the tears in his eyes no longer self-contained. And yet, five minutes later, there he was, thumbing the pages of a catalog of a high-end clothier, asking Alana if women were turned on by matching ties and silk handkerchiefs. People are complex.

"Just coincidence," he said, sounding confident, defiant.

"Nah, I told you — you jinxed us!"

"What the hell are you talking about?" asked Captain Felton, his eyes darting back and forth between the two detectives.

"Not twenty minutes ago, Desi was talking about how dead things seemed today — something we used to say in the homicide division, by the way, whenever we got busy. Anyway, I told him not to say it because he'd jinx us and we'd get bombarded with work. And now here you are, dropping a case on us."

"Pure coincidence, sister," Desi retorted. He'd recently started referring to Alana as "sister," which she found off-putting, even sexist until she began to wonder if it was maybe his way of reaching out to her, establishing a bond. Was it a police thing, you know, `brothers-and-sisters-in-blue'? Or was she — and other women he was close to — filling the role of the missing sibling in his life? Was it guilt? Good-heartedness? Or was he just a troll? Well, it wasn't her job to solve every mystery in life, just the ones that came in manila folders with file numbers taped onto their tabs that got dumped on her desk.

"So, what's today's matinee?" Desi asked as Alana opened up the file. She scanned the report, then glanced over the file at Captain Felton as if to ask why this was being handed off to hate crimes."

"The vic isn't gay or a minority — straight white male. Looks like a robbery gone wrong. What's the catch?"

"Check out the notes attached to the tear sheet."

"Friend to Man?"

"Oh, shit!" Desi blurted out. "Those fucking Jesus freaks?" Desi was already at his laptop computer, punching up a social media website. "It's a group of crazies that put out these totally dope videos. Costumes, music, puppets, real artsy shit."

"Film students?"

"Evangelists. At least that's what they call themselves."

"You don't agree."

"Check the notes," Felton said. "When they're not busy spreading the whacked-out Word online through their groovy-vibes videos, they're sending threats to heathens. The vic was one of them. He got a few damning letters from them, one as recent as a week ago. Now he turns up dead — shot in the face."

"Whoo-hoo! The righteous sword of retribution, baby!" Desi said, quoting something he'd heard from one of their videos. "Our Lord is not a meek Lord!"

Alana looked at Desi and then at Felton, who shrugged his shoulders.

"Arroyo has been looking into their operation for the last few months. We've known about them, but they haven't stepped over the line."

"Until now?"

"That's for you and Arroyo to figure out."

Alana looked at Arroyo, who had a cat-that-just-ate-the-canary look on his face.

"What are you so giddy about?"

"I hate to be played."

"So, who's been playing you?"

"These fuckers," he said, flicking the file case. "I went over to their office about six weeks ago. They're in the old tannery building in Hoboken. Kind of a dump. They use it as a headquarters and a studio for their… what the fuck did that guy call it? `Homiletic montages.' Whatever. When you watch a few, you'll probably be weirded out like I was. Anyway, I get there, expecting some acid-washed Scorsese wannabe, and instead, I met this guy who runs the whole Friend to Man thing with his sister, and he's like a bookkeeper from the 1950s. I mean, brush haircut, white shirt and skinny black tie, horned-rim glasses, but acting like David Bowie and talking like a parody of some TV evangelist. "Thee" and "Thou" and "Take heed, brother!" Couldn't get a real clear read on him — except that he was dirty. That much, I'm sure of. Something was going on, something beyond sharing the saving grace of our Lord Jesus Christ. They're playing Mary and Joseph, but they're more Bonnie and Clyde."

"Did you bring him in?"

"Couldn't. I had nothing."

"But if they've been threatening people?"

"They threaten people," Felton interjected, "the way every minister in America threatens his congregation on Sunday. Sin and you're going to hell."

"Yeah — but they make it personal," Desi said. "They send dozens of letters every week to all kinds of people. Doctors, lawyers, atheists, sex workers, anybody soiling the message of deliverance. Still, the letters are vague enough to get them off the hook — legally. But I knew they'd fuck up, eventually. Looks like they did,"

"At this point, it's just a theory," Felton said. "Don't rule out other possibilities."

"It's them. I know it," Desi said. "This guy, what was he… lemme see the file."

Alana handed it over to him. Friend to Man… where had she heard that name before?

"Oh, baby! Triple word score! Check this out: the vic wrote porno films!" Desi ejaculated. "Friend to Man snuffed him out." Desi seemed a bit too elated. When Alana shot him a questioning look, he simply repeated, "I don't like to be played."

"Just a theory, remember," Felton said.

"We'll look into it," Alana said, while Desi continued in an almost religious reverie, waving his arms, bowing his head, and chanting, "I'm coming for you! I'm coming for you, fuck yeah!"

Desi went over to his desk and grabbed a file filled with photocopies of letters Friend to Man had sent to various heathens. "I'm going to go read some scripture," he said, grabbing his jacket and slinging it over his shoulder. "If you want me, Sister Alana, I'll be at Antoinne's, changing wine into water."

In this instance, "sister" didn't seem inappropriate — kind of pithy, in fact — so she just smiled and nodded as he bounded off, convinced he'd already collared the culprit. But Alana was more careful, more judicious. She had leaped before she looked too many times in the past. Friend to Man sounded like a pretty creepy enterprise, but the world was full of creeps, and at this point in the investigation, Felton was right — it was too early to narrow down the possibilities. Alana needed to get her feet wet on this one, and even though her shift was ending, she knew that she'd be getting very little rest. The first few hours on a new case were like the formation of a bruise, the initial shock and pain morphing into recognizable contours, colors emerging on a blank, fleshy canvas. She needed to get a read on the victim, Augustine Hiatt. She pulled out a notepad, logged back on to her computer, and then reached out and hit a number on her speed dial.

"Hello, Lee?"

Li Qiang, proprietor of The Golden Chopsticks, recognized her voice immediately.

"I'd like the usual, please. That's right. Thanks."

She hung up the phone, the taste of fried pork dumplings tinging her mind's palette. Chinese food meant she'd be at work for several more hours. She reached into her purse to grab her wallet and excavated a $20 bill ("Keep the change," she heard herself say). In a few hours, when the nearly empty oyster pails of Chinese takeout decorated her desk top, Detective Alana Stamos would have a slightly better sense of who Augustine Hiatt was — and who might have wanted him dead, a roster of dark intent filled with the names of friends — and foes — to man.

***

The lanky, saturnine-looking man stood at the iron gate and simply leaned back and stared up at the house on the hill. It didn't look like a clinic, though upon closer inspection, he noted a few features that distinguished it from the upper-class homes where he sometimes had been invited to tea. There were bars on the windows, and at the end of the curlicue driveway that led to the French doors adjacent to the carport, there was a stocky man in a brilliant white uniform and hat, standing with his arms crossed, an anxious bearing forming his whole existence. He was waiting for something, impatient but resigned. The slope upon which the house looked down was tended artfully, hydrangeas columned like sentries along the well-manicured lawn of dwarf perennial ryegrass and trimmed neatly in primrose. The man at the gate lazily stuck his hands in his pockets, thinking about what to do next. There was a sign indicating that all visitors must use the intercom system to communicate with the admitting office, but the man at the gate had never used one before, didn't know what an "intercom" was. There was a button, but he didn't realize, apparently, that one had to press it and then lean forward to speak into the small, wired grid. Someone from inside the clinic must have noticed him standing there because they eventually buzzed him, which caused a fleeting moment of astonishment, this voice from nowhere asking him who he was and what he was doing there.

Regaining his wits but unsure where to deliver his answer specifically, he spoke as if he was talking to an invisible person standing next to him. He was very cordial when he spoke.

"Samuel Beckett."

He heard a brief shuffling of papers, and then the voice told him that his name was on the visitor's log and that he may enter. Next, he heard a rumbling, and a metallic scraping, then the wrought-iron gates he was standing in front of slowly swung open, and he walked up, hands stuck purposefully in his trouser pockets. Several paces before he reached the front door, he saw her sitting in what was called the "sunroom" — even though only the very early morning sun illuminated the space. The rest of the day, the room was in the shade, though the young man ambling toward the sunroom was grateful for the tint of darkness. He hadn't really wanted to come, though he knew he had to, mostly for her but also for him.

When he reached the front entrance, he paused, unsure if he should just walk in or wait to be told what to do next. This time, an actual person came out to meet him and ushered him inside.

"Any packages?" she asked, not looking at him, staring down at a piece of paper clamped to a clipboard.

"No."

"One moment." She returned to her station behind a glass partition, told him to proceed, and he heard another buzzing sound. He pushed the door open, and soon he was in the sunroom at St. Andrew's Hospital for the mentally unsound.

"Samuel!" The intensity of her greeting unnerved him, but he tried to maintain his poise. He offered a wan smile as she embraced him, and soon they were sitting, facing each other across a small wooden table, her hands extended, grasping his. "I'm so happy to see you. I've been so dreadfully bored here. You can't imagine what it is to spend all of your time waiting."

"Waiting for what?"

"You don't know. That's the worst part."

He nodded and laughed lightly to himself.

"But now that you're here, I don't have to wait any longer," she said.

He fidgeted a bit before replying.

"I don't understand."

"Now that you're here, we can leave. You can tell them it's going to be okay; you've come to get me."

"Lucia," he said, staring into her eyes, misty portals of goodness and terror. "Nothing's changed. I'm not here to take you away. I'm here just to say goodbye. I'm leaving for France, and I just wanted to—"

"Liar!"

She dug her fingernails into the palms of his upturned hands, leaving little red crescent moon marks in his pale flesh.

"Monster!"

Later, the doctors would describe her as "hysterical," just as she had been described by her mother when Samuel Beckett had come to her Paris flat to end their relationship. He had no idea it would be the catalyst that began her final downward spiral, nor had he realized it would herald the end of his relationship with her father, who in many ways had become his own father over the last several months, sitting at the foot of his bed while the nearly blind writer dictated passages of a work that seemed as private in its language as the secret lingua franca that father and daughter used to communicate with each other.

He sat like a shadowed stone now, the sun having moved into lighter and happier spaces.

"I'm sorry," he said. "I never meant for things to get out of hand."

Lucia put her head on her crossed arms on the table and looked sadly out of the barred windows.

"I always hoped you'd see it, but you never did. You're as blind as they are."

"See what?" he asked.

But she didn't answer. Her eyes filled and refilled with tears, a look of resigned melancholy fighting something deeper, a quality of goodness that mere saltwater could not wash away.

***

The readers at Phalanx publishing were told to always remember that their job wasn't to select the books *they* would like. Their job was to find the books the *public* would like. Personal taste was not to be mistaken as a barometer for publishing success. That was rule #1. But there were other rules as well: Read deeply before deciding a book lacks merit. Scan for potential — if this particular book doesn't have potential, does the author? Can the liabilities of the story be redeemed by re-writing? (Phalanx publishing maintained a lucrative side business of "editorial consultations" — essentially an ego-stroking for insecure authors who wanted to sit down for an hour and go through their manuscripts "with a seasoned publishing professional" for a hefty fee that was advertised as "highly competitive.") These rules, and many others, were written down and given to the interns and manuscript readers in an in-house publication referred to as "The Gospel" — that's how seriously these guidelines were taken.

Except by Holdena Straithorne, whose unorthodox approach to unsolicited manuscripts comprised a completely new testament. Holdena was *always* guided by her personal taste. If a work didn't appeal to her after a couple of pages — maybe it was the writing style, maybe a character failed to register with her, maybe it was simply a quality of voice she found inexplicably grating — she gave it the old heave-ho. If the writer didn't grab Holdena early, there was no hope for either of them. In the amount of time it took most manuscript readers at Phalanx to read the typical un-agented submission, Holdena would have thumbed through half a dozen works. Even her bosses — who claimed to have great respect, awe, even, for her almost prophetic powers of intuition — would have been surprised to learn just how hastily she formed her opinions about the worth of a manuscript. Frequently, she never got past the first couple of pages before registering a verdict.

"The writer deserves a fair chance," Holdena remembers Jules Cirro telling her and the other new employees during her first training session. "After all, you wouldn't want someone to make snap judgments about you."

That didn't make any sense to Holdena. In fact, the only reason any of them were there in that room listening to Jules was because *he* had made a snap judgment about each of them. Snap judgments determined the course of many people's lives, and the world seemed to get along just fine. She made a mental note to pretty much disregard what she was hearing and to just do what she had always done when she read a book: give yourself to it *fully*. You'll know right away if it's a book you are supposed to find — if the writer is a friend — or just posing as one. Why would you spend time with people who don't get you when you could be alone instead? That was her philosophy, though she'd never stated it explicitly. Holdena would much rather be alone with her own thoughts than spend time trying to find compatibility with a stranger. But sometimes the stranger turns out to know you almost as well as you know yourself. That familiar feel of the psychic tumblers turning happens seldom, but when it does, you don't have to be convinced. You don't need copious notes or marginalia or a marketing strategy. Bells ring, coins clatter, and you feel lost for a moment, swept along by the rush of recognition. When that happened, Holdena would whisper "Jackpot" to herself and set aside that submission for the next editorial meeting. And almost always, her private jackpots became winners for the house.

As Holdena stretched out on the daybed in her office, a small stack of unread manuscripts balanced on her stomach, the afternoon held the promise of discovery. Her Bluetooth speaker blared the usual mix of classic country that put her in the most relaxed state (though inducing widespread smirking through the offices of Phalanx publishing, whose executives found such music rather unsophisticated).

Holdena took a deep breath, closed her eyes, and randomly pulled one of the manuscripts from the gently undulating stack. "Let us pray," she said, pulling on her reading glasses and grabbing her #2 pencil. The next hour saw Holdena cycle through more than a dozen manuscripts, none of them destined to make it to her boss's desk. Was she being too harsh? Maybe. But whether the pages she let fall on the floor unmarked would have earned a similarly quick shut-down from her more empathetic colleagues never entered Holdena's mind.

There was a novella-length ghost story called *Shivering Timbers* about the spirit of a seventeenth-century pirate who had been executed but was now terrorizing a port village in Florida whose town council was trying to build a luxury condo development. The construction site was plagued by inexplicable accidents — raising the interest of the president of the local historical society, who discovered the legend of a local pirate who swore vengeance on the land just before his hanging.

There was a non-fiction book called *Golf Widow Syndrome — How to Put `Fore'-Play Back Into Your Relationship*. It was a whimsical guide to living with a man who thinks chasing birdies with his friends on the golf course every Saturday afternoon is preferable to trying to score with his wife at home. Holdena wondered how much mileage the writer could get out of the golf puns that filled the first page, but she wasn't committed enough to find out. "This book will help put the `drive' back in your hubby's libido without you having to get too `catty.'" the preface began. Holdena wondered if the author even realized that the word was spelled "caddie."

There was a memoir by a man who left his job as a subway motorman to become a Buddhist monk. The book was called *Engineering Goodness*, and instead of chapters, it had "station stops." There was a fantasy novel called *Winger* about a young girl who could communicate with dragonflies and a detective story called *Follow the Dough* about a baker who moonlighted as a private detective, using his baking skills "and his rye sense of humor" to help solve crimes "for those kneading his help." Reading that made Holdena hungry. She decided to take a break and go out for a doughnut, trading the afternoon's half-baked ideas for something she genuinely craved to consume.

***

"And make sure you've got the klieg light shining directly *into* the camera. We need a lens flare right as the cross is being lifted — you know, the setting sun over the shoulder as Christ expires. Gonna be a beautiful thing. But we're only going to get one shot at this, and I'm gonna be in no condition to shout `cut' if we get it wrong. *So get it right!*" Todd Lawson said sharply, but then he softened. "I'm so sorry, brother. Here, give me your hand." He reached out and grabbed the director of photography's hand with both of his. "Forgive me my impatience, brother. I know not what I do." Todd smiled, and the DP nodded, clasping Todd's hand in his own. This would be Todd's last chance to direct the scene before mounting the cross. The idea had come to him a month ago to actually have himself crucified.

"But, that would mean you… what, die?" his sister asked, concerned but intrigued when he first proposed it to her.

"Well, no. I think we should take it right up to the death. You know. Nail me, hoist me up there, taunt me, crown of thorns, the whole deal. What do you think?"

Beth Lawson pondered for a moment, thinking about how genuinely excited their online followers would be if Todd were actually crucified. She could practically hear the donations pouring in. Devout evangelicals love intensity; they love suffering. *Well, let's give it to them in high definition*, she thought. Yes, let's do this! But what she said to her brother relayed more of a pragmatic concern.

"Where are we gonna get a crown of thorns?"

They had solved that problem and lots of other little details that came up along the way as they worked out the logistics of the scene (including having a doctor standing by, a requirement put forward by the lawyer they kept on retainer). Once they had convinced a local demolition company to donate the lumber for the cross — an old exposed ceiling beam from a vocational school for the blind that was being renovated to create luxury condos — they were home free and heaven-bound. For weeks, Todd had been preparing for today's shoot, including several additional sessions with his sister, bringing him manually to near-sexual climax and helping him block out feelings of physical urgency. He'd also been practicing meditation and self-hypnosis to overcome pain. Today, he'd take it to a whole new level. And if he felt pain — which he was sure to do when the centurions used real spikes to nail his hands to the cross — well, that would only add to the authenticity of the scene.

Is it crazy to agree to be crucified? "The early Christian martyrs didn't think so," Todd told the crew at a production meeting when he finally decided on this course of action. "In fact, they thought it was crazy *not* to. They weren't going to deny the Lord and miss out on eternal salvation just to save their own miserable skins. But that lesson has been lost on people today. They need a reminder. Let's *be* that reminder."

Fear of the Lord is the beginning of wisdom, Todd told himself. And in truth, he was afraid. Afraid that his director of photography — a recent convert named Billy Vale, a former philosophy student and small-time drug dealer who was "saved" while attending his recovering meth-addicted girlfriend's evangelical church — would fuck up the shot. So he pulled his sister aside just before he laid down to be bolted onto the cross.

"You've got to stay on the monitor the whole time. Make sure he gets the close-ups. I don't want people thinking we're using special effects. Show the blood, show the tearing flesh. Billy's squeamish. He'll pull away. You won't. Make sure when they nail me, we nail the shot. Don't lose heart. Everything we've worked for the last three years. It all comes down to today." He lifted her chin with his hand. Goddamn if she didn't *really* look like Mary, the mother of Jesus. "You've got to be strong today, for everybody. Stay on the monitors. Our followers need this. Humanity needs this. Don't let the devil weaken your resolve."

She took his hand and pressed it against her cheek. She pulled his head gently toward her to offer her own final words of comfort and adoration, whispered with love into his ear, which she lovingly cupped.

"Don't stifle your screams. Make sure you really yell out in pain," she said, a tear starting to roll down her cheek. "That will add significantly to the dramatic impact." She leaned forward, kissed him on the forehead, and then shouted "Places!" to everyone in her typically businesslike and no-nonsense manner.

***

Investigating a crime is a lot like driving someplace late at night that you've never been to, without a map and sometimes without even headlights. You have a vague idea of where you're going and possibly what you'll find when you get there, but you don't know how many wrong turns you will take and how much doubling back will be required. Some crimes — they're called "cold cases" — are never solved because the investigators simply lost their way. Too many roads flitted by in the darkness, avenues that might have led to a lead but were so poorly lit or hidden away by nature or design that they never were explored. Alana Stamos knew that every crime had a perpetrator but that sometimes the road to discovery was too fraught to make capture a realistic possibility.

At other times, *too many* roads presented themselves to the probers of a criminal act. Thinking back to her conversation with Captain Millner, she was reminded of the JFK assassination. Millner once told her that the reason so many questions remained after the crime was the number of possible assailants, all of whom seemed to have a good reason for wanting JFK out of the way: the Mafia, the Cubans, the Russians, Lyndon Johnson, the military-industrial complex, J. Edgar Hoover — the list seemed to be endless. And sometimes, having too many suspects is as bad as having none at all. So instead of driving along on a one-lane highway, hoping to connect to another road, you're lost in a spaghetti bowl of possible exits, each putting you firmly on a path in one direction but moving you further from every other direction.

As Detective Alana Stamos of the Hate Crimes Division began her background research on Augustine Hiatt's apparent murder, she wondered which category this would fall under, no real suspects or way too many. It wouldn't take long to discover this was more spaghetti-bowl than lonely highway. Initially, the list of possible assailants seemed pretty garden-variety: burglars, ex-girlfriends, drug dealers maybe. There also appeared to be a recent rift between himself and an employer, Tongue-in-Cheek productions. Then there were the letters from the evangelical group, Friend to Man. What to make of those? The victim had been kicked out of grad school — had he done something to piss someone off? Maybe a fellow student? Could revenge be a motive? His girlfriend moved out of his apartment recently — did it end badly? Alana had enough experience in homicide to know that sometimes people just get killed for the wrong reason — or no reason at all: mistaken identity, wrong-place-wrong-time, some random act of *un*kindness.

Of course, sometimes cases turn on factors that aren't uncovered by investigators, things that seem to come unbidden: letters sent in the mail, photos that mysteriously appear on a detective's desk, an anonymous phone call giving a tip, sometimes a name. These revelations are often the result of a guilty conscience: a witness sees a murder, decides at first not to get involved, thinking *it's not my business... why should I get involved?* But then a few sleepless nights, maybe a few sleepless weeks, and suddenly the desire to "do the right thing" becomes undeniable. Some very high-profile cases have been broken not by the work of intrepid investigators but by a nosy neighbor or cheating husband who simply couldn't keep the lid on the pot. The motives of most of these 11th-hour testifiers are usually pure: *gotta do the right thing*. But sometimes, it's tainted with the residue of self-interest or revenge. Alana knew this — she'd been "played" many times in her career. Every detective has. But despite the strong case that can be made for staying cynical *all* the time, if you're in law enforcement, you've got to trust people.

So when Alana got a call from a young woman named Monique Tyson saying she had information about Augustine Hiatt's murder, Alana started the process of sifting. What does she know? What's her relationship to the victim? Can she be trusted? What's in it for her? Alana was experienced enough to know that sometimes even the perpetrators of the crime will come forward, hoping to throw the police off their scent, implicating others to cover their own guilt.

"Where would you like to meet?" Alana asked the somewhat nervous-sounding young woman on the phone.

"Meet me at Catnap," Monique said.

"The pet store?"

"It's next door to where I work. I don't want to talk around my co-workers. I'll meet you in the reptile section. I'll be there during my lunch hour."

That's a new one, Alana thought. Usually, informants want to meet at a diner or a bar — though sometimes they'll pick a more clandestine location, a strip club, maybe, or an underground garage. *They've seen too many spy movies*; she always figured in those instances. A pet store? Hmmm. *Not sure what to make of that.*

About forty-five minutes later, Detective Alana Stamos found herself face-to-face with a leopard gecko, a gorgeous, lithe, reptilian throwback, dappled brown and purplish, under the warming UV light of a 30-gallon aquarium tank. The gecko was sunning himself (herself?) on a simulated rock cave, a nervous-seeming cricket hopping wildly about on the other side of the tank.

"They're beautiful but fragile." Alana turned around and found Monique Tyson staring at the tank. "They're also very high maintenance. Five degrees too hot, or too cold, and it's feet up in the morning."

"You must be Monique. I'm Detective Stamos."

"Thanks for coming to meet me."

"My pleasure. Sorry about your… friend, was he?"

"Augie? Yeah. He was my friend. We used to date, but after we broke up, we stayed friends."

"That's good. A bit unusual, in my experience."

"Yeah, mine too," Monique said, wandering past the cages of bearded dragons and iguanas to a small alcove where exotic birds chirped gleefully.

"I sometimes come here just to be around animals," Monique said. "Animals make the best people."

Alana nodded. Monique seemed to her a little like a rescue animal herself, wounded and mistrustful but in need of love.

"So, what can you tell me about Augie Hiatt?" Alana said, trying to return the conversation to the human animal.

Monique exhaled.

"I know who killed him — and I want you to nail the bastard."

"You have my attention."

"It's going to seem crazy when I tell you. I know you're not going to believe me, but I promised myself I wouldn't keep it to myself. No matter what he might do to me, too?"

"Who, Monique?"

She bit her lower lip.

"His name is Zale. He's a professor, a bigshot. You can check him out online — lots of publications, all that shit. But he's a prick, and he killed Augie."

"And why would he do that, Monique?"

A scarlet macaw in the aviary alcove unleashed a throaty chirp, flapping its wings furiously inside a wire mesh cage hanging from the ceiling.

"Because Augie had him by the balls."

***

"Cheater!"

Professor Russell Padget looked over his shoulder. The voice was familiar, but he couldn't immediately place it, and he simply didn't see anyone he knew. Probably it was directed at one of the students standing in the long line snaking its way toward the cash register. This was the worst time of day to come to the cafeteria, he knew. But he'd just finished placing his book orders for the coming semester next door at the bookstore, and he didn't feel like walking across campus to the food truck. He figured he'd save a little time by ducking into the cafeteria and grabbing a quick bite before class. As he stood there, eyeing the dozen or so students in line in front of him — and the lone work-study student looking puzzled as she tentatively punched the electronic keypad for the cash register — he realized he'd miscalculated. He'd be lucky to have time to get to his office and eat before class. He'd probably have to actually eat in the cafeteria, a prospect he generally dreaded. The cacophony of student conversations, the raucous music, and the inane overheard cell phone conversations all served as an appetite suppressant. But here he was in line, committed.

"Thought you didn't eat meat!"

Camile Danforth, his math-loving colleague, had sidled up next to him, wagging a shameful finger at him with one hand and holding a styrofoam clamshell filled to the starchy brim with onion rings in the other. Typically, anyone trying to cut in line — even a professor — would have been subject to the taunts of the hungry, waiting mob, but Camile was one of the most popular professors on campus, and the students behind quickly returned to their banal conversations without so much as a raised eyebrow in her direction.

"I'm not as moral as I seem," he admitted, caught red-handed with a grease-stained paper plate holding a thin slice of pepperoni pizza. "But in my defense, I've eaten much worse."

"Hmm. Some defense."

He would have remarked on the fact that they always seemed to run into each other at the various food dispensaries on campus, but they had long ago acknowledged that odd fact. Math and English were like the academic equivalent of the Crips and the Bloods, two distinct gangs whose territories almost never overlapped.

"Still eating healthy yourself, I see," he said.

"Have you had these onion rings? They are so delish! Want one?" She plucked one from the stack, held it aloft like some kind of delicate creature, wiggling it gently before him.

"Thanks. I'd like something more substantial. I don't like to dine on food I can see through."

"Your loss," she said, taking a healthy chomp out of the ring, turning the crispy O into a capital C.

"You realize you haven't paid for that yet, right?"

"I'm counting on the rule of associative property. Zoe is a math major."

Zoe, unbeknownst to Padget, was the name of the beleaguered work-study student currently weighing a take-out salad container.

"Associative property. I can't remember. Does that have anything to do with committing fraud?"

"Russ, no offense, but when it comes to math, you're an absolute zero."

After they'd worked their way through the line, they found a couple of spaces at a Formica counter that ran the length of the back wall of the common seating area in the student cafeteria.

"So tell me," Camile said, tracing her finger around the perimeter of the styrofoam container to salvage any of the crumbs that broke off from her deep-fried delicacy. "Whatever happened with that wild story your former student told you? About the secret manuscript. Did you look into it?"

So much had happened on that front since he first casually mentioned it to Camile that he didn't really know where to begin. So he abruptly changed the subject.

"Camile, do you ever think about retiring?"

"Me? No way. They'll have to carry me out of this place."

"Keep eating those onion rings, and you'll get your wish."

But he could tell she was sincere. As he surveyed the lunchtime crowd, all he saw were reminders of his own growing frustrations, students far more interested in using their hand-held cells than their brain cells.

"What about you?" she asked. "You thinking of giving up the ghost?"

"No, I just… I just haven't been myself lately. I've got a class shortly, and I'm just not sure I'm up to walking into a classroom full of students who think Hamlet is an item on the breakfast menu."

He took the final bite of his pizza, a half-moon of crust lying in a small silhouette of grease on the flimsy paper plate.

"Sounds like a classic case of burnout. Maybe you need a sabbatical. Ed Dobbins — you remember him, taught accounting? Anyway, he took a sabbatical three years ago and it changed his life."

"Really? How so?"

"He went to Tahiti, met a cocktail waitress there, and never came back."

Padget sighed.

"I'm not much of an islander," he said.

"There's lots of ways to combat burnout. Onion rings, for instance."

"I don't worry about becoming burned out, exactly. I know that's a common complaint. But I think the opposite poses an even greater threat. The more one spends time in a particular discipline, reading, writing, researching, whatever, the more one knows about that subject, right?"

"Hopefully, yeah."

"Right. So each year, a teacher is learning *more* about the subject he teaches. But each year, students come in knowing the same as every other group of students, or maybe even a little bit *less* than they used to know. And so the gap between the teacher's knowledge and the students' knowledge grows. Eventually, the gap becomes too great, the chasm too vast to traverse. At some point, the parties will barely be able to even talk to each other. The knowledge divide becomes canyon-esque. That's not burnout. That's Babel."

"Wow. If eating meat has this impact on you, I think you're wise to avoid it."

Padget laughed lightly, picked up his plate, and slid off the Naugahyde stool.

"I've got a class. Great to see you, Camile."

"You too, Russ. And don't forget, our students have things to teach us."

"True. They're really good at finding stuff online. Maybe one of them can find me a really cheap flight to Tahiti."

***

For a bunch of people who still didn't really know what they were doing — on a purely technical level, that is — the crucifixion video was shaping up to be a marvel of amateur cinematographic achievement. The lighting, the sound, the costumes, even the camera work seemed, well, divinely inspired. The centurions (a couple of box boys from a local grocery store called FoodVilla who agreed to wear some cheap leather gladiator outfits Beth Lawson had found online) were really getting into their parts. One of them actually spat on Todd Lawson as he laid down on the cross, a move that seemed to take all the players by surprise ("This is awesome," Billy Vale said quietly to himself as he watched the action unfold on the monitor). Beth had explained to the box boys what they were expected to do. They were highly skeptical at first — who the hell would want to actually *nail* another person to a piece of wood? Who could? So in their pre-performance rehearsal in Beth's office, she did what any casting director might do to calm the nerves of any would-be role seeker: she gave them drugs. Once they had moved past the initial giggly stage, she told them that what they were doing had cosmic consequences. "Cosmic? *Really?*" And just like that, the drugs kicked in, and the actors bought in. Now she could only hope that when Todd's reflexes did what human reflexes do in the presence of unbearable pain — the screaming, crying, and of course, bleeding ("There's gonna be blood? COOOOL!") — that they would still think things were cool. All it took was one flinch, one "I'm sorry, Dude!" one hesitation with the mallet, and the shot would be ruined. Beth could feel her heart racing under her virgin's robe. Todd appeared to be focused somewhere far away as one of the centurions/box boys knelt on his forearm, and the other grabbed a handful of nails.

"This is it," Beth said, biting her lips so hard she could taste blood. Just imagine an *actual* crucifixion — captured forever on video, to be replayed again and again in times of personal doubt. How many souls would they save? How many weak-willed sinners would find the strength to persevere once they saw what Todd Lawson had done to his flesh, willingly and in the name of the Lord? *Holy Hosannah!* Everything they had worked for, all the promises they had made to others and to each other, were all about to come to fruition with that first "thwack!" of the mallet as the iron nails pierced Todd's flesh. Camera Two was close on his hand, Camera Three on his face, the principal camera was holding the long shot.

The centurions — still appearing to Beth to be pretty stoned, were not only *not* getting squeamish — they seemed to be getting into it. "Where's your fucking father *now*?" growled the actor kneeling on Todd's arm. "Maybe he can't *hear* him!" said his partner, getting into the savage act. "I guess he needs to be a little louder. Maybe *this* will get his attention!" The actor with the hammer showed Todd the four-inch nail he was about to drive into his flesh. "See this, savior boy? This is one of my best nails. But I'll tell you what — *you* hang onto it for me, okay?" Derisive laughter, delivered right on cue.

These guys are unbelievably good, Beth thought, biting down even harder on her lip. *Todd is gonna flip when he sees this.* When she was auditioning them in the office prior to the shoot, she sensed that their natural crudity and irreligious nature might be an asset, but she had no idea that they could be so convincingly sadistic. They were really getting into it. These guys would have actually made good centurions. She cleared her head and tried to focus on the shot, making sure each camera was deployed correctly. And that's when she noticed the tear rolling down the side of Todd's face. His eyes were open, his mouth muttering what appeared to be a series of silent prayers, that one lone tear just glistening on the side of his face. Beth waved to the young woman on Camera Two — a former veterinary-assistant-turned-holy-roller after she said a cat she was putting to sleep actually *spoke* to her, urging her to get right with the Lord ("You had to be there") — and then pointed to her own face, indicating the tear. The young woman nodded, and the camera moved in as close as possible to the track of the tear. This was going way better than she had imagined.

"Well, Jesus Christ, I've really got to hand it to you." The centurion (there was nothing about him now that said "box boy") lifted the hammer, pausing just for a moment to giggle at his own pun. Then he drove home the nail with demonic ferocity.

***

Dearest Papli,

Something wondrous strange happened to me. Earlier today, I asked Enid to take me into the garden because I wanted to draw some pictures and the smudges on my window looked like a ghost (and he kept ruining everything I was drawing by sticking his stupid ghost-face into all the pictures). Enid is a sweetie, but I had to beg her because she says if I get in trouble, she gets in trouble. The evil magicians who run this place create trouble when there is none, just so they'll have an excuse to practice their dark magic. But Enid must know the secret word because sure enough, she got me out! I spent almost an hour there (I think it was an hour, but it could have been five minutes or five hours. There are no clocks here, so we never know if things are moving as fast or slow in the real world as they are in our minds) Just imagine — the rose garden all by myself! The sun wasn't even setting yet, but the moon on the other side was waiting for her turn. I had my pad and tried to draw, but then I decided just to stare at the flowers and try to remember them later. And that's when the strange thing happened.

Remember when I was little, and we were walking by that church with all the beautiful windows, and I didn't know what a church was, and we saw all those people going in, and they were dressed so fancy, and I asked you why they were all going in, and you told me that they think they are going to God's house, but then you laughed, and I asked you what was funny and you said: "God is a shout in the street." Do you remember? Well, I was sitting there in the garden, and a honeybee flew over from one of the roses, and he landed on my hand. Enid wasn't watching, or she would have shooed it away, but I just let it stay there, and it climbed from my hand to my wrist and then up my arm, and I tried to be very still, very flowerlike because I was very happy and honored to have this little bee thinking that maybe I was a flower too! As it approached my shoulder, I turned to get a better look, and I spoke to the little precious little thing and said, "I think you are more glorious than the roses," and it looked at me — I swear Papli, it looked right at me — and then it lifted off so so so slowly and then buzzed away gently and landed on some rose in the flower bed, but I could still feel the tickle of its fuzz on my arm, and I held my hand up to my face, and there was this very very fine dust on my hand where the bee landed, and it smelled like flowers (but it was a little sticky). And then I thought, "God isn't a shout in the street, God is a trickle of sweet-smelling dust — and the bees are his angels."

Your loving one

***

Preface

The thing you miss most is toilet paper. I would have thought coffee. We all drink coffee, right? Heck, I couldn't get through my morning — couldn't even *start* it — without a cup of Joe. But dependency is a funny thing. Lots of the things we think we need to get through our day — caffeine, texting, Haagen-Daaz, hot showers, bourbon, sex — are actually negligible. It's true: change your thinking, change your world. Of course, I was changing more than my thinking. I was changing, well, *everything*.

It all started when I met Nathaniel at an eco-fair during a summer of volunteering for an environmental activist organization. My job was to walk around with a clipboard and get signatures on a petition to urge the state legislature to provide funding for a census for the yellow-bellied sapsucker, a fetching little songbird whose numbers had been tumbling due to suburban over-development. Nathaniel was sitting behind a card table that was strewn with beadwork: necklaces, bracelets, earrings, bandanas, beautiful stuff, really. His grandmother made them, and he went to fairs and sold them. (His grandmother was in her mid-90s, bless her heart!) Nathaniel's grandmother is a member of the Ojibwa tribe, one of the most important and long-dwelling Native American tribes from the Upper Midwest. Like most Ojibwa, her native lands were seized generations ago by the government in their campaign to relocate Native American nations (there are more than 500 separate Indian nations. Did you know that? I didn't!) But she continued to practice the traditional native handicrafts she had learned as a girl from her grandmother, and so on, and so on, hundreds of years back into the past.

I asked him to sign the petition, but he just looked at it and kind of smirked. Then he handed it back to me. "Don't you care about the earth?" I asked him in the practiced tone of indignation that the organization taught its petitioners. The look he gave me — I tell you; it froze me right where I was standing. But I had to find out more about him. Just *had* to. It was one of those situations that romance novelists call a "sentimental imperative" (get me, ladies?) Anyway, we talked for the rest of the fair (I never did turn in my petitions… sorry, Gail and Jesse!). And yes, we fell in love, eventually. Along the way, I learned a LOT about the Ojibwa tribe (and even met his grandmother before she died — she made me a beaded leather belt that I'm wearing as I write this). But Nathaniel said the only way to *really* understand the Ojibwa — or to begin to reckon with the horror of the Native American holocaust (not *my* word, folks: read the stories! *So* sad!) Is to live like the Ojibwa. He challenged me to spend a month on an Indian Reservation. No, not as a Keno girl in a casino (though I've been in Indian casinos, and they are *lots* of fun) but actually on the land — outside, I mean. Well, there's tipis, of course, but most of the time you're outside. You live on the land — but you also live *off* the land, if you get my drift. Everything you use — food, shelter, clothes, tools — is supposed to come from nature. That's where the toilet paper situation comes in. The Ogalala Lakota (that's who I was with for my month on the reservation) don't buy *anything* at the store. Want to know what they use instead of toilet paper?

Not enough to read further.

Holdena scrawled a few other notes in the margin of the manuscript: "Reads like a junior high school girl's report about what she did during summer vacation. Send the author a note to read *Bury My Heart at Wounded Knee.*" What the world does *not* need are the shallow observations of Gabrielle Naismith [if Holdena had made it to Chapter Six, she would have learned that Gabrielle earned the Indian name "Sister Quill" from the other tourists and "searchers" spending their vacation on the reservation]. Even the title, *Love and Other Reservations* seemed derivative. Was this the way the rest of the day was going to go?

"Nap time," Holdena said, casting aside the manuscript and settling in for a guilt-free afternoon deep sleep.

***

"Someone here to see you."

Students. Sheesh. How do they always know just when I want to be left alone?

"All right. Send 'em in."

Russell Padget gathered himself. His afternoon had been spent vainly trying to introduce a group of students to the intellectual underpinnings of the Protestant Reformation — another exercise in frustration for him, for them, for the heirs of Martin Luther, a circular discussion in which concepts like *Pre-destination* and *Grace* seemed to have as much relevance as the "No Talking" sign in the school's library. But soon, he'd be home. He had no more classes this afternoon, and his mind was already stretched out in his recliner, buried in one of the leather-bound books that were his refuge, a buoy of intellection in a tidal pool of pop culture that washed over him but left him dry. *How could they have never heard of Wittenberg?* When he asked one of the students about Martin Luther's "95 Theses," the young man shifted uncomfortably in his seat and then suggested, "Maybe that's what got him shot," confusing the sixteenth-century reformer for the twentieth-century civil rights icon.

"Mr. Sanderson, are you suggesting the Protestant Reformation happened in the nineteen-sixties?"

"Um, well, I wasn't born yet, so I guess it could have been then, yeah." A surprising number of students nodded in assent. Why not? They weren't born yet, either.

"The Protestant Reformation was one of the defining events of Western Civilization. Its impact shattered Europe."

"Isn't this *American* literature?" a brave but flummoxed soul volunteered from somewhere in the protective miasma of the back row.

"Yes, of course, but we cannot talk about the Puritans without understanding *who* they were, *what* they were reacting against, *what* they were seeking to do in the New World." His tone was more pleading than exasperated. He really wanted them to understand this.

"Mr. Sanderson — what would it take for you to leave the land you grew up in, the people you knew, everything you had ever known, to travel to some place that was completely unknown — might not even *exist*, for all you know? What would it take?"

Roy Sanderson processed the question, but he needed a bit more data.

"You mean like for Spring Break?"

Russell Padget stared at the blonde, bulky Sanderson for just a second and then bit his lower lip, turning back toward the front of the class. The clock showed him he was seven minutes away from being free of his students. If his students could conflate the sixteenth and twentieth centuries, it was surely no crime against chronology to pretend that it was time to end class.

"Continue reading John Smith's diary," he told them, rousing a bit of life by signaling class was ending. "We'll talk more about the Reformation next week."

That exchange was still looping through his mind when he heard the knock on his office door.

"Come in." *And let's make this quick, shall we?*

"Hi. Professor Padget?"

Not a student, she. A parent of a student?

"Yes, that's right. Please, come in."

"Thank you."

He gestured for her to take the seat facing his desk, but she remained standing, thrusting her hand into her pocket and then removing the small leather billfold that housed her badge.

"I'm detective Alana Stamos, an investigator with the Hate Crimes Unit. May I have a few moments of your time?"

"Why, yes — certainly. Won't you sit down?

"Thank you."

Alana settled herself comfortably, removing a notepad from her canvas shoulder bag and placing it on the desk. It had several lines scrawled across the top half of the page, but Padget couldn't make out the writing.

"I won't take much of your time."

"Oh, that's quite all right," Padget said, trying, like most people who are confronted with a police detective at their door, to sound as non-defensive as possible. "I'm done teaching for the day."

"I see," she said, picking up the pad, looking at her watch, and then making a few quick notes before placing it back on the desk. Then she looked at him. "I'm sure you must be wondering why I'm here."

"Of course. 'Hate crimes' — that sounds pretty serious. Are you sure you don't want the math department?" He chuckled awkwardly, reminding himself to share that one with Camile the next time he saw her at the food truck.

"Professor Padget, I believe you know a Monique Lawson?"

"Oh no! Please tell me nothing has happened. I just saw her a few—"

"No, she's fine. Well, a little upset, actually, at the death of Augustine Hiatt."

"Oh right, right. Monique recently gave me the news about him. I could tell that she was distressed."

"Yes. Distressed — and angry. I met with her earlier today, and that's why I'm here. I'm hoping you can help me clear up something."

"Of course. How can I help?"

"Well, the investigation is still in the very early phases. We're not even sure Augustine..."

"Augie."

"Hmm?"

"Augie. He preferred to be called Augie."

Alana leaned forward, jotted a quick note, and continued her explanation.

"Monique seems to have known this Augie pretty well. And she believes he was murdered."

"You don't say."

"She also thinks she knows *who* murdered him. That's where you come in."

Padget felt like he was in one of those hour-long television cop shows where the murdered party was introduced and killed by the end of act one, the murder investigated during act two and solved by the end of the third act. The three-act structure — he'd taught it dozens of times during his Introduction to Dramatic Literature course.

"Let me be candid. Monique thinks Augie was murdered by a professor named..." She scanned her notes. "...Professor Zale. Monique said something about jealousy — he was bitter about some discovery Augie had made?"

Padget was fascinated with what he was hearing — a mild sense of déjà vu sending a shiver through his body. He remembered the same sense of skepticism and wonder when Augustine Hiatt sat in that chair, telling the story of the discovery of the lost James Joyce manuscript and lodging his accusations against Zale. He didn't dare mention to this detective sitting across from him that he had already, in his way, begun to investigate the crime and that Zale should indeed be considered a suspect. Not yet.

"I see," he said, nodding in that practiced and thoughtful way that so many actors have used when playing an academic on screen.

"So I was hoping you could help me figure out all of this academic jealousy stuff. Monique told me how highly she thinks of you. She says you're a great professor and that you were working with Augie on some project of his? So maybe you can help me out here. Is it conceivable that a professor would actually have someone killed? That seems more the stuff of detective fiction than real life."

"That's what I was thinking."

"So it's not plausible?"

"Detective..."

"Stamos."

"Detective Stamos, there's a well-known saying among professors: 'The fights in academia are so intense because the stakes are so small.'"

"Meaning what, exactly?"

"Well, there's this notion that we members of the academy are rather... spoiled. Being a tenured professor is a rather nice lot in life when you think about it. There are worse, anyway. And most professors get seduced by the trappings of the job. Think about it: every time you walk into a classroom, students revere you as some sort of authority, they write down everything you say, they rarely challenge you, and when someone in the media needs an expert, they usually go to an academic. After a while, it can get to you — give you kind of an inflated sense of self-worth."

"I see. And if one's sense of superiority were threatened, that could be...?"

"Devastating. Ego is what drives the profession. Puncture that, and all of you've got left is someone who often has never done a real day's work their whole life."

Russell Padget — friend of the working man.

"And was Augie threatening this Doctor Zale? Was it something that could have compromised his authority?"

"There's a lot of competition in academia to come up with the next big idea. So it's unnerving if you've built your career on one belief and someone comes along and reveals that — *pffft!* — your idea no longer obtains."

"Ok, I get that — but would someone actually be driven to murder? What exactly did this Hiatt have on Zale?"

"Well, nothing concrete. At least that I'm aware of. I don't really know all the specifics. But if what Augie told me he found in his research is, in fact, true, it could be pretty ground-breaking."

"I'm going to take a few notes if you don't mind," Alana said. Finally, a student who was paying attention. "Can you tell me what Augie had found — and why it's so important?"

Padget was only too happy to play the role of expert. He explained to her how important a figure James Joyce was to the academic community and the groundbreaking nature of his writings. Joyce's life's work had fueled innumerable dissertations and academic promotions. And by now, the "experts" had cemented the narrative, poured over all his works, letters, biographical shards, anything that might cast some light on the complexity of his writing. The results of their research could be found in the most prestigious academic journals and learned literary presses.

"And then here comes this academic wannabe, an uninvited wanderer in the intellectual forest with an axe, about to hack into that narrative and fell a few sacred trees in the mystic grove of we-know-best."

"You mean Augie Hiatt. But what exactly was his… discovery?"

"That there's a hidden Joyce manuscript, a lost work written at the end of his life, when by all biographers' accounts he was creatively spent. Joyce spent the last couple years of his life fleeing war-torn Europe, dealing with some debilitating health issues, and desperately seeking help for his daughter — who was said to be mentally deranged. None of the research even *hints* at a final work. To unearth such a document is akin to finding the Dead Sea scrolls or a new tomb for King Tut. It could change the way Joyce is viewed by future generations."

"So, it's a big deal."

Padget nodded. "The biggest."

Alana stopped writing and looked right at him.

"Was he right? Does such a lost work exist?"

The man of words suddenly found himself unable to speak. What should he say? That Augie was an angry ex-grad student whose thesis was fueled by animus? That Augie was tricked into believing some documents — possibly forgeries — were the real thing? Or that Augie had found the Holy Grail and that Padget himself had come to believe such a manuscript existed? Should he tell her he'd *seen* the manuscript pages? He resorted to the cheapest way out that he could think of.

"*Est autem mysterio*"

Stamos stared at him.

"Yes. It certainly *is* a mystery."

"You speak Latin?"

"Twelve years of Catholic school," she said.

"Then you're acquainted with some mysteries of much greater import."

She flipped her notepad back to the first page, capped her ballpoint pen, and stood up.

"I had a nun who used to tell us that when we're confronted with what seems like a mystery, it just means we're asking the wrong questions."

"So what's the right question? In this instance, I mean."

Alana stood up, shouldered the strap of her portfolio, and cocked her head slightly.

"That's an easy one. How do I find this Zale fellow?"

***

Man, I've seen the future, and that ain't it. Detective Desi Arroyo walked past the security desk in the basement of the converted warehouse where Friend to Man had their offices. Desi had been a cop long enough to know that many of his brothers and sisters in law enforcement spent what little downtime they had daydreaming about their next hitch after they got their twenty in on the job. Most of them went into "private security" — a euphemism for sitting in some anonymous kiosk in a mall, college campus, or outside some off-the-beaten-path warehouse, staring at a black-and-white monitor, juking your nervous system with caffeine and Boston Cream donuts, waiting for the Powerball numbers to be pulled and the relief shift to send you back into semi-retirement.

In this particular case, the "security officer" had simply given up all pretense of professionalism, slumped in the chair behind his industrial gun-metal gray desk, eyes closed, mouth open, a copy of *The Racing Form* sprawled across his lap. *Naw, that ain't gonna be me.* Desi still felt the pulse beating beneath his thickened skin. He was closer to rookie than twenty-year-vet, but even now, he knew he could never mail it in. Not like that. He'd seen burnout mask itself in lots of different ways during his time on the force, and he knew the dangers of taking the job home with you. But he still felt it, the gnawing in his bones and blood, the zeal to fix the broken things in the world that needed fixing. He took one last look at the somnambulant constable, wakefulness's foe, and he mounted the stairs, ascending to the holy empire of the deranged.

The spartan and silent corridors unnerved him a little. The videos he'd been watching of this so-called religious organization were carnivals of sensory overload, vibrant, noisy, tearful, jubilant, fueled by the manic energy of barely-controlled fanaticism. But this place? Quiet as a nunnery. Desi remembered when he was in the academy, a recruit told him he joined up because he was a fan of the Sherlock Holmes stories of Arthur Conan Doyle. Desi had never been much of a reader — his parents put a lot more stock in physical activity. Reading was seen as being idle. Why sit and read about the world when you can be out in it? But Desi was curious — he'd never read any of the Sherlock Holmes stories, so the guy loaned him a book. He didn't remember any of the plots (and he remembered feeling frustrated at never being able to figure out the solutions to the mysteries before the great detective himself explained it all), but he did remember one particular moment from the book. Holmes and Watson were riding through the countryside in a horse-and-buggy, and Watson (who resembled in Desi's mind the sleeping sergeant one floor below, currently dreaming of hitting the trifecta at Aqueduct) said something to Holmes about how lovely and peaceful the countryside looked, but Holmes reprimanded him, telling him that the quiet places of the world are where the darkest and most extreme dangers lurk. "The dirtiest and most noisome London slum has nothing on the treachery that lurks behind the manicured shrubs and moonlit moors of the country," Holmes told Watson. Desi was surprised he remembered that, but it was a lesson that was reinforced by much of his career. Beware the things you cannot see, the sounds you cannot hear. There *are* things in the dark that aren't there in the daylight. Desi paused outside the door with the charred cross burned into it. He cocked his ear and closed his eyes, Holmes-like, trying to feel what might be going on in the silence behind the door. But just as in the mystery stories of Arthur Conan Doyle, the answers would have to await further explication.

The force of his knock shattered the silence and brought him back to himself. *These people are not owed reverence.* He'd been at first mildly intrigued, then positively transfixed, and then finally repulsed by the group's latest video. Purporting to be a re-enactment of the crucifixion, Desi was intrigued to discover how far they would go. At the time he logged in, the video had only been posted the previous day, yet more than 10,000 people had already viewed it. He wrote down several of the comments that people like "SinKnowMore" and "fu2Satan" had shared, a fulsome eruption of religious fervor that surprised Desi with its vehemence. "The blood of the lamb don't come from a bottle of stage blood," one commenter posted. "It gotta come from the lamb itself. You done right. Healing prayers brutha!"

It was an act of violence that led Desi to become a cop and daily acts of violence that brought him to the brink of despair about the goodness of his fellow man.

But here was a situation that challenged the divide between righteousness and evil. If Desi was accurate in his professional assessment, the video really *was* a crucifixion. Anyway, it looked real. He couldn't detect any trick photography, fancy editing, or fake blood capsules being crushed to create the sanguine illusion of sacrifice. If what he thought he saw is what he really saw, should people be cheering it on? And yet, isn't the sacrifice of Christ on the cross what ushered in 2,000 years of Christianity? The amount of goodness that emanated from that one historical event is imponderable.

Theology, schmeology. Desi was there to interrogate Friend to Man to discover what role they might have played in the death of Augustine Hiatt. Surely any group that manifested the public savagery in that video had the stomach — and maybe even the zeal— to dispatch a non-believer, a contributor (in the words of the letter they sent to Augie weeks before) "to the moral rot that corrodes Christ's Kingdom on Earth." Friend to Man sat atop the first-draft list of suspects with means, motive, and opportunity to commit the murder. And that crucifixion video seemed like Exhibit A in the case Desi intended to build against the perpetrators. But would a group clever enough to fool tens of thousands of followers with a fake crucifixion video — *it had to be fake, right?* — be stupid enough to walk right into a murder rap to announce their bloodthirsty intentions to a worldwide audience?

Desi knocked again. His instincts told him there was someone inside, but he also felt that patience was what was needed here. No need to bust down the door — not that he ran the risk of rousing Rip Van Winkle one floor below. That guy's days of running upstairs two at a time to investigate an unfolding situation were as far away as post-prandial consciousness. Instead of jamming his shoulder against the door jamb, Desi pressed his ear against the door, and when he did, he heard what sounded like a small child, or maybe even an animal purring. His protective side took over.

"Are you all right? Can you hear me? I'm with the police. Can you open the door?"

He pressed his ear to the door again and heard a soft scraping, a gentle scratching. It wasn't frantic, not like an animal trapped and fighting for escape. And it got a little louder the more he listened. Someone, or something, was crawling toward the door.

"If you can hear me, say something!" His voice was louder and more insistent now. There was definitely something on the other side of the door, on the floor, coming towards him, insistent, patient, but unafraid. Desi was reconsidering his plan to bust the door in when he heard a light click, and then the door slowly slid open. He peered into the darkened entryway and noticed something wrapped in a white bed sheet. Underneath it was a figure writhing gently, mumbling to itself.

"Police. Don't move." He didn't know what else to say, but it seemed to work. The lump quieted.

"I need you to remain still. I'm going to pull back the sheet. Don't move."

As he leaned down, he became aware of his heart beating. He reached out, grabbed a corner of the sheet, and began pulling it towards him. It unspooled like a smooth, fleecy skein, unraveling one body part at a time until Desi found himself standing over the naked body of a young woman, unharmed but her face and torso lined with what looked like finger-painted streaks of blood. Desi knelt beside her.

"Miss, are you okay? Do you need medical assistance? Can you speak?"

She glared up at him and grinned disconcertingly, her eyes round with wonder, summoning him closer to her with a curled finger, her smile a sinister, otherworldly smear drawn across her face.

As Desi knelt down, his ear close to her mouth, she whispered to him in a husky, jubilant murmur: "Ten thousand views in twenty-four hours. Fucking *unbelievable!*"

***

"Y'all know I keep it real for you. I might not have the biggest audience out there, but those of you who tune in know I don't sugarcoat things. Ain't my way, ain't in my nature. When I started Nique's Peeks, I was just hoping to spread some sunshine and find a way to highlight the good that's going on out there. Trying to be about love. Too much hate in the world, too much. But I still believe you can fight off the darkness. Today, though, I'm not so sure of that. Not anymore. Not after what happened to a friend of mine. His name was Augustine. We were close — used to be real close. We had a connection, you know? He was special. And he died. He was murdered. The police are looking for who did it — might have been a robbery, or maybe drug-related, but that's unlikely 'cause Augie wasn't into that anymore. I'm in pain because I lost my friend, and I'm pretty sure I know who did it, one of those people who don't ever seem to pay for what they do. I'm telling y'all — this time, he's gonna pay."

***

"I thought you people didn't drink."

Desi had helped Beth Lawson off the floor, re-wrapping her in the bed sheet that hung on her like a death shroud, and now, propped somewhat unsteadily against the desk in her and Todd's office, she pressed her head in her hands as if trying to reboot her skull.

"Wrong, wrong," she said, though Desi couldn't tell if she was speaking to him or chastising herself. "There's drinking in the Bible. Lots of it. Jesus drank."

"Well, here, drink this," he said, handing her a cup of water from the cooler. "I'm sure Jesus drank water, too."

"It started out as water," she said, taking the cup and draining it in one gulp.

"So what's the story — why the bender?"

"Who are you?"

"My name's Desi Arroyo. I'm a detective — Hate Crimes Unit." He showed her his badge.

"Since when is drinking too much a hate crime?"

"So exactly *why* were you drinking last night?"

"I was celebrating. My brother — he's been in the hospital, but he's gonna be okay. The doctor called me last night and told me Todd's out of the woods."

"What was wrong with him?" Desi knew — or at least he had an idea. He had seen the video of the crucifixion. Shortly after what appeared to be real nails going into his hands and being raised up, Todd Lawson seemed to go into a kind of shock, suffering a convulsion, and then — all recorded live as it was happening — a man appearing to be a doctor came onto the set and began trying to revive him, stabilize him. It was hard to tell exactly what was happening— it was pretty chaotic. And none of it seemed staged.

"People think it was the nails, but it wasn't," she volunteered. "It was the fasting."

"I'm sorry?"

"The fasting. I didn't know — none of us did — that Todd hadn't eaten for several days. Like Jesus fasting in the desert, Todd was trying to purify himself. But the stress, the adrenaline, the shock of actually being nailed, the glaring lights, it all got to him. His body couldn't take it. Glory be to God." She reached out, throttled an uncorked champagne bottle by the neck, held it up to the light, turning it sideways to see if there was anything left inside, and then frowned and put the bottle down."

"I think you've had more than enough, don't you?"

"A celebration," she said. "We knew this could help the mission, but ten thousand views in less than one day? *That's righteous!*"

"You're Beth Lawson, then. Your brother, Todd — you and he run this… operation, right? Friend to Man?"

"By the grace of the Almighty."

"Well, that's fine. I need to ask you some questions about a recent homicide. Your name came up in the investigation?"

"My name?"

"Friend to Man."

Beth laughed, a satisfied and genuine expression of joy, a rapid pivot into sobriety that surprised the detective.

"That's not my name. That's Jesus's name." She held the empty bottle up again, this time studying it, contemplating its emptiness. "It's so funny you thought that was my name."

"It's the name of your organization," Desi said, unfazed. "And it's been mentioned in connection with a murder."

"Murder? *And on the third day, he rose*," she said absentmindedly.

"Yeah, well, this guy won't be rising anytime soon. And I need to talk with you about it. Why don't you go get dressed, clean yourself up, and we can talk further?"

"Friend to Man is godly. We don't kill," she said, almost mystified that someone would make such a charge. "We create. We're all about *love* — don't you see? That's why Todd did what he did — to show compassion with our Lord Jesus Christ."

"Nailing someone to a board and plunging them into shock doesn't seem too compassionate to me. And if you could almost murder your brother, I don't see why you wouldn't—"

"*It wasn't murder,*" she shouted, angry energy animating her gaze, the glassy-eyed look of the hungover penitent replaced by an evangelical furor. "It was a sacrifice. Todd was trying to show people that all their worldly possessions, money, cars, family, even personal health — mean nothing if you haven't been saved. It was the opposite of murder. It was *salvation.*"

"Well, fine. Call it what you will, but I still have some questions you need to answer."

Holding the folds of her sheet tightly in front of her with the fist of one hand, she walked behind the desk where the empty Champaign bottle lay on its side like a sleeping sentry. She opened the top drawer, pulling out a card.

"Here you go," she said, handing it to Desi. "Talk to him about earthly matters. I'm only concerned with the afterlife."

"Your lawyer. Hmmm. You feel you need a lawyer, Miss Lawson?"

"I feel I need a shower," she said, picking up the paper cup Desi had handed her at the beginning of their interview. "Thanks for the drink." She walked out of the front office and into one of the back rooms where she and her brother had so often plotted the salvation of the world's unclean.

***

"You gotta message — he said it was urgent."

"He *who*?"

"Some egghead. They routed the call down here."

"Oh, right. Thanks, Mooch."

He had a nickname for everybody. Maybe that's because everybody called *him* by his nickname, Mooch. *What is his real name?* Alana had always meant to ask, but the answer seemed unlikely to tell her anything. Mooch was like most of the cops she knew, most of the good ones, anyway. He lived a kind of double life, affecting a cynicism on the job, a hard-shell that seemed impenetrable but also gave him a strength, a resilience that she had come to rely on. But she also knew that there had to be a softer side. One can't maintain that kind of emotional distance twenty-four hours a day and still lead a normal life. Then again, did Mooch — did any of them — maintain "normal" lives? A "normal" person might have welcomed Alana back to the homicide offices — even if it was just to pick up some files pertaining to the Augie Hiatt murder. Maybe a "Hey, how's it going?" Or "What's your new partner like?" Or even a nod of acknowledgment. But he didn't even flinch when she came through the door. Mooch had seen too many of his brothers and sisters on the job come and go like paperwork, like some file sent to the D.A.'s office: maybe it would come back, maybe it'd be gone forever. Yesterday's problems. But Alana couldn't overcome the temptation to try to generate a little warmth, however manufactured.

"So, Mooch, have you missed me?"

"Yeah, I was just telling Sweater yesterday how empty I felt, you know, deep inside," he said, without once looking up from the tabloid newspaper he was reading. "And yet, I somehow found the strength to go on. Please don't ever abandon us again — I haven't got time for the pain."

"Since when have you started taking life advice from Carly Simon."

"I got all her albums — chick's got a great rack."

Still not making eye contact, he flipped the page of his newspaper with studied indifference.

"Well, thanks for the phone message anyway." She settled back into what was her old desk, though it was clear from the detritus strewn across the stained desk-top calendar that someone had made good use of her former workstation. She was tempted to simply upend the calendar and send the Ring-Ding wrappers, fortune cookie crumbs, and coffee stirrers toppling into the un-emptied trashcan, but then she remembered that it wasn't her place, wasn't her mess. She had other messes to clean up. Maybe the "egghead" — Professor Padget, she presumed — would help her do just that. The number he left was his office number at Hackett Community College, and though he had phoned several hours ago, he picked up right away when she called back.

"Hello? Professor Padget? This is Detective Stamos. You called?"

What he told her ensured that her return to the office of the Homicide Division was a short one.

"I'll be there in about twenty, twenty-five minutes."

"Well, that was a short visit," said Mooch, who though still focused on his newspaper, had clearly eavesdropped on her conversation. "Hot date?"

"Maybe a break in the Hiatt murder. We'll see." As she got up from the chair and slung her bag across her shoulder, Mooch lifted his gaze from the sports section.

"Need back-up?"

"Why Mooch," she said, with exaggerated affection. "That's the nicest thing you've ever said to me. You're worried about me?"

"Don't moisten your panties, detective. I was going to call Sweater and tell him to go with you. He hasn't gone on a call since the Lindbergh baby. Figured he could use the practice."

"Mooch, don't worry. I can handle myself."

"So can Sweater. I think that's what he's doing right now in the men's room. Pound on the door if you want him to ride along."

"I love you, Mooch. Don't ever change."

She was gone too quickly to see the beginning of a wry smile tweak Mooch's stony, hard-boiled countenance. But getting to the college took a little longer than Alana thought. There was a water main break on the road she'd normally take, so she had to grind along bumper-car style with the other three lanes of traffic squeezing into the one-lane detour. It took almost 45 minutes to get to the college's visitor parking lot. She asked the guard in the semi-circle protective kiosk if Padget was still in his office, but he shrugged. He seemed far too young to be a cop — he looked more like a work-study student. *God help this campus if there's a real police emergency.* She pulled her car into one of the visitor slots and stepped out with more-than-usual urgency. Approaching Padget's office, she could see pale light from underneath his door fan-tailing the linoleum hallway floor, and she relaxed for a moment. Knocking gently, she stood there like so many of his students must have over the years, expectantly, nervously, hoping for validation or guidance. Before she could imagine the wide variety of scenarios that would have brought Padget's students to the same threshold of expectation, he yanked open the door and looked immediately relieved.

"Hello, Professor. What's happened?"

He waved her in, sat down, and began shaking his head.

"I had to call. I didn't know what else to do," he said, seeming far less assured than he had during their previous interview.

"Of course. Tell me what's going on."

"Well, I taught my usual class this afternoon. American Romanticism. We were discussing the transcendental movement and its relationship to British nature poetry. You know, Wordsworth's "*Clouds of Glory*," etc."

"Something happened in class?"

"What? No, No. I'm sorry. It's what happened after class." He had a faraway look that told Detective Stamos she might be in for a long story.

"Can you just focus on what happened, Professor?"

He nodded and then pushed a manila envelope across the desk toward her.

"This. It was in my mailbox when I got back from class."

Her instinct to pick it up was checked by the humbling recall of many chastisements by her colleagues in the police lab for having corrupted evidence. She reached into the inside pocket of her coat and pulled out a pair of what looked like latex gloves.

"What is it," she asked, inspecting the outside of the envelope.

"The Holy Grail."

She cocked her head and then lightly unfolded the clasp that held the flap in place and then gently removed the sheaf of papers that appeared to be handwritten, much of the writing in small columns running down the front of the paper. The pages were clearly photocopies, but the original appeared to be a bit weathered and, in places, almost indecipherable.

"That's it," he said. "*Archimedes at the Gear Fair.*"

"Help me out, Doc."

"The work that Augie found — the James Joyce manuscript. There it is. You haven't been able to find it, right?"

"Well, we assumed it was taken after he was killed."

"Of course."

"So what was he doing sending it to you?"

"I guess he trusted me."

She removed her notebook, looked again at the envelope, and then flipped a few pages of the notebook.

"Hmm. This can't be a coincidence."

"What can't be?"

"According to the postmark on this envelope, Augie mailed this the very day his body was discovered. That's odd."

"Maybe he put it out for pick up the night before."

"It's possible. Why'd it take so long to get to you?"

"Oh, that's easy. Campus mail. They mean well. But it takes forever. Things can sit in that mailroom for weeks. I once ordered a copy of Bloom's *Anxiety of Influence*, and it took at least—"

"Ok, I got it."

"There's more. This was paper-clipped to the bundle." He handed her what looked like a fresh piece of copy paper, folded in half. She opened it and found a brief, typewritten note: "Professor Padget, I no longer feel this is safe in my possession. Hang on to it for me. Will explain when I see you." And then, in cursive, the signature "Augie H."

"This was in the package?"

Padget nodded.

"Types a letter but signs it in ballpoint?"

"Actually, that's a fountain pen. Pretty sure anyway. Augie and I talked about fountain pens when I first met him."

"The lab will check this out, of course," she said. "Has anyone else handled this package?"

"Well, let's see. The department secretary. The mailroom staff — probably two or three people down there. And of course, the postal service people."

"And the contents?"

"Just Augie. And me."

"Any idea *why* he sent you this?"

"Well, just what he said in the letter, I guess."

"Right." Alana closed her eyes for a minute and tried to gather her thoughts. "I'm going to need this," she said, holding the envelope. "And the letter."

"Oh, right," he said, handing it over to her.

She was about to stuff the pages back into the envelope when he spoke up.

"Don't you want to look at it? I mean, if it really is what Augie said it is, you're holding one of the rarest documents in English literature."

"But it's a photocopy, not the original."

"If the original even exists anymore. This could be the only evidence of what Joyce wrote. Aren't you even a *little* curious? I mean, my God — James Joyce!" Padget's enthusiasm was genuine — his voice lifted when he named the writer, and his whole frame seemed more animated. She removed the contents and laid them carefully on the desk."

"What did you call this? Ark-something?"

"*Archimedes at the Gear Fair.* That's what Joyce called it, a long poem, childlike in its simplicity. It's about the sea. It was written for his daughter. Well, she wasn't a child when he wrote it for her; she was already an adult, a young woman. But she had a very childlike way about her. Some thought her mad — mentally ill. But Joyce had a special connection to her, and so far as can be told, she's the only person who ever saw this."

"Is it any good?" That was Alana's sly way of getting Padget to reveal whether he looked through the pages.

"Well, it's silly. Lots of wordplay. Joyce had just come off a 17-year-labor, writing a book called *Finnegans Wake*. His eyesight was poor, his health was in decline, and his spirits needed lifting. But he seemed to have relished the chance to put some foolish rhymes together, just for his daughter, not for publication or posterity."

"Yet here it is."

"Yes," Padget said, smiling broadly. "Here it is. Though it's far from complete, as you can see. Maybe there were other pages, or maybe he decided to abandon the work. But what's here — my God — if it's from Joyce, then yes, it's an exquisite find!"

Stamos looked through the short stack of papers.

"You'll see some of the poems are part of letters he wrote to Lucia — that's his daughter, Lucia — with some notes in the margins or at the bottom. Joyce loved footnotes."

"Yes. I read *Ulysses*. Or tried. Mostly the footnotes explaining what the hell he was supposed to be saying. To tell you the truth, I didn't really understand anything I was reading."

"You sound like my students. They're still so young."

Insult? Compliment?

"Take your time. You're holding literary history. Here," he said, reaching over, picking up the first page. "Start here."

***

[In tightly cramped and slanted handwriting]

Archimedes at the Gear Fair.
For Lucia,
My favorite creature of the Depths,
a private Ody-SEA

[There are a few lines erased that appear to be indecipherable. The legible text begins after several smudge marks. It's not clear who did the erasing.]

'Plash! Tiny fins make a plesh! ploosh! plish!
Tail propels tale of Archimedes – a fish!
And the swirly curlicues of Archie (to his friends)
Life for us portends, wat'ry cells round their bends.

Long, long ago in that cold depth of time
washed away from our mind though our species did climb
up the ladder 'til sadder and wiser we rose
right before we had toes – only flagellum knows!

When the land and the sea weren't knit yet as host
for the life which was rife drifting nearer the coast,
in the dark it was stark how much teemed in the wet
vast expanse, Neptune's Manse! (Prelude to Earth's not-yet.)

Little fish!
How'd we miss
Your upgrade from lone cell,
When you moved
And you grooved to the ocean's upswell?
Now you've fins!
And a tail!
What you propulse to do
Is create
Human fate
With a wiggle or two!

[There is a break in the manuscript here — perhaps the end of one of the letters. The next section begins after a brief explanatory note from Joyce: "The Ancient Greeks believed there were seven seas: The Mediterranean, the Caspian, the Adriatic, The Red Sea, The Black Sea, The Persian Gulf, and the Arabian Sea (part of the Indian Ocean). So *Archimedes* will have seven parts — with one adventure set in each part. You remember the secret I told you about the number seven, right Lucia?" The next section appears to be more of a mini-drama, with the characters Archimedes and Molecule (a Lady Shrimp), somewhere in the Mediterranean.]

Molecule (singing):
Oooh Whee! Look at Meee!
Primping in the undertow!
Wow-Wee! Slap that sea!
Shrimping in the thunder-so!
(The Lady Shrimp does a kind of frantic water ballet, like a Cuban Mambo Dancer)
Molecule (still singing)
Pffit pffaw – I see it all!
Evolution, won't you wait?
Gotta date with fate – and thus the call
Can't be halted. I'm ex-ALL-ted!

(She flips dizzily, tail overhead, creating tiny whirlpools of bubble and foam as Archimedes applauds with his fins.)

[This section of the manuscript also ends abruptly. Unclear if the scene continued or if there are pages missing. What appears next seems to be the start of another episode, this time set in the Indian Ocean, and with a new character called Mozambique]

The Indian Ocean's Sprung a Leak!

"'Andyman'll be here soon
He's coming from the Andaman lagoon!"

Archimedes sighed a bubble stream
As Mozambique shrieked: "Leaks won't sink our team!"

Indian Ocean (nice and warm!)
Hindi notion (Kharma swarm!)
Boo-dah life forms (heir to breed!)
Some moon-drunk goddess (in seaweed!)*

[*Joyce's manuscript includes this brief margin note to Lucia: "Some moon-drunk" = "Samudra, the Hindi word for Ocean." Joyce also wrote in the margin, "Several additional verses in which the fish frolic nervously amid the widespread rumor of a leak." But those verses don't appear. The only remaining verse is the last one.]

'til Archimedes commandeered the deep,
atop a spine of coral rock quite steep.
"My friends, this frenzy must now cease! Here's why:
A leak's not bleak – we'll get more wet than dry!"

[The next brief section commences in watery parts unknown, and with new characters introduced]

*Glaucus Atlanticus**
wearing striped pant-iccus
(Just more of his anticus)
hoping he could land a kiss!

[Joyce's note: "'Glaucus Atlanticus,' a type of sea slug sometimes called the Blue Dragon, has a bitter sting. Cleverly, they float upside down, their blue bellies blending in with the water, invisible to their victims. Crafty devils!"]

Fell upon a mantis shrimp
(in your day that puts a crimp!)
Just imagine your frustration
tumbling o'er some crustacean!

Harry Frogfish tags along
dangling algae for a song
(Is he frog – or is he fish?
Anemone – or friendly-ish?)

Barry-cuda caught his eye
Glaucus upturned 'gainst the sky
Harry leaped while Shrimpy creeped,
leaving Barry very piqued!

[The rest of this episode — what looks like several more verses — are too light to be definitively transcribed.]

***

"I don't.... I'm not sure what to think. You think it's real?"

"You mean — are there really talking sea creatures?"

"No. I mean, is it Joyce?"

"Hard to say. It's got his playfulness. We know he wrote silly children's stories for his only grandson, Stephen. He included them in his letters. Wait a minute."

Padget reached up to a bookshelf and extracted two very slim volumes, *The Cats of Copenhagen* and *The Cat and the Devil.* "These were published from Joyce's letters. It seems he enjoyed writing silly rhymes. I guess seventeen years of working on *Finnegans Wake* left him exhausted. Children's stories might be all he had left."

"Have you researched the handwriting?"

"Right down to these little curlicues," he said, pointing to the ends of some of the lines in *Archimedes.* "That's Joyce. And see these misplaced dots over the i's? Joyce's vision was failing. This is common in the correspondence of his last few years."

"Ok. Well, thank you," she said, rising. "I'll turn these over to the lab."

"I need them back. I mean, it looks like I've become the caretaker of Joyce's legacy."

"You mean Augustine Hiatt's legacy, right?"

"Of course. But please be careful. That's literary history right there."

"Thank you for turning this over." She put the envelope carefully in her bag and got up to leave.

"Do you think this will maybe help you crack the case?"

Crack the case. *The learned professor has watched too many TV crime dramas,* Alana thought.

"Very likely. This might be just what we needed. Thank you, Professor."

"Please, call me Russ."

She nodded. "I'll be in touch if we need more. Thanks for your cooperation."

"*In Arbitrio Tuo*"

"Ah, more Latin," Alana said. "The language of wisdom and treachery."

"Is that from Cicero?"

"No. The Dead Eye Dicks. A punk band from the 70s."

Padget nodded. "Wisdom can be found everywhere, as they say."

"Yes," Detective Stamos said, pulling the door open and stepping across the threshold. "Treachery, too."

***

Bunch of sick motherfuckers. Religion? Torture porn. Sometimes, you can smell when someone's guilty. And that place stunk to high heaven.

Detective Desi Arroyo felt strongly that Friend to Man was involved in Augustine Hiatt's murder. His interview with Beth Lawson earlier in the week left him at first puzzled. Still, the more he thought about his interrogation with her — and watched more of their videos — he became angry. How could so many people be so stupid as to be taken in by that brother-and-sister freak show? And their masochistic commitment to the salvation of all of the unsaved who were surfing the internet at 3 a.m., trolling for epiphanies, activated his police radar. In his experience, anyone *that* blinded by ideology is usually deluded — and dangerous. But instinct is one thing — and evidence something else altogether. So he continued to investigate Augie's murder by the book, meaning interviews with anyone else who might have been involved, which is what led him to Hiatt's residence. According to the rental agreement on the property, he shared the place with a roommate named Jaquelina Courson, though Desi knew no more about her than her name. As he approached the screen door of the small house, he could already detect the aroma of a controlled substance.

Jesus, it's 10 in the morning. Who gets high to start their day?

He knocked, but no one answered. Peering through the door, he could see someone sitting in a chair in the middle of the living room, spooning something out of a bowl (a *Spaghetti-O's* knockoff called *Tasty Tomato Rings*) and bobbing her head methodically.

"Excuse me, Ms. Courson?" he said, though she ignored him. Desi saw the curlicued cord of the headphones snaking from the stereo receiver, and he cut her off at the source, turning the volume knob as far left as it would go. She stopped in mid-spooning, tapped the headphones with her palms, and then grimaced, unsure why the music stopped. She still hadn't noticed him in the room, lit only by the louvered mid-morning sun.

"Excuse me, Miss Courson?"

She turned and eyed him like someone she had been expecting to see.

"Don't have it," she said casually.

"Have what?"

"The rent. That is, I have half. I don't know how you are going to get Augie's share. He certainly didn't have any savings that I know of. And I haven't had time to advertise for a new roommate."

"Miss Courson, I'm not here for the rent."

She put down her fortified macaroni O's and stared at him.

"Oh, shit — you're *evicting* me? Aw, come on — I'll find some way to get the money."

"Miss Courson, your landlord didn't send me. My name is Desi Arroyo. I'm a detective with the Hate Crimes Unit."

"Oh shit. The smoke? I can explain, detective. The vent on the dryer unit doesn't work. It backs up into the house."

"Miss Courson, that's not ventilated steam. That's marijuana."

"Oh shit. Yes, of course. It's my neighbors. They're exchange students from Jamaica. I left the kitchen window open, and what must have happened is—"

"Miss Courson, relax. I'm not here about your recreational activities. I'm here to talk about Augustine Hiatt. I'm investigating his death."

"But you said 'hate crimes.' You think somebody hated Augie enough to kill him?"

"Well, that's what I wanted to talk to you about. May I?"

Desi walked over to an overstuffed couch and sat, sinking deeply into the puffy cushions stained with spilled beer, salsa, and ranch dressing, cat claw marks engraving its tapered walnut legs.

"Did Augie ever mention anything to you about a group called Friend to Man?"

"Friend to Man — is that like, what, a gay group? I don't think Augie was gay. Or if he was, he hid it pretty well."

"No, they're not a... they are a religious organization."

"Oh, then definitely not. Augie wasn't at all religious. I had a paper due once on Nostradamus. You know, the prophet? Anyway, I asked Augie if he had a Bible that I could borrow, and he just laughed."

"I see. I understand he had an ex-girlfriend, someone he met in a creative writing program, and that the relationship might have ended on less than good terms. Did she ever come around or call?"

"Not that I know of. But I sort of keep to myself. I've got my music, and my, well..."

"Recreation."

"Right. But I'm pretty sure he never mentioned her to me."

"Ok. Did he ever talk to you about his work with a company called Tongue in Cheek?"

"You mean the pervy movies? No, not much. I once told him — I was joking, of course — that I needed to make some extra money and that maybe he could help me get an audition."

"What did he say."

"He told me I didn't want to ever have anything to do with that place. He called it a sewer."

"Right. So, is there anything else you can tell me about who he might have, you know, had words with?"

"Augie was a pretty easy-going guy. The only person he ever talked about with what you might call anger was this old professor of his, some guy Augie worked with in graduate school. Augie called him a first-class prick."

"Do you remember the name?"

She squinted as if trying to peer back into the past.

"Sorry," she shook her head. "My memory isn't that great. Probably too many Spaghetti-Os."

"Yes, I'm sure that's it," he said, getting up and taking out his card and handing it to her. "If you think of anything else, just let me know. In the meantime, can you tell me where Augie's bedroom is?"

"He mostly slept out here on the couch. He didn't have a lot of stuff. That's his desk over there. He spent most of his time sitting there, writing."

"Writing what, exactly?"

"Not sure. Like you said, he used to be in a creative writing program. Maybe he was writing a book? He also liked poetry. He gave me a Dr. Seuss book for my last birthday."

"Dr. Seuss?"

"I'm an early-childhood ed major."

"I see. Well, thank you for your help — and call me anytime if you think of something that might help."

The future of education in the hands of people who smoke weed and eat canned pasta rings for breakfast. How lovely.

"I will. Like I said, though — I don't remember so good sometimes."

It was only a moment or two after he drove away that Jaquelina Courson settled back into her Papasan chair, somewhat rattled by the interruption of her morning routine, and reached for a recreational sedative. In no time, she'd forget that Detective Arroyo had ever even dropped by.

***

After his first few years of teaching, Russell Padget settled into a rhythm dictated largely by forces beyond his control, the churning academic calendar nudging one phase seamlessly into the next: back-to-school enthusiasm becomes mid-semester ennui, final exam adrenaline fuels the glide toward the holiday break, and the cycle repeats. Savvy professors learn to schedule their own individual freak-outs — book deadlines, conference presentations — during the fallow periods of the school year. Camille Danforth was a savvy professor. Her math students loved her because she was a calming influence in their lives. They saw her as unflappable, but Russell Padget knew better. She could be as insecure as they were, but she knew how to pick her spots. But she was also great at picking lunch spots, which is why the eminent Doctor Padget found himself awaiting her arrival at Sage's Place, a diner just a few blocks off campus. When Padget first started eating here, he assumed the establishment was named in honor — however ironically — of the local college. But then he actually met Sage, the man who owned the place, a former stuntman who worked out West performing in historical re-enactments of famous cowboy versus Indian battles. A towering Native American, Sage had forsaken the life of tourist showbiz glitz for the grittier reality of grill and grind. "I traded New Mexico for New Jersey," he told Padget during their first meeting. "I used to ax cowpokes. Now I ax for directions."

When Camille arrived, it was clear the wait staff knew her. Everyone smiled and nodded. How did she become so popular *off* campus?

"Hi, Camille."

She took off her trench coat and sidled into the booth.

"I've got 45 minutes before I'm Skyping with my publisher."

"Skyping?"

"Oh Russ, stop living in the past."

"Hey, I'm more `with-it' than you think," Russell retorted. "I'm all about online. Just last week, I ordered a brand-new VCR from eBay."

She rolled her eyes but reached out to pat him on the hand.

"We'll have to eat fast. I can't miss that call."

"Sounds important."

"Didn't I tell you? I signed a book contract! I'm writing a test prep book for Axiom. They're a Math publisher. If the call goes as well as I hope, future lunches will be on me."

Camille Danforth, author. Good for her. That's what professors do — they write books, right? Padget wrote a book. A couple of books. They just, well… he never actually finished them. The timing wasn't right. This was back in the early days of his teaching when he hadn't yet figured out how to time his freak-outs with the circadian semester's rhythm. He would have finished, but other things kept intruding. He couldn't ignore his students after all, right?

"So what's happening with you? What's going on with that fellow who you were helping. The one who died."

"Yeah, well, the police are investigating. I'm actually helping."

"Wow! That's kind of exciting — in sort of a gruesome way. Hey, maybe there's a book in this. A detective who's also a professor of literature. Might be a whole series."

"I'm sure it's been done."

The waitress arrived.

"How's the seafood?" Padget asked. She just raised an eyebrow.

"Never order seafood at a diner," Camille said sotto voce, hiding her face behind the menu of daily specials.

"Ok, never mind. Bring me the avocado salad."

Camille shook her head.

"Meatball sub. And please put a rush on it. I have an appointment."

"I'll tell the chef to go to Code Blue," she deadpanned, turning away with practiced indifference. Camille laughed.

"I fucking love this place."

"So tell me about the book." Padget folded his hands in front of him and appeared to listen to his colleague talk about her forthcoming book — how she pitched the idea, wrote a proposal, met with an agent, all the usual author stuff, but he couldn't focus on the words. His mind kept going back to those long hours he had spent, what seemed like wasted hours now, trying to come up with just the right phrase, the pithy critical aphorism that would help establish his reputation as a discerning young critic. Didn't he still have those pages around somewhere? Maybe they are worth dusting off. Sure, they'll need updating, but that'll just offer an opportunity to work in the latest scholarly catchphrases, give the book some cultural currency. Help it, you know, trend.

"Anyway, I'm sure this is all very boring to you," Camille said.

"No, it's not."

The waitress arrived with Padget's tea and Camille's diet Coke.

"On second thought, can you just wrap it up and make it to-go? Russ, are you okay with that?"

He nodded.

"Thanks."

The waitress headed back to the kitchen to encase Camille's meatball sub in a styrofoam clamshell case.

"Russ, I'm really sorry. I just don't want to miss this call. If I blow this, who knows if I'll ever have a chance to publish a book again, you know?"

"No, you're right. You know what they say about opportunity."

Yet, in the back of his mind, he heard a light knocking as well.

***

Holdena sipped her chamomile tea from a Betty Boop coffee mug, licking the cup's edge, savoring the trace of honey stranded in the warm liquid's retreat. This was her golden time. Most people in the word trade do something else, *anything* else, when they are done with work to get their minds off of language. They jog, they play video games, they garden. But Holdena almost never left her apartment. And at night, she wrote. But instead of notes in the margins of other peoples' works, *this was all for her*. And when she felt the work was finally ready — not just garden-variety ready but literary-prize-stun-the-world-best-selling-notable-book-of-the-year-ready, she'd release it to the world.

Her eyes scanned the lines on her computer screen, squinting, shaking her head, treating her work like she would treat the most promising manuscript at Phalanx, savagely attentive. In creative writing classes, students are cautioned not to put on their "editor's hat" too soon. It destroys the flow, the creative process. There's a time to write and a time to correct what one has written. Harsh self-criticism has kept many an aspiring writer from ever producing anything. The Muse doesn't abide a scold. But Holdena didn't care. She'd often edit herself *in mid-sentence*. If it didn't sound right, sound *perfect* in her ear, she'd stop and stare, think, revise, replace, supplant, terminate, reinitiate, evaluate, amend, or abandon. To pass the time once while she was stuck on a city bus in a traffic jam caused by a crazy man chasing a squirrel on the concrete median of a two-lane highway, she calculated that she had deleted three words for every word she had finally allowed to exist in her own work. For Holdena, it wasn't about flow. That was a touchy-feely concept peddled to mediocre writers who lacked the requisite skills to produce great writing. Easy writing made for easily forgotten writing, she knew.

But Holdena's Achilles heel wasn't her rigid writing ritual but rather her lack of faith. She didn't trust her imagination to take her to the right places. It wasn't that she put on her editor's hat too soon. It was that she put on her writer's hat not at all. She was extremely distrustful of any thought that began to gallop across her mind, racing faster than her censorious editorial sensibility could corral it. As a result, her writing was polished but bloodless. Technically adept, she often found that she had written pages of the most un-involving prose, replete with precise descriptions, deft metaphors, the shifts in point of view, and time handled with supreme expertise. But what the hell did it all mean? She hadn't yet found a way to marry the seriousness of purpose she felt when she wrote with the lightness of heart and mind that lubricated thought, turning world-weariness into wonder.

Take, for example, the story she was laboring over this particular evening, a short fiction titled *Suicide, with Musaka.* The story was about a docile and forgettable middle-aged woman who worked in the town she grew up in as a secretary for a small travel agency, but she herself had never traveled anywhere in her life. She decided one day to book a train trip for herself on the famed Orient Express after one of her clients, a handsome and successful owner of a chain of funeral parlors, booked a trip on the train as well. In fact, she booked the same train, the same cabin, even. A long train trip through exotic locales with an alluring acquaintance — didn't she deserve this? But as it turned out, the handsome funeral parlor owner was traveling to Budapest to die, heading there specifically to proclaim his love for a girl he knew in high school — his first love, though she never knew it — who fabricated Christian figurines in chocolate: chocolate Jesus, chocolate Moses, chocolate Eve. He planned to tell her that he always loved her and, now that he was going to die (of a terminal illness he received from an insect bite while embalming the wife of a mountaineer who lived among the wild elk of the Dakotas), he asked her for one last kiss.

Holdena had all of this sketched out in painstaking detail in the journal she carried with her to and from work. She was about twenty-five pages into the story, right up to the point when the train was leaving the Vienna station when she realized that the funeral parlor business was all wrong for the handsome stranger because it was her protagonist, the forgotten middle-aged woman (who wasn't even given a name) who should be symbolically linked with death and that the stranger should be given an exciting job that, the reader will discover, failed to excite him despite great wealth and fame. No, it was the prospect of a kiss from his high school sweetheart that had always held for him the greatest appeal. So Holdena decided to make him a symphony conductor, one of these globe-trotting maestros who jet-sets into major world capitals with a leather portfolio of Brahms' scores tucked under the sleeve of his Burberry.

"He conducted other people's worlds beautifully, but he couldn't conduct his own life," she wrote. Then she immediately changed "worlds" to "masterpieces," and she added the word "even" between "couldn't" and "conduct." Then she changed "He conducted" to "Conducting," and she deleted the word "beautifully." Then she changed "conduct his own life" to "orchestrate his own life." She took another sip of tea and squinted at the revised sentence. She shook her head, bit her lower lip, and then deleted the entire sentence, the Word graveyard gobbling up another night's effort.

"Not good enough," she said, draining the dregs of the tea, tonguing the tiny wilted flowers that snuck through the tea infuser. "Try again tomorrow," she thought, closing her laptop, the symphony conductor and lonely woman stranded between Sofia and Istanbul, chocolate Jesuses left uneaten, and chocolatiers left un-kissed.

***

As detective Desi Arroyo pulled into the parking lot of Tongue-in-Cheek productions, he had one thought on his mind: *try not to touch anything*. The place looked as sleazy on the outside as whatever it was they were filming on the inside. He still felt strongly that Friend to Man must somehow be involved in Augie Hiatt's death; that bizarre scene at their offices just confirmed what a bunch of crackpots the whole cult was. But he'd spent enough time around vice cops to know that hardcore pornographers play for keeps. "It's not a field distinguished by a high degree of conscience," one of his Vice colleagues once told him. Would someone at Tongue-in-Cheek have actually resorted to murder? Well, they ain't making cupcakes here, he reminded himself, removing a silk handkerchief from the pocket of his Italian hand-made buttoned-down dress shirt and covering the exterior entrance's doorknob as he turned it and went inside.

The receptionist looked up at him and, deciding he wasn't there for an audition ("The talent wears much tighter pants," she had once told Augie), gave him a cursory "Be right with you" and continued staring at her computer screen.

"I'm Detective Arroyo, and I'm here to see Bobby Devlin," he said after a few minutes of being ignored.

"Can I tell him what this is about?"

"No, Ma'am."

"Oh. Well, I'll let him know you're here."

"Thank you, Ma'am."

While he stood there waiting for an audience with the "Pope of Pussy Pounding" (or so read the inscription to Devlin on a photo of someone named "Ramington Steel" hanging on the stained and faded walls of the reception area), he thought about all of the runaways he'd found over the years who'd made their way to the port of porn for what they took to be a temporary safe harbor. And he thought of how many he never found who didn't manage to stay afloat before he found them.

"Mr. Devlin will see you now."

Detective Arroyo straightened himself and, checking the urge to wrap his hand in his handkerchief yet again, simply knocked on Devlin's door, which had the word PRIVATE written in block letters with a Sharpie marker.

"Yeah, yeah," a voice inside battered back. "I ain't got all fuckin' day."

The detective pushed the door in gingerly and stepped on the gray-green Berber carpeting.

"I'm Detective Arroyo — Hate Crimes Division. I'm here to talk to you about Augustine Hiatt."

"Oh yeah? What's the little prick done now? Gone on Jerry Springer and told the world our men's room is out of towels?"

Arroyo cocked his head and asked, "I'm sure you've heard."

"Heard what? I haven't seen him since he came in for his last paycheck, which I should have shoved up his ass. Did you hear what that dickless wonder said about us online? Made us look like we cater to a bunch of mouth-breathers and perverts."

"Well, it was just a local podcast."

"Local? Tell that to my distributors — this fucking interview he did with some stupid bitch went viral, and now I have to deal with retailers who say I'm bad for business. *Me!* Are you fucking kidding me? I *built* ninety percent of their businesses, the ungrateful cocksuckers."

"Sounds like a pretty strong motive for murder."

"Goddamn right. If I see that fucking turncoat, I'm gonna wring his pencil neck."

"Mr. Devlin. I'm here to investigate Augustine Hiatt's murder. He was found dead in his apartment. It's been ruled a homicide."

Devlin paused.

"No shit? Somebody offed the motherfucker? Hmm. How about that?" He cocked his head and grunted to himself. "You got any leads?"

"The only one who made any direct physical threats against him that I'm aware of is…." He leafed through his notebook. "You."

"What the fuck you talking about?"

"You just told me you'd like to wring his neck. That sounds like a motive to me. Wouldn't you agree?"

"Blow me, Sergeant Bilko. I never laid a finger on the kid."

"But you agree the interview he did with 'Monique's Peeks' hurt your business. You just said—"

"*Fuck* what I just said. I'm telling you; I never touched that smart-mouthed son-of-a-bitch. In fact, I bent over like Tracy Tickle to help the guy out."

"Tracy Tickle?"

"What, you don't watch porn? Tracy Tickle — she's one of the biggest stars we got. Oh, you gotta get out of the squad room more often, Detective Poindexter. There's a whole world out there. You oughta loosen up." He pushed himself away from his desk, the rolling metal casters on his desk chair groaning in well-rehearsed distress. He reached behind him, grabbed a DVD, and flung it at Arroyo. "Here — try this out the next time your book club meets. This'll harpoon your Moby Dick."

Arroyo inspected the package. "TRACY TICKLE in POP GOES THE WEASEL — an interactive fable for adults. In 3-D!"

"Interactive?"

Devlin made an up-and-down pumping motion with his fist. "And make sure you watch the deleted scenes. Killer stuff."

Arroyo shook his head and suddenly wished he *had* used his handkerchief on Devlin's door.

"Yes, well, speaking of 'killer,' Mr. Devlin—"

"Of, for fuck's sake, I did not kill that ungrateful cunt. You think the pornography industry needs *more* bad publicity? Between the religious nuts, the ball-less politicians, and the mothers-against-whatever-the-fuck-might-make-their-husbands-hard, I'm up to my neck in a shit storm already. Murder? Jesus, no way." He reached into his drawer and pulled out a cigarette that appeared to have a lipstick smudge on its unfiltered tip. Lighting it, he leaned back and inhaled deeply, discharging smoke like a dirty dragon. "There's a saying in this business, Columbo. 'If it ain't on the sheet, it ain't worth shit.'"

"The sheet?"

"The contact sheet. The proofs. The fucking negatives. We make films here, you know."

Films. Arroyo always thought "film" was a fancy dress word for movies — especially pornographic movies. *The Maltese Falcon is a film. Pop Goes the Weasel is… something else entirely.*

"Nonetheless, I'll need your whereabouts on the night of the murder."

"Yeah, yeah, whatever the fuck you want. Talk to my secretary; she handles all that shit. I can't take a piss without her knowing about it."

"All right then. Thank you for your time. I'll be in touch."

"You pop in that DVD, Ace, and I *guarantee* you'll be in touch." For the first time during their meeting, Devlin smiled, but it was a greasy, nauseating smile.

"Trust me." He continued grinning like some larcenous Cheshire Cat, delighted at his own debauchery. Arroyo stared at that nicotine-stained enamel reef and realized Devlin probably wasn't a murderer. His impure motives seemed too pure. He was far more excited by cum shots than by gunshots. But he'd check out his alibi nonetheless. He reached for his handkerchief this time and grabbed the doorknob to leave.

"Keep that hanky handy, baby," Devlin chortled as Arroyo opened the door. "You're gonna *need* it!"

***

It had been almost a week since Detective Alana Stamos had met with Russell Padget. The lab report on the manuscript, which came back earlier this morning, was inconclusive. (Trying to deduce the authenticity of a particular author's manuscript from photocopies is almost impossible, it turns out.) This case wasn't becoming any clearer to her, the list of suspects neither expanding nor narrowing. Her colleague Desi was itching to arrest the brother-and-sister operation behind Friend to Man, but Stamos demurred. In her mind, the case against them was little more than speculation. Could it have been the pope of porn? Again, just speculation. How about Hiatt's ex-girlfriend, the one who appears to have left in a huff. What was she so angry about? Stamos knew how temperamental artists were. Could something have driven her to contemplate homicide? Then there was Zale, the eminent literary critic whose reputation would be upended if Hiatt's find turned out to be authentic. And Zale was certainly *acting* like a suspect — ducking calls, missing appointments, traveling out of town suddenly. Desi had made yet another date to interview Zale, but Stamos wasn't too confident. Would an academic superstar *really* be insecure enough to murder just for his own reputation? It seemed unlikely to her, but she was insulated from that world, and so here she was, on her way back to Hackett Community College to talk to Russell Padget, trying to hone in on how the whole academic hierarchy operated. There was something about Padget that she found appealing. He seemed confident but not cocky, and Alana had learned in her undercover days the importance of confidence if you want to make a mark in the world. Yes, she thought, Padget can help me. *I feel sure that he can.* Was there also the slightest stirring of, well, desire? Alana would have laughed off such a notion, more the kind of trash talk from Sweater or Mooch during a slow night at the precinct. But there was something there, a flicker of more than professional interest, a fascination with a life of the mind and the purity of intellectual pursuits. He doesn't have to roam through the gutter. He just has to read about it. But Alana knew that book learning could only get you so far. Yet, it also seemed to elevate you above the squalid, protect you, fortify you in some noble way, filling your head with fanciful concepts, forsaking the benighted world of homicide detectives for a utopia of well-turned phrases by well-spoken characters. Padget was well spoken — but as far as Alana knew, he was not yet spoken for. *Oh, stop it, for heaven's sake. It's the sleep deprivation talking.*

They spent the afternoon together, talking about James Joyce, Augie Hiatt, and the unexpected life turns that brought each of them to their current positions. Padget talked about his idealism when he first got into teaching and how when he was a graduate student, he lived in the library, turning over pages of forgotten manuscripts by forgotten writers in the hope of resurrecting the career of some forgotten genius. "Mostly though, I was hoping to make a career for myself," he admitted.

"And the genius — that would be you, right?"

Padget didn't correct her.

"Let's just say I had a pretty high opinion of myself back in the day."

They were sitting on a bench in a courtyard outside the building where Padget had his office, a small garden filled mostly with withered plants and painted rocks occupying most of the parcel. Amid the rocks was an imposing piece of sculpture, a kind of giant curving archer's bow aimed at the sky, reaching up several stories. Padget often stared down at the statue from his office window when he was feeling reflective. A bronze plaque caked with the dirt of many neglected seasons of tending said the statue was called "Daikyu" (which Padget knew was the Japanese term for longbow). A handful of students wandered past the bench as they spoke, and the detective in Alana noted that none of the passing students said hello to Padget. And he didn't take any notice of them.

"So did you always want to, you know, do literary work?" she asked as they made their way from the courtyard to Padget's office. "Even when you were a kid?"

"I never really was a kid," he said cryptically. "What about you? Always want to be a cop?"

"Oh, no. No way. I didn't even really know what a cop did."

"Everything I know about cops comes from watching TV."

"We didn't have a TV when I was a kid. My parents were Greek immigrants — first generation — and they didn't really understand the America they saw on TV. I was once with my parents at a department store, and they had a TV there. It was tuned to a sitcom, and I remember after every canned laugh, my parents both looking at each other with a perplexed look, like they had no idea why anyone was laughing."

When they got to Padget's office, he keyed in but kept the lights off, the midday sun filtering through dusty Venetian blinds, an amber glow smooching the spines of dusty book jackets.

"All the kids at school used to talk about what they watched on TV. I never had any idea what they were talking about. But I didn't really care. I had a radio. Someone gave it one to me as a present when I was eight or nine years old, a transistor radio with one of those earplugs that only goes in one ear. I discovered music. Not, like, heavy music, you know. Not classical, or anything that serious or deep. Rock and roll. Which can also be deep, of course."

Padget shrugged.

"Not a fan?"

"As a discipline, I always found rock music to be, well, rather undisciplined," he said.

"That surprises me."

"Why should it?"

"Well, you teach Romantic poetry, right? Rock and roll is the romantic poetry of our generation."

"I liked the Beatles for a while," he said. "But when I got into the serious study of literature, I came to realize that most pop culture provides only superficial delight. Real art doesn't yield its secrets so readily. A pop song has to be understood the first time you hear it, or it won't be a hit. But real art takes a long time — years, decades, before it yields up its treasures. Rock music cons people into thinking it's deep."

"Cons? Whew, that's pretty harsh."

"I don't think so. Talk to my students. They can't make it through a Wordsworth poem without taking a break to text their friends, order a chai latte, and post a photo of themselves on some silly website while drinking it. The Romantics — now *they* were deep."

It was Alana's turn to shrug.

"Punk rock got me through my teenage years. My adolescence was one long Blitzkrieg Bop."

Padget looked at her blankly.

"The Ramones?"

Blankness still.

"It's all right, Russell. I think it's kind of charming you never heard of them."

Russell? She called me by my first name? What's happening here?

"So, how do you go from punk rock to arresting punks?"

"We call them juvenile offenders, by the way. And it's a complicated story. Well, complicated emotionally. On the surface, it's actually pretty simple."

"Like a Keats poem, hmm? Now you've got my attention."

"All right. All right."

Alana brought her hands together in one interlocked fist and raised them to her forehead, a gesture of preparation or absolution. She sat there in Padget's office like so many others had, looking a little desperate. She exhaled and then opened her hands, unfolding them, staring at them like they held a secret text to be deciphered.

"Like I said, my parents were Greek immigrants. So — surprise, surprise. When they came here, they opened a diner. It was their whole life. Both my mom and dad worked, like, 18 hours a day. It was really tough on them. But for me, it was actually fun. I grew up there, hung around after school, weekends, basically, when most other kids were home, or with their friends, I was there. But I loved it. The cooks, the waitresses, everybody was always so nice to me. It was like diner daycare. Ajax." She had a faraway look that suggested she was no longer on the third floor of Eider Hall. She nodded very slightly and looked at him like he had become her confessor. "That was the name of the diner. Ajax."

"Right," he nodded. "Son of Telamon. From the *Iliad*. Makes sense."

"Huh," she said, nodding as if this was news to her.

"And?"

"And... so I got pretty comfortable there, and as I got older, I'd help out whenever I could. I think my parents thought I'd take over the place one day. I guess I sort of figured I would, too. I never really thought about the future, actually."

"Were they disappointed you didn't follow in their footsteps?"

The faraway look got even a little farther away.

"It was a weekend night. I was in tenth grade. I was supposed to have gone on a weekend field trip with my class to Gettysburg, but it was President's Day weekend, and that's a busy time for a restaurant, so I stayed behind to help out. Around nine on Sunday night, as we were getting ready to close...." She just stopped talking, suddenly lost to the past.

"Alana?"

Hey, why not? She called me Russ.

"Anyway, we're closing up, and this... this guy comes in — and he pulls out a gun. I'm in the kitchen, and I hear somebody yelling, so I walk up to that little window in the two-way door to see what's happening. So I'm standing there, watching through this grease-smeared window my father, fumbling with the cash register, my mother with her hands clasped to her face. I see my dad hand this guy all the cash from the register — and there was a lot because it was a really busy day, and then the guy grabs the money and sticks it in his pocket, and then... *he didn't have to shoot them!* They *gave* him the money. But he did. He fucking did. *He shot my dad.* And my mom. He shot my mom, Russ! Just because she was fucking *there!* And I saw them fall to the ground. And they both died. Right there, on the floor of the fucking Ajax diner. I *watched* it, Russ." She looked at him directly, her jeweled eyes telling him everything about her pain and guilt and anger, still alive, still a force within her. "And I've watched it every day since." She wiped away her tears with the back of her hand. "So yeah, that's pretty much when I decided I wanted to become a cop."

He felt a desire to comfort her, but what could he do? What should he do?

"Alana, I'm so sorry. That must have been… well, yeah, I can't imagine anything worse."

"Yeah, I couldn't either. Until I took this job."

"Right."

Alana collected herself, regained her composure and her focus, almost seamlessly transforming back into Detective Stamos. "This case — the Augie Hiatt murder — it's a puzzle, Russ. I'm totally perplexed, and I need your help. Who do you think killed him?"

Her pleading eyes begged an answer, but all he felt at the moment was a desire to kiss her. So he did.

When he pulled back, her eyes were closed. He waited for the rebuke he was sure was coming, but all she did was pull him back toward her, and they kissed again.

"Whatever happens next, let's not analyze what *just* happened, okay?"

"Occupational hazard, Alana," Professor Padget explained. "I make my living analyzing."

"Yes. But fiction, not reality."

"This seems almost unreal — I mean, I never kissed a cop before."

"Not one of your life ambitions, huh? So tell me — what are your life ambitions?"

"Ah, this is the part where I open up to you, is that it? Spill my secrets, tell you my true feelings? Hmm. Was that kiss just a clever interrogation technique?"

"You found me out," she whispered. "Let's interrogate some more."

And they kissed again, but it was more like two kids exploring the world of adulthood than two adults exploring each other. Alana had spent so much of her life recently immersed in the grim and grisly that she had forgotten what spontaneity and excitement felt like. Padget was so used to being in charge of his every waking emotional state that it felt liberating to give himself over to what Byron called "the volcanic plume of passion."

"You still didn't answer the question."

"I guess, when I used to have ambitions, it was to write a book. I remember the awe I felt in graduate school when I used to walk among the stacks in the school's library, just staring at the names on the book jackets, names of people I didn't know, would never know, most of whom were dead anyway — but there they were, lined up, waiting to impart some secret knowledge. Their lives had meaning."

"Just because they wrote a book?"

"Yes."

"Do you feel your life has meaning even though you never wrote a book?"

"Now, who's doing the analysis, huh? I thought we weren't going to overthink things."

"You're right," Alana said. "I should probably go."

"And just when you were starting to break down my defenses," Padget said. He ripped a piece of paper from his notebook and wrote something on it. "You asked me who killed Augie. Here you go."

She opened the paper and saw a familiar name.

"We've been looking for him," Alana said. "In fact, I'm hoping to talk to him tomorrow."

"I'm sure you'll get what you're after. You're a very persuasive interrogator," he said. "But does that mean our interrogation is over? Don't you want to know any more of my secrets?" he said, pulling her towards him again, vertical sun streaks lining her dark hair, falling in stripes on the shelves of books whose long-gone authors lived on in Padget's admiration and envy.

"This is not the proper location for further probing," she said.

Several hours later, as Padget left Alana Stamos's apartment, a light rain began to fall, dampening his Ascot hat and trench coat but not his mood.

***

Distinguished Professor R. Lancaster Zale wasn't to be found, Alana discovered. She had driven to his office, the piece of paper with the single word "Zale" in Padget's handwriting open on the seat next to her, a catalyst for thinking about what had happened the previous night. On the way to see Zale, traveling through the Holland Tunnel, Alana felt like she was in a mental tunnel, the world around and outside her obscured, blocked off by enclosures that had slowly moved in on her over the past several years, her career frustrations, her non-existent social life, the darkness of her daily labors. And then the flashpoint, Russell Padget lighting the fuse. She didn't have strong feelings for him, she knew. He just happened to be there during her surrender to temptation. But she could feel his weakness, too. And also — the detective in her speaking now — she felt he was trying to mask something in his own life, a secret that their make-believe interrogation would never have uncovered.

It would be two weeks until she finally cornered Zale. He was scheduled to meet with a producer for public television who was doing a story about Bloomsday, the annual global celebration of James Joyce's *Ulysses* in which fans of the book gather in public to read from the book — and even recreate the movements of the book's protagonist, Leopold Bloom (hence "Bloomsday") as he wanders around Dublin on June 16, 1904. Zale, being the leading authority on Joyce on the East Coast, was a highly sought-after "talking head." Alana had heard about the appointment from an informant-journalist acquaintance of hers who moonlighted writing scripts for video features for the station. She decided to stake out the production facility and after he concluded his interview, confront him as he walked to his car. There was a nearby plaza with a cafe that she hoped he'd agree to visit. *Maybe if he's relaxed,* she thought, *he'll be more inclined to speak to me. If not, I'll just arrest him.* Detective Stamos was becoming impatient with the lack of progress on the case, and she decided it was time to rattle a few cages, no matter how lavishly gilded.

In his interview for the Bloomsday video segment, Zale was charming, funny, self-effacing, and well-spoken. But as he left the studio and was confronted with Detective Stamos, a different side of the eminent professor emerged.

"Just who the fuck do you think you people are, harassing me day and night with some horseshit story that I had anything to do with that nut case's death?" Alana had no sooner pulled out her badge when Zale launched his tirade. "If you want to arrest me, I recommend you do so. Otherwise, all of you, stop it!"

All of you? Alana would later learn that "Monique's Peeks" had begun a fairly unrelenting campaign telling her listeners to call and email Zale, urging him to turn himself in to the police and confess to Augie Hiatt's murder. She also didn't know that Padget had tried to sandbag him at an academic conference, making the same accusation. Still, Zale's reaction seemed a bit extreme, she thought. *Guilty conscience?*

"Dr. Zale, if you could just—" But then he was gone, nestled securely into the limousine that awaited his departure from the television studio. She could have pursued him, she knew. Or called for backup. Or even sent a squad car to his office to arrest him at work. But she also knew she had very little to go on, other than the hunch of a fellow academic and a history of enmity with the deceased.

So she let him drive away, and then she climbed back into her car and popped in a CD from a band called *The Mishapen*, an Indie punk outfit whose members she had befriended when she was undercover as a rock-and-roller. Whenever she felt rattled by life, punk music settled her down. The energy, the fury, the passion reconnected her to a source of meaning and power that stretched back to her teen years. The madness of the music had *form* — unlike the madness of the world, and the tumult of the instruments achieved a kind of bristled, jarring harmony. Anyway, it helped her think. Her CD player was set to random, and the song that started was the only slow song on the album, a dusky and dissonant ballad called *Won Too Many*, about a high school kid who takes revenge on the Homecoming King and Queen by sneaking into prom and poisoning the punch. The song is sung just slightly off-key by the lead singer of *The Mishapen,* who called herself Cheri Pie. As Detective Alana Stamos stared out the windshield at the purpling early evening sky, wondering what her next move should be, she lost herself in these words:

The lowly never get a chance
for holy ordination.
They're too busy eating shit.
The machinations never quit.
Time to yank the plug.

Alana remembered hearing that song in the clubs, and she remembered how when Cheri Pie sang that last line, it became a kind of mantra that bounced off the dingy walls and found a full-throated embrace in the swaying and sweaty crowd. They'd raise their fists and intone "Yank the plug! Yank the plug!" turning a dark, whispered verse into a shared truth that filled the space, a specter of aural comfort and communion. Sitting there in the car, feeling a little lost, she mouthed the words again herself — "Yank the plug" — and then pulled out into the street, joining the rush hour dance heading home, hoping to spend the evening unplugging more completely from the bristling live wire that hummed in her head whenever she couldn't shake her job. And as *The Mishapen* continued to play, Alana changed her mantra to three other words, hoping they too had a talismanic power: *solve this case.*

Part Three

Human Voices Wake Us, and We Drown

Dearest Papli,

Oh, fangs! Did I tell you what THEY did to me? They took YOUR letters! Mister, the Man who has started coming around every day to ask us, do we like the tapioca pudding or the bread with butter and the pungent cheese remember we had at the cafe Tromp L'oeil with that very strange little man with the moustache that tied behind his ears and spoke with a Bavarian accent und simply couldn't complete a single sentence without bowing convulsively. He said the rules about "unhealthy stimulus" (which is what he called YOUR letters), took them and told me they'd be safe in a file with my name. Papli, I know the truth of things even though my being here seems to suggest elsewise. Once they have a file on you, there's no escape. They never show you your file, and they can put anything in it THEY want. Never surrender your file. But they didn't know that I have a secret file RIGHT HERE (tapping my noggin) and that all your letters are already a part of my permanent file, by which I mean my mind. I love the story about Archie the fish, but I wish I had paid more attention to ancient history in school. If you can, please send me a book about Archimedes because I would like to know more. I remember that he built something, but I can't find in my permanent file what the blazes it was! I've drawn a bunch of pictures of the story from your letters. They let us decorate our rooms with pictures (good thing — this place is weary dreary), and in fact, sometimes Dr. Polk comes around and looks at the pictures we've drawn and asks us about the things and the people in the pictures. He seems to believe that the pictures I've drawn of Archie and his friends reveal something important about my inner self, but I tell him — and I told them again when they came to take your letters — that the pictures are just a story that Papli is telling me and they asked me who was that, who was Papli, but I DARE NOT tell them that is our secret name for you and I dare not tell them especially what your secret name for me is, and that's why I never ever write it so that it can only be in one file and that's the one in my head.

I do wish you would come to see me. I thought you were coming last week when during quiet time they came to me to say that my parent had come and wished to see me. I got SO EXCITED, but it was only Mam, and she brought with her some papers she said I needed to sign so she could continue my treatment. And I told her and told her and told her that I didn't need any treatment and that the reason I was in here was because of her in the first place, and she got very upset when I yelled at her that I wouldn't sign and she took the papers and rolled them up, but I'm still in here, so I don't know if they were real papers and she left, and I told her not to come back. That night I had a dream that Mam was walking back from the butcher with a fresh kidney wrapped in brown paper in her hand, and a giant black and gold bird swooped down and grabbed the kidney and flew off — and Mam was still holding it! And she flew all over Dublin, and the bird said to her, "Don't be afraid. It's beautiful in the clouds," and Mam said, "That's what Lucia used to say when she was little and before she got violent," and then the package with the fresh kidney ripped and Mam started falling and I was lying on the grass slope by Dluglaz's, and I saw this odd shape shooting across the sky, and I said to myself "That looks like Mam!" and then she turned into a bird herself, and one of the Pogue boys shot the bird with a slingshot, and the bird fell to the ground, and then I woke up.

I hope you'll keep writing the story. I have a lot of space left on the walls of this room, and I don't like to look at the blankness. This whole place is a giant blank, and when I'm here, I become, if I'm not careful, a giant blank, so I have to close my eyes and remember what it was like to get ice cream and cakes and what the music sounded like when we were in Paris and how the people in their fancy clothes looked and sounded like and the perfume and bakeries and cigarette smoke smelled, and what the people said or the blankness takes over and then I have to squint and press my fists into my eyes to make kaleidoscopes just to remember what real colors look like.

Can you get the papers from Mam and re-write them and put "Out" where it says "In" and "Fine" where it says "Diseased" and drive up here in your tweed suit and sunglasses and your walking stick and give a hard sweet to the nurse and tell her you're here to take your daughter away and we can escape on the road and in the river and then through the sky because it IS beautiful up in the clouds and you can tell me about Icarus and Dedalus again, and I won't be afraid to fall because I know you'll always catch me.

Can you?

Lu

***

Detective Desi Arroyo very rarely evidenced feeling any kind of strong emotion. Most cops learn to keep their personal feelings under wraps, and that's especially true of cops in the Hate Crimes Unit. Their daily lives entwine with so much emotional devastation that it's either give in and drown or keep treading water. They learn early (if they want to stay on the force) to let the hideousness of humanity wash over them like an unexpected deluge. Change your clothes, dry off, forget it ever happened. So when Desi thrust the sheaf of papers at Alana and yelled, "I got the sons of bitches!" she knew this was kind of a rare event.

"And which particular sons of bitches would these be?"

"Take a look," he said. "This just came over from the ATF."

Alana studied the document, which appeared to be an application for a permit to carry a handgun. Along with it was a bill of sale from a gun dealer in Arlington, Virginia, for two Walther P99 AS semi-automatic handguns. The applicants were Todd and Beth Lawson.

"Friend to Man," Alana said, looking over the document.

"Check out the date of purchase."

Alana flipped the page and saw the date, which Desi had highlighted with a bright yellow streak.

"Two weeks before Augie Hiatt was killed,' he said. "Sons of bitches. Let's see them pray their way out of this."

Alana recognized the vibe — she had felt it often enough in her career. You stumble along in the dark looking for anything that might help solve a case, and you keep coming up empty. Then for a moment, the lights flicker briefly and you see what you've been missing. Sometimes, though, it's a trick of the eye, and you don't really have what you think you do. Alana had spent too many hours in her captain's office explaining why her smoking gun turned out to be a water pistol. Even the most judicious cops can let their desire to crack the case override their sober selves — a fact she tried to remind Desi of, to little purpose.

"We don't have the ballistics from their guns, so maybe let's take a step back," she said. "We don't even have proof they ever fired their guns. We don't even know if these guns exist."

"Oh, they exist. One of them was used to kill Augie Hiatt. I'm sure of it. These Jesus freaks are all `Life is Sacred' until it's in their interest to snuff out dissent. This was a message killing, Alana."

"And the message was?"

"We're not going to let porn corrupt the soul of America. If you're aboard the perdition express, you're gonna be derailed."

"Perdition express?"

"Augie Hiatt was a smart guy. Literate, cultured, maybe a future scholar. And instead, he turned his talents towards porn. A guy like that could really make a mark. Friend to Man couldn't let that happen. Scumbags like Bobby Devlin you can't do anything about. There was never any hope for depraved people like him. But Augie should have been on the side of the angels — and when an angel falls, look out."

"You've really got this all worked out," Alana said.

"I spent the first half of my life soaking up this shit," he said. "I know how religious people think. People like Augie who turn from the light represent a legitimate threat. Watch the videos, Alana. Friend to Man has made no secret of their belief that we're in a holy war. Hiatt is a casualty of that war."

"Thou shalt not kill."

"You think the 'flaming sword of the Lord's wrath is supposed to be used to slice pizza? Alana, open your eyes." He took his gun out of his shoulder holster, flicked open the chamber, squinted as he sized up the rounds inside the chamber, and then pushed the cylinder back in and tucked the gun into its cowhide sheath. "I'm going to bring them in."

Alana still felt it was premature, but Desi was headed out the door before she could register one final objection.

"Desi!"

He turned, giving her his best "what now?" look.

"Be careful."

His impatient grimace turned into a shy smile. He nodded and then headed out the door, another angel ready to play his part in an unfolding holy war.

The holy war at Friend to Man looked more like an unholy mess. When Desi arrived, Beth Lawson, her brother Todd, and their acolytes were finishing the set-up for a video shoot in the studios of the industrial building where they had their offices. The title of today's short video was "Knowing Rot from Wrong," and Beth and Todd were taking a literal approach. They had strewn the floor of the studio with garbage. Brother and sister had been secretly retrieving bags of garbage from the massive dumpster outside their building for the past week, and the result of their putrid pilfering was evident to Desi Arroyo well before he actually arrived on the set.

"What the hell…?" As he tiptoed toward the trash, he saw Beth Lawson, looking much more composed than the last time he saw her, her hair pulled back in a ponytail, holding a clipboard and giving some sort of instruction to an overweight fellow in a too-tight striped polo shirt that made him look like a lopsided bumble bee and plaid Bermuda shorts with the "XL" tag still clinging to his left glute, holding a light boom, and sweating profusely. Arroyo, unseen, stepped back gingerly amid the cameras and tech equipment and positioned himself behind a wrought-iron support beam. Perhaps he'd see something during the filming that would bolster his case. At the very least, the more evidence he had that Friend to Man was crazy, the easier his case would be, he thought. And shooting a video amid a pile of putrid refuse certainly seemed crazy. *Don't they realize their viewers won't be able to smell the garbage?* Well, *he* could, so he removed the neatly tri-folded paisley handkerchief from his jacket pocket and held it over his nose. Out of sight, out of smell, he hoped.

Beth Lawson shouted at everyone for silence, and then she counted backwards from ten. By the time she got to one, a hanging bank of tungsten halogen wash lights had lit up, bathing the garbage in an otherworldly aura. For the longest time, nothing seemed to be happening, but then slowly, slitheringly, the garbage began to move. In different places beneath this sea of slop, semi-recognizable body parts began to emerge: a quivering toe, an elbow, what looked like a forehead.

Jesus, there are people under that shit. Desi Arroyo was disgusted but also captivated — and a little awed. From where he was, a couple of dozen feet from the pile of putrescence, the smell was nauseating. He could only imagine what it was actually like being inside it. Friend to Man was committed to their mission. Of course, he had known this since watching the crucifixion video. As he witnessed the nails pierce the flesh of Todd Lawson's hands and feet — stopping, re-starting, zooming in, playing it all back again and again, looking for evidence of trick photography — he began to develop a genuine respect — and fear — of the group. Someone who will mortify his own flesh for a cause might be insane — very likely *is* insane. But you've got to respect that kind of commitment.

"Code Blue," someone shouted, and immediately the lights went out, and Beth Lawson quickly removed her headset.

"Where?"

"Here!" shouted a production assistant, now standing directly behind Detective Arroyo.

Beth Lawson raced over to Hanley Drodge, Friend to Man's director of social media and — given his bear-like physique — the group's unofficial bouncer. He had grabbed Desi Arroyo by the back of his suit jacket and was actually lifting him up off the ground, not completely airborne, not yet, but Desi was bouncing uneasily on the balls of his feet. When Beth saw who Hanley had collared, she yelled "Stand Down!" and, with a perplexed look on his face, Hanley released the tottering detective. Then Beth turned toward the entire production team and yelled, "Not a Code Blue!"

"Code Blue?" Desi asked, straightening out his lapels and giving Hanley an indignant stare.

"It's what we say when spies break in and try to get intel on our operation."

Intel? Stand down? Code Blue? These people use an awful lot of military language — another red flag, Desi thought.

Hanley remained directly behind the detective, arms crossed, returning every inch of Desi's icy gaze.

"He's police," Beth explained to Hanley in lieu of a more formal introduction. Then, turning to Desi, asked, "Why are you here?"

"I have a matter to discuss with you and your brother."

"Well, as you can see, this isn't a good time. We're just in the middle of—"

"Ms. Lawson, you and your brother are under arrest. I need you both to come with me."

"Under arrest? For taking garbage from a dumpster? Are you kidding me?"

"For murder."

Five minutes later, as he drove to the precinct with Beth and Todd Lawson handcuffed in the back of his car, he concluded that it would probably take several weeks to get rid of the putrid smell of the garbage that still clung to Friend to Man's co-founders, griming the back seat, reeking of rot, as deep-seated as sin.

***

When Holdena Straithorne finally opened her email — smartly, not at the beginning of her workday but at the very end, as was her habit — she discovered, amid the usual and highly deletable messages, a piece of correspondence rather unexpected. It was from a former professor of hers at Hackett County Community College — one of those professors she considered a mentor. In fact, it was this professor who first recognized her literary acumen ("Quite frankly, you're way too good for this place," he told her early in her academic career there, surprising her with both his assessment of *her* character and *his* workplace). She transferred from HCCC the following semester, but they stayed in touch the way most people today do: without ever actually seeing each other. When it came time to apply to graduate school, she reached out, and he responded with a glowing letter that must have helped — she not only got accepted by her first choice, but they offered her a teaching assistantship. It took Holdena less than one whole week to discover that she didn't enjoy teaching and that she was actually quite lousy at it.

"If students are so disinterested in what I have to say, why did they even *take* the class in the first place?" she lamented to him on the phone after a particularly sobering class. "I mean, they are *paying* to be there, right?"

Padget simply let her query hang there, intermittent static punctuating the quiet. *I ask myself this question every day.* Holdena's gifts did not extend to interacting with other people. She was a loner — a personality type Padget had identified early in his own life as helpful for the mastery of close reading and literary analysis — so he wasn't surprised that teaching wasn't for her. But they continued to exchange virtual greetings, and Padget even recommended her to Phalanx publishing after one of their textbook reps told him they had an opening for an editorial assistant.

It had been more than a year since she had last heard from her former professor, but Padget had thought of her many times since they last corresponded. He regularly picked up a copy of *Publishing Week* when he was in the library that HCCC subscribed to, and he noted with more than passing interest that Phalanx Publishing occasionally brought out books on literary criticism and biography. He found it somewhat ironic that Holdena was reading manuscripts written by distinguished scholars while he was stuck reading Freshman Comp 101 essays. In fact, he had once considered contacting her to see if they needed any additional readers — but then he realized just what he was asking: she would become his boss, a reversal his ego would simply not tolerate, no matter his respect and affection for his former prodigy.

Holdena took a sip of her tea and opened the email, expecting to find the usual "I thought I'd drop you a line to say hello" cursory catch-up. But what she found was far more surprising:

> Good day, Holdena. I hope this email finds you well. If I know you — and I feel I do — I'm sure you have spent the last several hours substantially improving the world's prose profile through an investment of your considerable intellect. You might not always be cognizant of it, but the work you are doing is the most important work that can be done. Oh, I can just hear the objections to *that* were I to say it in class: what about doctors! Police officers! Lawyers, Teachers! On and on, the litany goes, and you can fill in the remaining slots with the usual roster of noble and necessary professions. So let's look at that, shall we? A doctor, for instance, does indeed serve a critical function in society, but let's face it: the work most doctors do has only a temporary value. Harsh, yes — but true nonetheless. A doctor can keep you alive today. But what of tomorrow? The most skilled physician can't prevent your death. He or she can only make you more comfortable while you're here. Now, let's imagine that the manuscript you just laid aside prior to opening this email does indeed get published. Five hundred years from now, someone might well encounter that work — and your contribution to it (though sadly, save for a mention in the Acknowledgements, your efforts will likely pass unnoticed). But that work, Holdena, and the substance of what the author is saying will continue to minister to humanity long after your local G.P. has taken his last pulse.
>
> My digression (is it perfume from a dress that makes me so digress?) isn't quite so arbitrary as it seems, as I hoped to steer our discourse towards the

subject of publication. In fact, I am delighted to share with you my hope that we will once again be united in the holy cause of literature.

Holdena, I've something special to tell you. Through some investigative work of my own, I've been able to uncover a lost work by none other than JAMES JOYCE. It's taken some diligence — and good fortune — but I am now in possession of a work by Joyce, a playful and lengthy poem about some frolicking sea creatures, and I have reason to believe that there is no one living who has seen this work. Except, of course, myself. And shortly, you. I would like Phalanx to publish this work. I think it could be one of the most important literary finds in recent decades. Holdena, this is why people such as ourselves get into this field.

I have attached to this email an introduction (by me) to the work and a few sample pages from Joyce's poem (which he called *Archimedes at the Gear Fair.*). My sense is you will be as excited by this find as I am and that together, we can do something that will make our names household words in the literary community. So shall we make a little history?

Yours in the continuing struggle to ensure literature's prominence,

Dr. Russell Padget, Ph.D.

Among Holdena's many intellectual gifts was near-total recall. Once she read something, it was there, locked away. During many sleepless nights, the previous day's reading cycled through her brain, words and phrases from discarded manuscripts vainly attempting to re-assert their worth in perfectly replicated verbiage encoring in her brain. So she didn't need to re-read Padget's email — but she did. Several times. A lost work by James Joyce? Her recollections of Professor Padget's class brought to mind a fairly sardonic sense of humor, but nothing in this vein. If this was a prank, it was out of keeping with what she assessed as to his character. But something didn't add up for her. Padget wasn't a major Joyce scholar — not even a minor one, really. To her knowledge, he'd published nothing of importance on the writer. He didn't even go to academic conferences (he could be quite cutting about academia in his comments to her over the years). It struck her as unlikely that Padget could have found a lost work by Joyce when he was so far removed from the front lines of active research. *But it's possible, I guess — why else would he be saying this?*

She opened the attachment and downloaded it to her printer. Later tonight, she'd set aside her own work to spend some time reading Joyce's words. *There is no one living who has seen this work.* That had an intriguing, sinister ring to it. The editor in her told her that it would make a very nice blurb for the cover.

***

"Can I get you something to drink? Maybe some holy water?"

Mooch was seldom so irreverent — at least to people's faces. But this guy — well, something about him just seemed to be asking for it. Was it the bow tie? The slicked-back hair? The white suit that made him look like a cross between Mark Twain and the Good Humor man? The alligator briefcase? Or the *Bible*? Yes, that was it: he held the *Bible* like it was an additional appendage, like it had nerves and feelings of its own. He looked a little bit like a cartoon character, Mooch thought, what with his rimless glasses and the oversized gold crucifix on a chain around his neck. His lips seemed pursed in a sort of having-just-sucked-a-lemon kind of way, and his oxblood wingtips were not just shined but seemed to be emitting light all on their own. He's what might have been called in another time, and by a more literate observer, a "dandy."

"No, thank you," he said in a voice Mooch would have described as "squeaky." Even his name — Ferguson Cree III — seemed made up. Everything about him seemed made up. But there it was on the business card he handed to Mooch when he entered the detective bureau, along with the words "Attorney for Christ."

"What the fuck's that mean, 'Attorney for Christ'?" Mooch asked after reading the card.

"It means I represent the righteous."

"Of course you do," Mooch snarled. "Doesn't every lawyer say that?"

"Yes, I suppose they do," he said, plucking an errant piece of string off of his French cuff. "But I mean it."

"Of course you do," Mooch repeated, lightly shaking his head and returning to his desk. "What act of God brings you here today, counselor?"

"I'm here to see Detective Alana Stamos."

"You're in the wrong place."

"The officer at the reception desk looked her up and told me—"

"Yeah, I know that's what the directory says. But she's been transferred."

He wrote down her location on a notepad and ripped off the top sheet.

"Upstairs. Here's the number."

Ferguson Cree III looked at the paper, folded it neatly once, put it in his jacket pocket, and just stood there, sweating lightly from his upper lip.

"Anything else?"

"Well, I don't wish to offend you, but—"

"Yeah? Out with it."

After a brief pause during which Ferguson Cree III closed his eyes and lightly rubbed the crucifix hanging about his neck, he looked at Mooch and smiled sympathetically.

"Our Savior does not look favorably upon sins of the flesh." He gestured with his chin to Mooch's "in" box, which sported an open and well-thumbed soft-core porn magazine called *Enchante,* the upturned page featuring a mostly naked woman sitting astride a barber pole, over the words "Close Shaves — A Gallery of Grooming Get-Offs."

"I see," Mooch said, in the tone of a seasoned detective who is constantly sifting for clues. "The Lord don't like the female body, huh? That seems a little odd, since he created it."

"He created it for His glorification."

"Well, that's one use," Mooch acknowledged.

"Yes, well…."

"Anything else, counselor?"

"No, I'll be going now. Thank you for your help."

He turned abruptly, the *Bible* firmly tucked under his arm, and left without further comment. Mooch was beyond saving, probably. (Even he would admit as much.) But since Ferguson Cree III hadn't come to the police precinct to save souls, it was no loss. What he had to share with Detective Alana Stamos wouldn't make a believer of her, either. Still, it just might create reasonable doubt about who killed Augie Hiatt.

Same business card, same reaction. Alana Stamos's eyebrows arched after reading the description "Attorney for Christ." Like Mooch, she just couldn't restrain an irreverent reply. "You must excel at cross-examination," she said. Ferguson Cree III betrayed no reaction whatever — no indignation, no humor, nothing. He stared at her blankly.

"I'm here on behalf of my clients," he said. "Todd and Beth Lawson."

"They're being held pending arraignment," Alana said.

He just nodded and reached into his alligator briefcase, removing what looked like a square, see-through envelope containing a DVD.

"No need," he said dismissively, handing the DVD to Alana.

"Home movies from Bible camp?"

FC3 ignored her comment.

"This is a copy of a video surveillance tape, taken the night of Mr. Hiatt's murder, right outside his residence."

"Who in God's name was surveilling Augie Hiatt?"

"My clients. They hired a private detective to keep the house under watch."

"I don't understand."

"You see, Detective, unlike most of the clientele you deal with, Beth and Todd Lawson are not violent or hateful people. They are all about love."

Alana couldn't keep from rolling her eyes.

"I see. Another non-believer. Regardless, they had nothing to do with Mr. Hiatt's death. And this tape proves it. Once it became clear to Friend to Man that Mr. Hiatt had become a threat to the morality of their constituency, they decided to place him under surveillance. It has been their experience that immoral people don't suddenly become moral when they leave their workplace. They believed it was likely he was engaging in some sort of illicit behavior in his private life — drugs, prostitution, fornication."

"Fornication?"

Ferguson Cree III picked up his Bible.

"There are more sins in heaven and earth, Horatio, than are dreamt of in your penal code."

"Pretty good," she said. "Go on."

"It has happened before that people on Friend to Man's watchlist often stumble — sometimes, quite spectacularly. At that point, I am usually dispatched to meet with the fallen party and discuss how to keep the record of their indiscretion from a wider audience."

"Oh, I think I get it," said Alana, who got it exactly. "Blackmail. You show up with a tape and threaten to put it on Friend to Man's social media channel for all to see. They get scared and — what — make a donation to the church? That's called a shakedown where I work."

"Where I work, it's called atonement. But regardless of the terminology, it's perfectly legal. No money is ever exchanged. I merely ask the offending individual to reflect on whether or not it might not be prudent to refrain from further indiscretions — perhaps pursue another line of work. In exchange for their promise to do so, I store the evidence securely in a vault, never to be seen by anyone."

"And what, exactly, did you have on Augie Hiatt?"

"Nothing. He appeared to be surprisingly virtuous in his private life."

"So what's on the surveillance DVD?"

"Exoneration. You'll see that shortly before the estimated time of murder, someone enters Mr. Hiatt's residence. It appears to be a man, average height, medium build, wearing a belted trench coat, wearing an Ascot driving hat, and carrying a shoulder bag. The footage is pretty dark, but you can clearly see his outline. He looks nothing like either of my clients. He emerges about 15 minutes later, moving swiftly. The camera didn't get his vehicle. It was focused on the entrance to the place. But it's clear enough. Find that shadowy figure. There's your murderer."

Alana was experienced enough to know when someone was trying to throw her off the scent. Given Friend to Man's experience with video editing, it would have been easy enough to create a fake security reel. And the Lawsons certainly weren't foolish enough to commit murder themselves. The blood on their hands was the blood of Christ, not Augie Hiatt's.

"You know that we will have to authenticate this," she said.

"Oh yes — we insist upon it. Here is the name of the private detective agency that recorded the footage. It was their third night outside Mr. Hiatt's residence. All their contact information, as well as the signed contract from Friend to Man, is here," he said, handing her an envelope. "Their detective will testify, under oath, that no one else entered or exited the premises that night. Here," he said, reaching into his briefcase and removing a thick, triple-folded sheaf of papers, "is his sworn affidavit."

It's all very tidy. But it also sounds like it could all be true. Alana began rehearsing what she would tell her partner Desi when he got back from lunch. How would she characterize this new wrinkle: Red herring? Minor setback? Or do they need to search for a new suspect?

"This proves nothing at all, no matter what's on the tape," she blurted out somewhat defensively. "All this security footage captures is your clients' hired assassin doing what he was paid to do."

For the first time in their conversation, Ferguson Cree III smiled. It was a disarming and unsettling expression, and Alana felt a slight chill. He reached into his briefcase.

"Detective Stamos, not only is Friend to Man of interest to you. You have become interesting to them." He picked up another DVD and held it between his index finger and thumb.

After a few seconds, it hit her.

"Don't tell me — they've had me under surveillance? Are you kidding?"

"You and your partner. Friend to Man likes to know who they are dealing with."

Alana was a little stunned by the idea that someone had been watching her.

"What possible value could that have?"

That unsettling smile appeared again.

"This disk is for your private exhibition. I don't think you'll want your colleagues at the lab to see this one. Just a hunch."

What in God's name could be on it?

"I don't understand," she said, taking the disk from him, holding it like some fragile artifact, turning it this way and that. "What could possibly be on here that is in any way relevant to this case?"

FC3 smirked — it was almost as if some devilish impulse had seized control of his face, and he was no longer able to maintain his stoic Christian demeanor.

"Oh, I think it's relevant. The footage taken outside your apartment shows you entering your residence a couple of weeks ago in the company of a man."

What she wanted to say was, "Fuck you." But what her professional training and experience said instead was, "I'm allowed to have a private life."

"Indeed you are," he said, closing his briefcase in preparation for his departure. "I just find it interesting — and perhaps the court will too — that the man who is accompanying you appears to be the same man — belted trench coat, Ascot hat, shoulder bag — seen entering Mr. Hiatt's residence on the night of his murder. Please don't take my word for it. Review the video at your own convenience."

As he left, Alana was simply too stunned to offer even a cursory "Goodbye." Belted trench coat, Ascot driving hat, shoulder bag. She didn't have to canvass her memory long to identify the only person she'd been with who matched that description.

...appears to be the same man.

She had no idea what she would say when Desi returned. Better yet, she wouldn't be there at all. She grabbed the two DVDs and raced out of the precinct.

***

The expression raced through Holdena's head like a freight train: *The Quick and the Dead.* As a lover of lexicography, she realized that almost everyone misinterpreted the word "quick" in that particular phrase to mean "fast." Still, she knew that the word, at the time William Tyndale, 16th century Bible translator, used that phrase, meant "alert, lively, sensitive to feeling." So as she found herself typing it in an email to the editorial board at Phalanx publishing, she was counting on all of them interpreting it according to its erroneous modern usage.

"I'm writing to you with a sense of urgency. As you are all aware, there are only two types of publishers: the quick and the dead. We must embrace the former — and if we do, the rewards, I believe, will be immense."

Holdena hadn't even finished Professor Russell Padget's preface before she flipped open her laptop and began furiously typing. A chance to publish a James Joyce lost manuscript? *Are you fucking kidding me???* If Phalanx didn't move on this with lightning speed, some other publisher would surely get wind of it and offer Padget a better deal. Holdena realized that Padget, for all of his education, was a babe in the woods in the publishing world. She assumed he had no idea how to bring this work to the attention of a truly major publisher. Instead, he was relying on his friendship with her. That's pretty stupid, Holdena thought. *But it works to our advantage.* She was staking her reputation on this book being the big deal she knew it would be, and she needed to impress upon her co-workers at Phalanx how valuable this property is.

"No one breathes a word about this manuscript outside of the Board," she said. "This is the most important thing we'll ever deal with, and if we play our cards right, it could also make us all exceedingly wealthy." After years of plowing through reams of pedestrian prose, Holdena would soon be editing James Joyce's work. This was a career-maker for everyone involved.

"Do you remember that book by Harper Lee that came out a few years ago? The `lost" work she never published? Do you remember how much money that book generated? Dear colleagues, if we handle this properly, this will be *big*."

She envisioned a modest-sized hardcover book — Padget's preface in which he tells the story of how he came across the manuscript, the Joycean pages themselves, complete with illustrations Phalanx would commission from some well-known children's book illustrator, and an editor's note placing the book in a historical-literary context (Holdena would write that part). After this, she could write her own ticket. Her name would be known to every publisher in America. And when it came time to submit her own novel for publication?

Bidding war, she said to herself.

Her email urged all of her colleagues on the editorial board to meet in an emergency strategy session at 8 a.m. the following day. She attached an excerpt of Padget's preface just to whet their appetite.

"Read it and reap," she quipped, unable to resist a bit of her own Joycean wordplay.

Preface

The work you are about to read was written by the undisputed titan of twentieth-century literature. Generations of literary critics have poured over every word that James Joyce wrote since his death in 1939, but these words of his have never been read, never been seen — *never even known about.* In the annals of famous "lost works" by great writers, this particular manuscript — *Archimedes at the Gear Fair* — may well prove to be among the most significant.

The story of the work's composition (which began more than 80 years ago) and its discovery are almost as unbelievable as the preposterous but heart-warming tale itself. Joyce wrote this work serially, including different sections in letters he wrote to his daughter Lucia, over a period of years while she was in her late 20s, institutionalized in what would be the first of several decades she'd spend locked away in a sanitarium. Joyce always felt a special connection to his only daughter, who many critics see as the inspiration for his playfully complex work *Finnegans Wake*. Lucia and her father shared a special connection and reportedly even a private language that they would sometimes use to communicate. It's no surprise that father and daughter continued to exchange letters regularly (though Lucia had a chilly relationship with her mother and her only other sibling, Giorgio, both of whom found Lucia's mood swings and occasional outbursts worrisome, even dangerous). And the tone of *Archimedes* captures Lucia's personality perfectly. She was a dancer, an artist, a visionary, and the only rule she seemed to follow was the rule to live every moment according to the dictates of one's whim. This work, the elder Joyce surely understood, appealed directly to Lucia's iconoclastic nature. Who better than an irreverent, fun-loving fish, slipping through the world's waterways and dancing to his own nautical nocturnes to represent Joyce's daughter, whom the world named mad? (It was a charge that was often leveled against the father as well.)

But there was a method to his madness — and to hers, he believed. It's unclear if he ever explained the significance of the title of the work to her or if he needed to. But modern readers might perhaps benefit from a bit of background about this particular act in Joyce's word circus. Joyce had just spent the previous 17 years working on *Finnegans Wake*, a massive, encyclopedic history of the world as encompassed in the ups and downs of an Irish family that regularly morphs into their mythic counterparts — and even parts of the physical world (a tree, a stone, a mountain). The river of time and the actual river that runs through Dublin, the Liffey, factor hugely in the book. After this exhausting effort, Joyce was reported to have commented to a friend that his next work would be a simple book and that it would be about the sea. Having covered human history, he now turned his sites on pre-human history.

Archimedes at the Gear Fair is a poetical, mini-epic about the development of life in the sea, right up to the time the first sea creature walked up onto the land. The historical Archimedes was an ancient Greek mathematician, the inventor of cogwheel gears. In Joyce's story, he's a catfish, and the "gear fair" is Joyce's term for the carnival of life that was evolving in the sea, creating the gears that would drive human existence. And in a lovely example of Joycean wordplay, "gear fair' is an anagram for "farraige," the ancient Irish word for "sea."

The entire work is told in a series of episodes with Archie the catfish getting into all kinds of wild adventures and encountering other bizarre and wondrous creatures in the deep. There appear to be several sections missing, and the entire work runs only a few dozen pages. What can be inferred from the letters in which he enclosed parts of the work is that Joyce was putting some real effort into this underwater odyssey and that there were many more pages that he either sent to Lucia but were lost or that he simply never sent. Whether Joyce ever had any intention of publishing the work is impossible to deduce. However, since his work was the principal driver of his life, it seems logical to infer that he intended the work to see the light of day — very possibly with Lucia as the illustrator.

How close this work came to never being read by anyone other than Lucia is breathtaking. After her lifelong confinement and subsequent death at a mental hospital in England, her few possessions were unceremoniously packed away in a cardboard box and stored in a dank hospital basement for decades until a researcher with whom I was working located them. Uncertain about their authenticity, he brought them to me for verification. After a painstaking and thorough review, I was able to assemble the story in the order Joyce intended and to verify through graphic analysis that the handwriting was indeed Joyce's. My experience and background in working with Joyce for decades paid off handsomely as I was able to collate and contextualize the work you are about to read. It is my intention to write a more comprehensive account of my involvement in the discovery and authentication of these texts for future publication. But for now, what matters is bringing this glorious work to the world's attention, which I'm delighted to be able to do. If, as some believe, all life came from the sea, then I commend you joyously to this account of our mutual ancestors' underwater antics, a gloss on human behavior that should remind us all that when turbulence threatens, there's nothing like a splash in the surf to revive one's spirit.

Russel Padget, Ph.D.

***

No doubt about it — it was him. Same coat, hat, bag. He even moved the same way. The man who was seen leaving Augie Hiatt's house the night of the murder and the man who was seen leaving Alana's apartment were the same man. Now that this was established, Alana did what any good detective would do. She began playing "what if?" turning over all the possibilities that would explain why Russell Padget was caught on camera coming out of Augie's place that night. And there were lots of possibilities — but none of them felt completely right.

Maybe he was there simply as a social visit? Maybe he was there to confer about some matter regarding the manuscript? Maybe Augie knew he was being watched and got nervous and called Padget to come over and calm his nerves? Maybe they were discussing possible paths to publication for *Archimedes*?

Or maybe....

The final possibility gave her a little shiver. She needed more data. Something didn't quite add up. She had the words but not the music. She picked up her phone.

"Hi, Russ. It's Alana. Sorry to call so late. I was just wondering if maybe you might like to get together for a drink or something. I've had a lot on my mind, you know, with this case and all, and I could really use a break. Call me if you want to get together."

So what was that — loneliness? Entrapment? Recklessness? Alana's instincts told her she was moving in the right direction and that the puzzle was coming together. Still, she resisted imagining the color of the final missing piece, though she could sense its contours. Another encounter with Russell Padget, and she hoped she'd have the clarity that currently eluded her. It wasn't long before he called back. They agreed to meet the next day at an Irish bar called Castle Rackrent. Padget hadn't been there for years — it was the site of a retirement party several years ago for a colleague Padget barely knew, but he went and had a pint just to be polite and then slipped out. His only recollection of the place was that it had a massive stuffed wild boar on a pedestal opposite the bar. He wasn't there long enough to determine the boar's significance, if any.

"Thanks for coming, Russ." She kissed him on the cheek. That's a good sign, he thought. He didn't feel the least bit guilty that he was there merely to pump her for information about the case. He had no idea she was there for the same reason.

"Well, the religious nuts are off the hook," she said, bypassing the obligatory round of small talk. "The ballistics came back on the gun registered to Friend to Man. It wasn't a match to the gun that killed Augie."

"So, where does that leave the investigation?"

Neither was making much of an attempt to hide their interest in what the other might be able to provide.

"Back to Zale. He's always been the number one guy, in my opinion. But I still can't figure something out."

She paused and raised her half-pint of hard cider to her lips, her eyes closed, the expression giving Padget an unexpected flashback to their brief encounter.

"May I ask what that is?"

"Oh, sure. In fact, you're probably the perfect person to ask because you know how guys like that think."

Compliment? Insult? Doesn't matter.

"Well, I'll help you in any way that I can."

She reached across the table and patted his hand.

"Thanks, Russ. Alright. So here's what I'm not getting. Let's say that Augie's manuscript is real. That Joyce, you know, was the actual author. Instead of booting the poor kid out of the Ph.D. program, why not collaborate with him, help him get it published, maybe even share the credit with him? I get that Zale is like this bigwig in the field, but wouldn't playing a part in this discovery, helping this kid out, be good for him as well as Augie?"

Padget didn't even try to repress a smile. *Alana, you know so much, but you have no idea how most academics think.*

"Guys like Zale didn't get to the top by sharing. The academic game, at the highest levels, is cut-throat stuff. And Zale is not going to admit that he was wrong — that no such work existed until this nobody found it."

"So it's ego?"

"It's self-preservation, Alana. Zale isn't going to be reduced to hand-holding some wet-palmed grad student who just made the discovery of the century. No self-respecting academic would allow himself to be put in that position. It undercuts a lifetime of one's own work. King of the hill, Alana — not 'kings' of the hill."

Alana was slightly alarmed at Padget's vehemence, but she tried not to show it. She could now sense the edges of the phantom puzzle piece coalescing, its shape sculpted as her mind turned.

"So you're saying that Zale would rather *kill* than share credit for a major discovery?"

"Zale's name will go down in history. Augie Hiatt is already forgotten."

Now it was Padget's turn to down his pint of ale as Alana prepared her next round of questions.

"But *you* were willing to work with him, right? You were going to give him the help Zale never would."

"Of course," Padget said, a bit defensively. "It's a terrible shame Augie died. Just terrible. But I know he would have wanted the manuscript to be published. So that's what I'm doing."

This time, Alana couldn't hide her surprise.

"You are going forward with publishing the work?"

"Damn right," he snapped. "Do you have any idea what this could mean?"

"For you? Or for posterity?"

He took another long and satisfying gulp.

"Both."

Detective Stamos played out the hand.

"But what gives you the right, Russ?"

"Excuse me, Madame prosecutor. Isn't there some well-known maxim about possession being nine-tenths of the law?"

"The work was Augie's."

"The work was Lucia's. And she died. *Then* it became Augie's."

"And *he* died."

Padget finished his drink.

"Exactly. Care for another?"

"No," she said, still processing what Padget had just told her. Had he always been this opportunistic, and she simply hadn't noticed? "Sorry. I can't stay. I have to go and check out a new lead."

"But I thought you said Zale is your man. Don't you believe what I told you about the egos in academia?"

Alana rose from the table and leaned over, her face close to her drinking companion, her whispered tone both seductive and defiant.

"Every word."

***

It was exceedingly rare for Dr. Morgan Staffordshire, the hospital director, to actually visit any of the patients. He was more of a ghostly presence: rumored, feared, almost never seen. His appearance outside Lucia's room must have been dismissed as a spectral occurrence by some of the patients. The hospital had become, in the years that he governed it, a reflection of his own personality, rigid and forceful. It wasn't that he lacked sympathy. In fact, he felt himself to be among the most sympathetic of souls. But he practiced a kind of medicine that, many years later and by clinicians far less disciplined than him, would be termed "tough love." He believed that allowing mentally disturbed people to circulate in "normal" society was an act of wanton cruelty, and he did what he could to keep that from happening. Over the years, some of the doctors on staff — and even, heaven forfend, some of the nurses — had come to him to suggest that such-and-such a patient might be better off back in the world. Staffordshire recognized this for what it was: misplaced sympathy. No, no, he'd tell them, they are much better off here. After all, the hospital he ran was designed down to the smallest detail to accommodate the needs of the mentally fragile. His failure to even consider the requests of his junior staff created the impression that he was some sort of heartless bureaucrat. Nothing could be further from the truth, he knew. In his mind, he was all heart.

Would a heartless administrator take it upon himself to do what he was about to do? No, indeed.

Unlocking the door, he then did something almost unheard of in the ward: he knocked. At first, Lucia thought the noise was caused by something falling, and she looked around nervously. It had been years since anyone had knocked on any of the doors, and the unfamiliar gesture created simple puzzlement. He knocked again, and still the memory of what that rapping sound might mean eluded Lucia, who sat stone still on the chair in her room.

"May I come in?" he said.

She turned to see a largely unfamiliar face. I think I know him, she thought. I think I should know him.

"Lucia?"

"Yes," she said, then bolted upright nervously.

"Oh no, please, you may sit down. Lucia, do you remember me? I'm Doctor Staffordshire. I run the hospital here."

She cocked her head and bit down on an errant lock of hair that fell across her face.

"Do you remember me?"

She continued looking at him, appearing somewhat lost. At least, that's what he took her expression to mean. But her verbal response revealed a far more acute mind than he would have ever suspected.

"Is he dead?"

"Excuse me?"

"My father? Is he dead?"

For all of his psychological training, Dr. Staffordshire still felt uncomfortable delivering this kind of news. As he walked to Lucia's ward from his office, he rehearsed several ways of delivering the news that her father, James Joyce, had died. He was taken aback — and somewhat relieved — that she had considerably simplified his task.

"Yes."

She looked at him wordlessly, still chewing lightly on the twig of claret-colored hair brushing against her face, curlicuing her chin.

"I'm very sorry, Lucia. He died two days ago in Zurich. There was an operation. Your father had been having stomach problems, and they were trying to repair a hole — what we call a duodenal ulcer — and the operation, that part of it, was successful, but during the recovery, he lost consciousness and never regained it. As I said, I'm very sorry."

Lucia looked at him, or actually just above him, gazing into some distant vista, sitting there quietly for almost a minute. Then she looked directly at him.

"My father once wrote that `History is a nightmare from which I am trying to awake.' I never really understood that until just now."

Doctor Staffordshire nodded, hiding his surprise at the depth of her thought behind the practiced insouciance of the medical professional.

"I'll have to read your father's works," he said. "I have heard they are brilliant."

"He was brilliant. His works are just paper and ink, the residue of genius."

"Residue of genius. Quite right," the learned Dr. Staffordshire said. He was surprised and a little unsettled by the turn the conversation had taken. This woman seemed possessed of a kind of intelligence, an acuity that didn't gibe with the context of this conversation. He pulled out his pocket watch.

"I'm sorry. I must go now."

He turned to leave, but a final question stopped him.

"Is Mam coming then?"

"Your mother? Well… she didn't say. If I hear anything, I will let you know."

Lucia nodded almost imperceptibly. That was it, then. With her father gone, her future was in the hands of her mother. So that was it, then.

"Goodbye, Lucia."

***

"Good morning, partner." And then he glanced self-consciously at his watch. "Make that 'Good afternoon,'" he said, smirking.

"Desi, not today. Please."

"Yeah, yeah. Ok. Tough night?"

"Tossed and turned until dawn. Then I finally fell asleep. Next thing I knew, it was noon. I jumped out of bed and raced here. I haven't even had my coffee yet."

Desi Arroyo hadn't been a detective for more than a few years, but he was experienced enough to recognize someone in distress. And also someone hiding something. But he gave his partner a wide berth. He decided to keep things all business.

"Lab dropped this off for you this morning," he said, handing her a large manila envelope. She looked at the label and then held it in her hands for a half minute before opening it. As she read the words, he noticed a look on her face that a more literate person might have labeled as mortification. He just thought it was an expression of surprise mixed with, maybe, disappointment.

The envelope contained a standard lab report. Paper-clipped to it was a short note: "Likelihood of match: 100%"

"What's up?" Desi asked. "Is that anything we're working on?"

Alana just nodded.

"Oh. Ok."

Too many closed doors. He went back to his desk and lost himself in some paperwork. Detective Alana Stamos glanced at the lab report but what she was really seeing was the final piece of the puzzle slide into place. After Friend to Man's attorney gave her the security footage of Russel Padget coming out of her apartment — and its similarity to the Augie Hiatt footage from the night of his murder — she knew she had to follow up, even if it seemed preposterous. She discovered she still had the crumpled piece of paper in her car (thank God for slovenliness) that Padget had given her on which he had written ZALE. She sent that paper to the lab, along with the envelope Padget received from Augie Hiatt that contained the Joyce manuscript. It turned out the ink used on both was the exact same: Diamine Shimmering Night Sky grey.

The same ink was used to address the envelope to Padget and to write Zale's name on the paper in Padget's office. It was all coalescing in a nauseating kaleidoscope. Yet she still chafed at reaching the logical conclusion. She felt she needed more evidence (even though she was sure that if she shared what she knew with Desi, he would have insisted on making an arrest right then).

"I'm going to go talk to the Captain and then step out and grab a quick bite."

"That's cool," Desi said. "Slow news day."

"In the meantime, can you initiate a permit search for a Colt Defender nine-millimeter handgun?"

"Sure. Under what name?"

"Russell Padget."

Desi gave her a perplexed look which she was simply too tired to notice. He wrote down Padget's name.

"Going to talk to the Captain about my raise?" He was still trying to break through her mid-day haze and establish some sort of patter with his partner, but she seemed locked in her preoccupation.

"No — I'm asking him for time off. I need to get away for a few days. Lots happening. Sorry to bail on you."

"Do what you gotta do. We'll still be here when you get back, me and the perverts."

She softened a bit and even laughed to herself. Turning to Desi, she smiled for the first time that day. "Me and the perverts. That'd be a great name for a punk band, doncha think?" She headed to the Captain's office, fondly lost in the memory of her poisonous persona, forgetting for a moment toxic thoughts of the present.

The Captain told her to take all the time she needed, but she told him it would probably just be a day or two. It turned out to be three weeks. And even though she joked with her partner about her punked-out past, she spent untold hours playing all her records from that era, reverting to her nocturnal ways, spending the nights rocking out in her apartment and the days shunning the sunlight. She kept telling herself she needed to wake up early, exercise, eat healthy, volunteer, learn a new language, and write in her journal. In her conscious mind, she had her reclamation all laid out, but her unconscious mind kept dethroning the better angels of her nature. This is what happens; this is *why* what happens happens. In the end, character is destiny, and you only become more neurotic if you deny your destiny. So she embraced it, made friends again with that teenage girl who sought comfort in the darkness of the music. She thought very little about the Augie Hiatt case, about any of her cases. She had teetered on the brink of burnout without realizing how close she'd come to falling over the edge, so she let this phase play out as it needed to. Three weeks of spinning records and eating junk food doesn't sound like a prescription for a healthy return to form, but it was just what she needed. In the words of one of her favorite punk bands, Ma Smeg, "Nobody licks the veggie plate clean."

But while Detective Alana Stamos was away regaining her mojo, someone else was watching theirs tantalizingly slip away.

***

[FOR GENERAL RELEASE]

Phalanx Books is pleased to announce the forthcoming publication of a major new work of literary scholarship — and the first appearance in print of Modernist master James Joyce's last work, *Archimedes at the Gear Fair.*

The work, edited and introduced by Joyce expert Dr. Russell Padget, is certain to shake the foundations of the literary world.

"For almost a century, the book on Joyce has been closed, so to speak. Well, this authentic, playful, and brilliant text opens another avenue of insight into the genius who was Joyce. Its importance cannot be over-estimated," writes Dr. Padgett in the introduction to the work."

Archimedes at the Gear Fair tells a delightful story — all in Joycean verse — of a group of sea creatures frolicking in the world's oceans long before humanity arrived on the scene. This panoply of marine life — from single-celled organisms to complex and clever crustaceans — is part Dr. Seuss, part Salvador Dali, and all James Joyce.

Advance copies available for review in both print and electronic editions. Inquire with credentials to Holdena Straithorne.

***

Reading *The Oculist* was, for R. Lancaster Zale, part of the accommodating routine of his inarguably successful life. Morning tennis, followed by mimosas at the club and a steam, then lunch, the daily *Times*, after which he'd steal a quick peek at the academic journals (he had long ago stopped thinking of his fellow writers as "the competition," though he still felt a small pang of jealousy when one of his fellow academics garnered a major award or positive review). So it was this Saturday as he settled into his leather wingchair with a small stack of recently published journals on his lap. Mostly, he scanned the ads — who was publishing what, by whom, and what were the publicity blurbs? (He had recently submitted on behalf of a colleague's work his own blurb — those glowing critical assessments of a book, hailing it as "brilliant and insightful," or some such smoke-blowing — though the book had yet to be published.) So when he came across the ad from Phalanx, he almost spilled his appletini.

Good Lord. They haven't.

But there it was, in black and white.

It took a lot to upset the daily routine of R. Lancaster Zale, but once he saw the ad, he knew what the rest of his day would consist of. At 5 p.m., the following email would appear in Holdena's inbox:

Dear Ms. Straithorne.

I am writing with regard to the advertisement in this month's *The Occulist*, p. 34, for a forthcoming work entitled, *Archimedes at the Gear Fair*, the purported "new" work by James Joyce. To cut to the chase, I regret to inform you that the work is a complete fraud.

How can I possibly know this, not having even read it? Ah, but I have. Here is the backstory — which I encourage you to fact-check. (It will not be difficult to verify what I am telling you.)

About a year ago, a Ph.D. student under my supervision submitted what he claimed was a lost work of James Joyce's under the title, *Archie's Irishy Sea Splash*. He claimed it was a work in rhymed verse about a group of impish sea creatures, all of whom exist before life emerges from the sea. He claimed to have found this lost work of James Joyce in the archives of a British sanitarium in which Lucia Joyce — James Joyce's only daughter — had been for most of her adult life, committed.

A compelling story — and one which merited further investigation. This student, named Augustine Hiatt, claimed to have found the letters that contained the story on a trip to England. The time he claimed to be in England coincided with the time, according to his application to the Ph.D. program, when he was also actively enrolled in a creative writing MFA program at Westmore Pacific University. In order to resolve this discrepancy, I contacted the program to see if he was, perhaps, on some sort of leave of absence. No, it turns out, he was there during the purported time he was abroad. I had a further conversation with his program advisor — and that's when I learned the truth. I explained to him why I was calling, and he said the work I was referencing — *Archie's Irishy Sea Splash* — was an original work Hiatt had been writing in his Children's Lit class. In fact, this professor (whose name I would be happy to supply you) said he gave Hiatt the idea to write about sea creatures because Hiatt was himself a water enthusiast (he told his professor one of the reasons he chose Westmore Pacific was because he was a scuba enthusiast and the school was close to the coast). "Take your knowledge of the undersea world and use it in your writing," Hiatt's professor advised him. The result of that was *Archie's Irishy Sea Splash*, an amusing but fairly amateurish effort. Once I learned of this — and after I received photocopies of the drafts of this work from his professor at Westmore Pacific — I called Augie Hiatt into my office and told him he was being dismissed from the program for fraud. Apparently (if I may infer from your advertisement), Hiatt was able to convince someone in your firm that the work was legitimate.

I write this to you, not with glee or indignation but merely to save you from further embarrassment should you proceed to actually publish this work. As I said, I can supply you with contact information and photostats of the work in question, should you wish.

R. Lancaster Zale, Ph.D.

It's over then, Holdena thought. The book would have to be withdrawn immediately. She didn't doubt for a moment that Zale — whose works she remembered reading as an English major — was telling the truth. She sent a brief, one-line message to her boss at Phalanx, subject line "Full Stop." The email read, "We need to meet to discuss damage control, and also my resignation."

After she briefed her boss, she figured she'd share what she learned with Padget, though her sense of loyalty to him was leeching from her with every word of Zale's email that she replayed in her mind.

***

"You look good. Way better than you did when you left."

"And you are just as tactful as you ever were," Alana shot back, though she smiled at her partner. "Tell me, Desi, how have you managed to stay afloat in my absence."

"Who says I did?"

As if to illustrate his point, he took a stack of mail from his desk and handed it to her.

"I never realized how popular you were," he said.

"Yeah, great," she said, quickly leafing through the stack. "Publishers Clearinghouse says I'm a winner."

"Well, they don't know you like I do."

Ah, the banter. That's one of the few things Detective Alana Stamos genuinely missed during her three-week hiatus. For a person as deeply engaged in her work as she was— and in fact, it was long hours poring over her caseload, at her desk and in her mind, that drove her to the brink of burnout — she was surprised how little she thought of work during her time off. There were dozens of cases she had put on hold, but their often-grisly details did not haunt her sleep as she expected. But the Hiatt case — that one didn't leave her alone. Once, after a night of a wee bit too much Beaujolais, she thought about calling Russell Padget. Their time together (and by that, she meant their night together) had helped soothe her wounded ego. It made her feel good to know not everyone had to be Mirandized to spend time with her. But it was, in fact, the jarring revelation that Padget was somehow involved — *might* be involved, she kept having to correct herself — that made her feel the need to get away, get some perspective. So as she leafed through the thick stack of correspondence, there was only one letter she was really interested in reading.

And there it was: From the Bureau of Alcohol, Tobacco, and Firearms, registration division.

Settling into her creaky wooden desk chair, she tore open the envelope. She had asked Desi to initiate a background check to see if Padget had ever applied for a permit to purchase a handgun, and now she had her answer.

"Holy shit," she said, loud enough to rouse her partner's curiosity.

"You being audited? I'm available to be a character witness. For a fee."

Ignoring his barbed endorsement, she grabbed the letter and said, "I need to see you and the Captain in the conference room."

"Ok. I'll see if he's free."

"I'm going to go splash some water on my face," she said, suddenly looking a little ashen.

"Right," Desi said. And then, just before she left the room, he shouted out to her.

"Hey, Alana."

"Yes?"

"Welcome back."

***

Vengeance has a rich Biblical provenance. The good book says vengeance is to be left to the Lord — and there are multiple instances of Him doing just that: smiting sinners, casting down fire and brimstone, baptizing the earth by opening the faucet for forty days. But turning the other cheek — that's what human beings are supposed to do. And that's exactly what Todd Lawson did while his sister Beth performed the long, slow dolly shot that focused, first from a distance and then, well, right up close, on his bare buttocks, upon which was written "We are imperishable" (left cheek); and Corinthians 9:25 (right cheek).

For the next couple of minutes, the camera simply lingered over the scripture, the fleshy revelation of Friend to Man's new manifesto. Todd and Beth were feeling vindicated, righteous — and vengeful. As Todd's hindquarters quivered slightly under the klieg lights, Beth read the voice-over to her brother's cheeky scriptural offering.

"To the members of the jack-booted Hate Crimes Unit, who persecuted us — *all* of us — for our belief, we command them to cast their eyes upon the body of Christ's people and remember that we are imperishable! Our spirits shall be uplifted even as the ugliness of the world intrudes upon our sanctity! We shall triumph — no buts about it!" Beth chuckled to herself when she wrote that line. Todd went along — they knew they'd have to address their recent, high-profile involvement in a pending murder case. The Christian message boards were buzzing, but Todd and Beth knew a thing or two about buzz themselves, so they decided to face it head-on, more or less.

"Our faith is being tested, sisters and brothers," Beth continued. "Persecution is nothing new. But neither is eternal damnation. And the Philistines who fanned the flames of this secular abomination shall taste the fiery fury of Satan while we ascend the angelic heights in the company of the Lord of hosts! We recognize no law but God's! We turn our backs on you, unholy keeper of man's covenant!! Defilers of true righteousness!!"

The sermonette ended, the camera slowly receded until Todd's posterior pronouncement, the consummation of an in-your-face rebuke to Detective Stamos & Co., was a distant blur. A final, tight closeup on a title card summing up the not-so-subtle subtext of the scene then comes into blisteringly clear focus:

YOUR EARTHLY AUTHORITY MEANS NOTHING HERE.
AND NOW YOU KNOW IT TOO.

Harsh words for the hardworking detective squad at the Hate Crimes Unit, but catnip to the ever-growing legion who considered themselves true Friends to Man.

***

The interrogation room was usually reserved for the questioning of suspects, but Alana didn't want any interruptions, and she knew how frequently Captain Felton's office phone rang or someone barged in. This was not something she wanted to dole out piecemeal. They needed to hear her out completely.

"This is about the Hiatt case," she began, dispensing with any chit-chat. "There's been a breakthrough."

Felton looked at Desi Arroyo, and they both kind of shrugged as if to say it was news to each of them as well.

"Very well," Felton said. "What have you learned?"

That I'm a fool. That a detective should not sleep with a material witness — it tends to cloud one's judgment.

"That we've been overlooking someone who — I now believe — is responsible for Hiatt's murder. Do you remember Russell Padget?"

"The professor you've been consulting with — the guy Hiatt sent the manuscript to?"

"Right — but that's not exactly right."

"What are you saying?" Felton asked.

Alana opened the manila folder and took out the piece of paper on which Padget had written "Zale."

"A month or so ago, while investigating the case, I was in Padget's office, and he wrote this down and handed it to me when I asked him who he thought the murderer was. On a hunch, I sent it to the lab and had it analyzed."

"What were you looking for?" her partner asked.

"I thought the color — and the handwriting — seemed somewhat similar to the writing on the envelope that Hiatt sent Padget. The one that contained the manuscript." She took out the envelope and held them side by side.

"I had the lab analyze both samples, and it turns out they both are a particular type of fountain pen ink. Not common at all. The graphologist also confirmed the handwriting in both samples as the same as well."

She could hear the wheels turning. They all could.

"So... Padget wrote his own name on the envelope, which means he sent the manuscript to himself, but he made it look like Augie Hiatt had mailed it to him."

"So it would appear."

"But that would mean Padget went to Hiatt's place and... what? Murdered him? Do you have any evidence he was there?"

Detective Alana Stamos bristled slightly. She took a deep breath and told them what the lawyer for Friend to Man had given her.

"There's a video of Padget — or someone looking very much like him - leaving Augie Hiatt's residence on the night of the murder."

"How do you know it's him?" Desi asked.

"Well... so here's the thing that kind of complicates the case, maybe. I recognized Padget's clothes and bag because he wore the same thing when he... um... came to my place."

"Elaborate," said Felton, peering over his reading glasses.

"The thing is, we spent the night together. And, well, the footage of Padget coming from Hiatt's place matches pretty much what he looked like leaving my place. The person matches Padget's build, and he has the same hat, coat, and bag that he brought to my place."

Felton took off his glasses and pinched the bridge of his nose.

"You had relations with a material witness in a case?"

"At the time, I didn't think he was anything more than, you know, a helpful source."

"Helpful," said Desi, smirking to himself until Felton shot him a look.

"Let's stay on point," Felton said. "Walk us through the timeline."

"Ok. Padget goes to Hiatt's place. He must have known where to find a key because there's no sign of forced entry, but he admitted to me he had been there previously. He shoots Hiatt, takes the manuscript, addresses it to himself with the pen he's carrying because he doesn't want to leave fingerprints on any of Hiatt's pens, then leaves and mails the envelope."

"But what about the gun?"

"That's the piece I was missing," Alana said. "But when I got back from my break, I found this letter from ATF waiting for me. It confirms that Padget was issued a permit to carry the same type of gun that was used to kill Hiatt. When Padget applied for the permit, he claimed he needed it for self-defense purposes because he taught at night and often didn't leave campus until it was mostly deserted."

"Ok," said Felton, adding it all up. "Handwriting, gun, and we've got him at the scene of the crime. But I still don't get motive."

"I didn't either — not until I got into this guy's world. Academia is a lot more cut-throat than I ever realized. Whole careers are determined by who is considered to be a `serious' scholar and who is merely along for the perks. And to be taken seriously, you need to publish."

"Publish or perish," Desi Arroyo said.

"In this case, both. Padget gets a whiff of what Hiatt has his hands on — a real career maker. A lost work by a modernist master. The chance to be the editor of an original Joyce manuscript, well, for a guy like Padget, who has spent his whole career on the fringes of academia, the temptation is simply too much. With Hiatt out of the way, Padget can spin his involvement in bringing the manuscript to publication. Hell, he can even claim to have helped discover it. Why not? The only people who can contradict him are Hiatt - who is dead — and another academic that Hiatt told about the manuscript. His name is Zale, the name Padget gave me, the one he told me was the real murderer. Zale gets fingered, his reputation sullied, Hiatt gets buried, and Padget gets his name on a book jacket. Which, I learned from my undercover work with him—"

Desi Arroyo smirked again.

"...which I learned was *the* most important thing to him. Padget desperately wanted to have his name on a book that would find its way into every Joycean's library."

"Joycean?"

"That's what James Joyce scholars call themselves."

"Cute," Felton said.

"So that's where we stand."

They all looked at each other and half-nodded.

"Nothing left to do but go pick him up, I guess," Desi said.

"I'd like to go alone - if you don't mind," Alana said.

She looked at Felton.

"Your case. Your collar. Handle it how you see fit. Just don't add any more... `complications'... got it?"

"Yes, sir."

Alana gathered the papers she had spread out on the table and put them back in the manila folder. Felton walked briskly out of the interrogation room and back to the dozen or so urgent messages that awaited him in his office. But Desi lingered.

"So tell me — did you have any hint this guy was guilty before you two, you know..."

Alana shot him a look of indignation.

"Would you *ever* sleep with a murder suspect? I mean, if you knew she was a murderer? Are you really that depraved?"

Alana gathered her papers and left the interrogation room, off to arrest a murderer, while Desi Arroyo was left to indulge hypothetical fantasies in the darker recesses of his imagination.

***

Holdena Straithorne paid little heed to the significance of the moment, even though this was the last email she would ever send from her office at Phalanx Publishing. There was nothing in her manner that suggested the kind of pathos that, say, a novelist might have found in the scene. Her posture, her facial expressions, everything about the way she sat perched in front of her laptop seemed to communicate business as usual. And in fact, the tone of the email she was writing was also business-like, even though the fallout of the message itself was to prove devastating. But to all appearances, Holdena was writing nothing more significant than a requisition for more toner for the copy machine.

"Hello, Professor Padgett. I hope this email finds you well. I'm writing to you to make you aware of some important developments regarding the manuscript you submitted to us, *Archimedes at the Gear Fair*, which, as you know, was what we call "in process." That is, it was being fast-tracked for publication and distribution (the details of which you'll find more comprehensively addressed in my previous email to you).

Our office is now in receipt of correspondence from Dr. R. Lancaster Zale (it's unclear to me if you and he are acquainted) that seems to indicate, fairly definitively, that *Archimedes at the Gear Fair* is not a work by James Joyce but rather by a former Creative Writing MFA student named Augustine Hiatt. We have investigated further and confirmed Dr. Zale's suspicions. Our Board has determined that the appropriate step to take at this time is to cease any further efforts at publication and to release to the media outlets in which the book has been advertised the following statement:

> We at Phalanx Publications have discovered that a manuscript we were presented with that purported to be by the Modernist writer James Joyce has, in fact, been established to be a forgery. Our editors relied on the expertise of an outside consultant, who, it turns out, lacked the proper credentials to authenticate the work. Once the work's true provenance was brought to our attention, we ceased all efforts at publication. We regret the error.

As you can imagine, Professor Padget, this incident has caused Phalanx considerable expense and embarrassment. Therefore, regarding your exposure in this episode, we request the immediate return of all monies advanced to you for your work on this project. In addition, our legal department will contact you shortly to schedule a deposition.

I regret the turn of events that have unfolded. On a personal note, if you wish to contact me further, you will be unable to do so through this address. I have been terminated from Phalanx and will not be reachable through any Phalanx-affiliated website or office.

Good luck going forward.

Holdena Straithorne,

[Formerly of] Phalanx Publishing.

She finished writing the email, read it through a couple of times, making changes to some of the wording. Old habits. She hit the "send" button, closed the laptop, and then tucked it into a box that contained her personal effects. The literary revolution she hoped to foment when she first moved into this office would have to wait for some other idealistic young wordsmith. She'd wagered everything she'd earned in her years in the field on a work that turned out to be no more written by James Joyce than the "Guinness is Good For You!" sign that she removed from her wall and slid into the box that now held all that remained of a once-promising publishing career.

***

"Hi, Russell. It's Alana. I wanted to come by and talk with you. Sorry I missed you. Call when you get this message."

She was calling from her car. She had just dropped by Padget's house, but no one was home. She thought he might be at the college even though class was not in session, so she decided to drive to his office. This could likely turn into one of the most awkward conversations Alana would ever have. *Russ, we have to talk — but you have the right to remain silent.*

She cranked up a song called "Spitting image" by a punk band called Toilet Water, nodding her head when the lead singer blared, "Every road a freakin' dead-end if you take things all the way." There were still some dangerous curves, and probably a few detours, in the road Alana found herself on, but for Russell Padget, she suspected he was about to hit a dead end.

***

It was outmoded, he knew, but Professor Russell Padget still liked the feel of chalk in his hand. It had been more than a decade since "smart boards" replaced traditional chalkboards in the classroom of Hackett County Community College. However, there were still a few on campus if you knew where to look. And on special days, when he was lecturing on a subject near and dear to his heart, he'd call a friend from maintenance and have him wheel a chalkboard into his classroom. Then Padget would start in, and after only a minute or two, that chalkboard would begin to fill with writing. It would keep on filling as Padget got worked up, becoming almost a living piece of performance art, students watching the professor do his thing, getting all excited, his voice modulating, his gestures exaggerated, his hand returning again and again to the board, filling in gaps, punctuating thoughts. By the time his lecture was over, there'd be a little lofty cloud of dust hanging over the chalkboard like a halo, sanctifying his inscribed insights. The students who paid attention to what he was saying — not many, it must be admitted — seemed more entertained than enlightened by the slightly unnerving spectacle of a college professor getting wound up like a manic nightclub comic. But he himself came to enjoy the rush of the performance.

"And where better to get a rush than in the most natural amphitheater of all — wide-open nature!" Padgett waved his arms like a magician, revealing the setting sun and the first twinkling of the stars, tentative gleams amid the dying light of day. He had found a chalkboard and hauled it up to the roof of the building in which he had his office. He didn't want to be entombed several floors below in his office, not tonight. Nothing for him down there except unwelcome emails from ungrateful former students, intrusive voicemails from scorned lovers. He'd had enough. He needed a change of scenery. He looked down from the rooftop to the campus below, the barely discernible footpaths, the bike racks, the scraggly hedgerows, the now-empty parking lot, and that lone piece of public sculpture, with its spire jutting skyward like some metallic petitioner for mercy.

"*Occupandi temporis!*" he wrote on the chalkboard with a flourish. "Live fully in the moment. Don't seize the day — seize the very *seconds* that make up the day!" He felt himself starting to get worked up again, felt the sweat of his hand glazing the chalk, felt his heart beating, his temples throbbing, and his blood pumping. "This is what it is to write!" he bellowed to the open air and the welcoming night sky. "This is what it is to create!"

The litany of his friends from other epochs crowded his mind: Donne and Virgil and Plato and Dickinson and Dunbar and Herbert and Rimbaud and Kafka and Rumi and Murasaki and Tennyson and Eliot and Plath and Aristophanes.

"Yes, Aristophanes!" he shouted. "That brilliant Greek who illustrated in his play *The Birds* the secret aspiration of all mankind, to ascend the heights, birdlike, to the very throne of God!"

He took off his blazer and hooked it on the corner of the chalkboard like a corduroy flag.

"Who says we can't? Hmmm? Who would deny mankind the right to know the mind of God? What — the law of physics? You think mere 'laws' have stopped the greatest creative minds in history? Nonsense!" And he turned again to the chalkboard and began writing furiously the names of DaVinci and Galileo and Curie and Hawking and Wright and a dozen others, chalk dust flying like smoke off the board, bits of the hard white substance cracking off, chipping like bark under a henchman's furious ax.

"And would you close your mind to the greatest literary adventure of all — the creation of *what-comes-next*? The afterlife? The next phase? The looking-glass Alice went through? This is WHY one writes — not to achieve immortality, but to create the *possibility* of immortality. Don't you SEE?!"

He was shouting now, feeling animated, excited like he used to be, back at the beginning of his teaching career, back when his future stretched before him like a sunlit roadway. If anyone was milling around below, they surely must have wondered what all that racket up on the roof was about.

"Bach's *I Know That My Redeemer Liveth* is a work of genius *precisely* because he did NOT know — he was willing the unknowable into the possible. *That's* what creative artists do — they make possible the unknowable; they give us a place to inhabit beyond the inadequate world we see and feel. They bring forth — to use Wordsworth's phrase — clouds of glory!" And here he turned to draw a large, puffed-out cloud on the chalkboard, but the force of his inscription caused the chalk to break apart, and both professor and cloud temporarily deflated, he paused and turned to face the imaginary class, the invisibles who were witness to his last and greatest lecture.

"To strive, to seek, to find, and not to yield," he said quietly, to himself as much as to the unseen creatures of the night. And then, showing his now empty palm with only the fragment of chalk, he shrugged. "The readiness is all."

He took a deep breath and collected himself, rolling down his sleeves and then buttoning his cuffs. He lifted his jacket off the chalkboard and put it on. He buttoned the top button of his shirt and then straightened his necktie. Then he turned his back on the empty rooftop space and climbed up on the roof's very ledge, looking down now at the campus, staring at the spire of the artwork several stories below, a twisted, conical metal horn that seemed to reach up to him from the gloaming.

He laughed quietly to himself and said, over his shoulder to the non-existent rooftop audience, "Do you recall the last words of Stephen Dedalus in James Joyce's *Portrait of the Artist as a Young Man*? Hmmm? Write this down: 'I go to encounter for the millionth time the reality of experience.' Well, brothers and sisters, make it a million and one."

And with that, he jumped.

Detective Alana Stamos was only half a mile away from the campus when she heard the police scanner blurt out *Ten Fifty-six, HCCC. Report of a body impaled on a public sculpture. Code 20. All units respond.*

She was perhaps the closest officer, but she didn't respond. Instead, she pulled her car over, flipped off the scanner, and put her head on the steering wheel, the sounds of sirens piercing the night like feedback from a grungy dive bar band.

***

"The next item of business," said Dr. Morgan Staffordshire, "is the matter of pendit arbitrium for Lucia Joyce." Since the death of her father, Lucia Joyce had sunken into a sullen, almost non-responsive state. The occasional glimpses of coherence, even joyfulness, had ceased. No one thought to address her natural grief through counseling, therapy, or time. Instead, they just increased her medication. "Having been here on an 'interim' basis — at the request of her father, who always believed she would improve, though sadly, she has not — it has now become necessary to finalize her status. Her mother has submitted a petition for life care by the state."

"And the cost?" asked one of the board members.

"To be paid by the estate, in perpetuity."

Satisfied nods all around. The hospital Board understood that James Joyce died a wealthy man, and they assumed his estate would be sufficiently able to provide for his daughter's care, even a lifetime of care.

"I remind you that this decision is permanent. Any discussion?"

"Well," chimed another Board member, clearing his throat. "Is she… well, you know. Is she likely to improve?"

"No, she is not. I have seen her myself," said Staffordshire, who was already calculating the monthly revenue from her long-term confinement at his hospital.

"Well then," said the questioner, now completely satisfied. If Dr. Staffordshire, the great man of medicine, has seen fit to visit the patient and personally examine her, well then, indeed.

"So be it," Staffordshire proclaimed. "I'll contact her mother, who is handling the estate. Miss Joyce will be relocated to permanent confinement. Our next order of business...."

Lucia Joyce was informed of the board's decision by an orderly who delivered a copy of the board's order to her. She barely stirred when handed the document.

"Do you understand?" the orderly asked. "It means you will be here forever." She looked at him blankly for a moment. Then her eyes wandered to a drawing she had made of a frolicsome little fish dancing with a shrimp in a whirling underwater ballet. And then she smiled, a lone tear trickling down her cheek like a drop of rain, a world of microbes at play within.

***

[Author's note: After James Joyce's death in 1941, Lucia Joyce spent the next 40 years institutionalized. She died in 1982 at St. Andrew's Hospital in Northampton. Stephen Joyce, James's grandson and only living heir announced at a literary symposium in Venice in 1988 that he had destroyed all of the letters of Lucia that were in his possession, infuriating and saddening the scholarly community. The record of her imaginative life during the half-century of her confinement — as well as any stories, poems, or riddles that her doting father might have sent her, such as the sea story he said he wanted to write — remains merely the product of sympathetic speculation.]

HISTRIA BOOKS

Addison & Highsmith

Other fine works of fiction available from Addison & Highsmith Publishers:

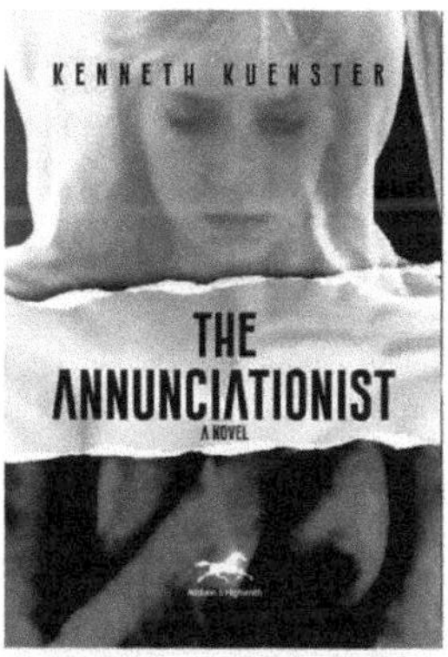

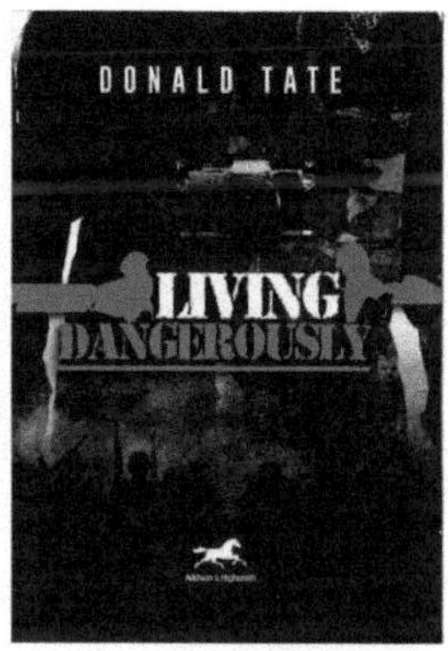

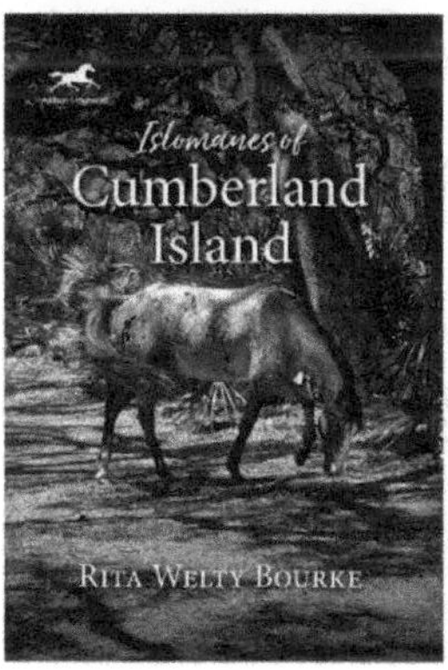

For these and many other great books visit

HistriaBooks.com